HALF THE
TERRIBLE
THINGS

HALF THE TERRIBLE THINGS

By Paul Legler

North Dakota State University Press
Fargo, ND

North Dakota State University Press
Dept. 2360, P.O. Box 6050, Fargo, ND 58108-6050
www.ndsupress.org

Half the Terrible Things, by Paul Legler

Copyright © 2020 North Dakota State University Press
All rights reserved. This book may not be reproduced in whole or part in any form without
permission from the publisher. For copyright permission, contact Suzanne Kelley at 701-238-6848
or suzanne.kelley@ndsu.edu.

First Edition
First Printing

Library of Congress Control Number: 2020943286
ISBN: 978-1-946163-18-9

Cover design by Jamie Hohnadel Trosen
Interior design by Deb Tanner

The publication of *Half the Terrible Things* is made possible by the generous support of donors to
the NDSU Press Fund and the NDSU Press Endowment fund, and other contributors to NDSU Press.

David Bertolini, Director
Suzanne Kelley, Publisher
Zachary Vietz, Publicist, Graduate Assistant in Publishing
Oliver West Sime, Graduate Assistant in Publishing

Book Team for *Half the Terrible Things*
Kalley Miller, Oliver West Sime, N. K. Routledge, Zachary Vietz

Printed in the United States of America

Publisher's Cataloging-In-Publication Data
(Prepared by The Donohue Group, Inc.)

Names: Legler, Paul, author.
Title: Half the terrible things / by Paul Legler.
Description: First edition. | Fargo, ND : North Dakota State University
    Press, [2020] | Includes bibliographical references.
Identifiers: ISBN 9781946163189 (paperback)
Subjects: LCSH: Tabert, Martin, -1923--Fiction. | Prisoners--Crimes
    against--United States--Fiction. | Women lawyers--United States--
    Fiction. | Nursing home patients--North Dakota--Fiction. | LCGFT:
    Historical fiction. | BISAC: FICTION / Historical / General. | FICTION
    / Small Town & Rural. | FICTION / Literary. | FICTION / Legal. |
    FICTION / Family Life / General.
Classification: LCC PS3612.E3524 H35 2020 | DDC 813/.6--dc23

♾ This paper meets the requirements of ANSI/NISO Z39.48-1992
(Permanence of Paper).

For Ali, Mark, & Sean

AUTHOR'S NOTE

The large events involving the main character in this novel, Martin Tabert, are real. Martin Tabert grew up on a farm near Munich, North Dakota. In December 1921, while traveling across the country, he jumped a train traveling to Florida. He was arrested by Sheriff J.R. Jones for vagrancy, sentenced to a convict work camp in Dixie County, Florida, by Judge F.B. Willis, and whipped to death by Captain Walter Higginbotham, an employee of the Putnam Lumber Company. The epilogue and cited quotations are entirely factual. The photographs used throughout the book are also real.

The other major characters in the novel, Nicole Knutson and Edna Knutson, are fictional, as are any minor characters connected to them, including staff of the Office of Legal Counsel, U.S. Department of Justice. Any incidents and dialogue involving them are the product of the author's imagination and are not to be construed as real. Any resemblance to actual persons, living or dead, is entirely coincidental.

I could not tell you half of the terrible things that happened down there.

> — Letter from John Gardner to John Tabert, January 29, 1923, Gudmunder Grimson Papers, records of the State Historical Society of North Dakota, Collection Number: 10120.

Chapter 1

MARTIN

Martin Tabert. Photo courtesy of State Archives of Florida.

1922, Convict Camp, Dixie County, Florida

A low, ashen sky loomed over the camp.

The men were dead, aching tired. The kind of tired that seeps through your flesh to your bones. They waited. Voices whispering in the dark.

"Maybe he won't call no ones out tonight."

"Maybe . . . but best not count on it."

"I ain't counted on it, but I prayin' on it jus' the same."

"Ain't nothin' the Lord takes interest in."

"Reckon you right, but never hurt to pray some."

The men watched the bonfire. He always had more pine thrown on before he called someone out. He knew the fire would draw the men's eyes in.

Gardner watched from the edge of the yard. He thought for a moment about making a run for it. Coming back with a gun somehow. It was black dark past the edge of the yard. But he knew they would be after him in the morning with the dogs.

He ain't me. He ain't me, he thought. *I can make it. Thirty-eight more days. I'll be out of this damn place.*

The men who had jackets drew the collars up. Thompson shivered. He didn't have a jacket and was still surprised how cold it got at night. Even here, where it was supposed to be sunshine and oranges every day. *Where was Martin? Maybe over by the bunkhouse.* He'd noticed him shivering earlier today, even in the heat of the afternoon.

Some of the men wandered out past the light to take a piss or shit in the dark, drifting back slowly, their eyes on the fire. Thompson watched the faces of the colored convicts sitting on the far side in the flickering shadows. They had their own sitting area, but they had the same fear in their eyes. *We all have the same fear.*

The men who were last to be fed edged back to the kitchen one by one to rinse their bowls and spoons and stack them. The cook was already finished for the night, and he stood by his door waiting for it to be over so he could get some sleep. It wouldn't be many hours before he'd be rising again to get the cornbread and coffee started.

It had grown almost entirely quiet, the wind hushed, and the birds silent in their roosts. Captain Higginbotham called for the bottle again. He took a long pull of the strong rank whiskey. The men could see the six guards on duty, their silhouettes against the fading fire. He turned and said something to them. The men could not make it out, but the guards laughed, and they took that for a bad sign.

"Jessup!" he yelled. The voice was like a shot fired in the dark. Then again. "Jessup!"

"Yas, sir."

"Stoke up this fire."

God dammit, no, Gardner thought. It was time.

Jessup threw an armful of logs on. The men watched as the flames grew, expanding the circle of light. The guards kept passing the bottle. Laughing now with a nervous excitement. This was what they'd been waiting for.

"Not Martin," Thompson whispered, half-aloud. "Oh Lord, please don't let it be Martin."

"Jessup."

"Yas, sir."

"You know what. Git it."

"Yas, sir. I gittin' it."

"Jessup. Pour syrup on it."

"Syrup?"

"You heard me, boy. You done it before." He stared at Jessup and Jessup ran. Then he turned to face the men outside the circle of fire. His voice rose to reach the edge of the dark. "We got us a Yankee been lammin' out. I aim to set his damn mind right."

"No, please no. Not Martin," Thompson whispered to himself now.

"Line up," Higginbotham barked out.

The men took their places and watched as Jessup handed him the long black strap. "Black Aunty" the Captain called it. He walked to his spot. The men could see by his gait that the liquor had taken hold. He always used the same sawdust-covered spot to stand on. He didn't like to slip once he got started. The area surrounding the spot was covered by sand. Even in the firelight, one could see its darkened red color.

He leaned over and dragged the Black Aunty through the sand slowly. First one side and then the other, inspecting it closely to make sure sand stuck to every inch.

The pine now crackled on the fire and cast an unholy light about the yard. Thompson could see Martin now, down at the very end of the line, trying to disappear behind a taller man. *That ain't going to save him.*

Higginbotham straightened up. He was not a tall man, but standing by the fire with that look, no man in the line could meet his eyes, and they all prayed he would not call out their name. The corners of his mouth curled into something between a smirk and a smile. He called out, "Tabert."

No one moved. He frowned, looking up and down the line of men. His voice exploded the silence. "Tabert. Martin Tabert. I'm callin' you out. Now!"

Life changes in the instant. The ordinary instant.
— Joan Didion

2003, City of Devils Lake, North Dakota

Edna fell asleep. Nicole sat in the chair beside her bed. She could hear the wind howling outside, whipping the bare trees. She wondered if she should take the photo from Edna's hand. She stared at it, thinking Edna would drop it, but she held it firmly. Her hand seemed impossibly thin — patchy with liver-spots. Some time went by. It was hard to say how much. It felt overly warm in the nursing home, with a dry stillness to the air. Nicole gently took the photo out of Edna's hand and kissed her forehead. She didn't wake, and Nicole put the photo in her purse and tiptoed out the door.

Nicole walked back to the nurses' station along the brightly-lit corridor. She could hear the small, hard clicks of her heels. Not another sound. Then, a cough from somewhere down the hall, and the sound of someone moaning. The air had that antiseptic smell that attempts to cover approaching death. She quickened her pace.

The nurse looked up and smiled as she approached.

"She's sleeping," Nicole said.

"That's good. They need their sleep when they get to this stage. Don't you worry, now. We'll keep her comfortable."

"I'll give you my card. Call me if there is any change."

"I will, dear."

"Don't charge her for the call. Call me collect."

"Okey-dokey. I can do that. Have a safe drive. Don't worry, the roads should be fine. The snow doesn't arrive until tomorrow. With the high winds it could get bad. You're lucky to be leaving today."

Nicole walked out to her rental car in the parking lot. The surface was slick with ice and she wished she had boots. She sat in the car a minute before turning the ignition, her head resting on the steering wheel. *Poor Edna. I had no idea.* She took a deep breath and started the car and headed east.

There were few cars on the road. She glanced occasionally at the North Dakota countryside as she drove. Although March, the fields were still cloaked in a dirty white. She watched as a single crow floated up from a stubble field and was swallowed by the sky. It was even more desolate here than she remembered. Nothing but abandoned farms and scrubby thin shelterbelts. Roadsides so empty that the occasional beer can in the ditch drew your attention. Now and then a wooden grain elevator in the distance, looking like a remnant from a faraway time.

She drove fast, thinking she would get to the hotel in Grand Forks early and have time for a drink. Maybe two or three. She knew she'd been drinking too much lately, but work had been stressful after 9/11. It was always lingering there in the back of her head. Like a spider in the dark. The alcohol helped her forget. And now this. *Why did Grandma have to ask me to do this?* she thought. *Now, of all times.*

She had an early flight the next day. It would put her in Washington D.C. by noon. It would still be possible to make it to the office and get some work done. She reached for her phone and looked at the call log. She perused through it quickly as she drove. It seemed like an endless number of calls to return. *Fuck.* She tossed the phone onto the passenger seat.

Nicole glanced out the window as her car sped along. The last words of Edna before she dozed off kept ringing in her head. It was a quavering, whispering voice that seemed to come from far in the past. "Find Martin's grave," she'd said. "Bring him back so he can rest in peace."

She knew the words would not leave her. She took a deep breath and glanced in the rearview mirror. No one was coming. She slammed on the brakes, made a sharp u-turn, and took the first turn south.

Chapter 3
E D N A

The light of love, the purity of grace.
    —Lord Byron

Edna woke up and gazed out the window. She could see the small, leafless trees in the parking lot swaying with the wind. Had she had a visitor? It annoyed her that she'd been having memory problems. Often she couldn't remember what she'd been doing just a short time ago. Then it came back to her. *Nicole. What a sweetie. Where is she?* She cried out, "Nicole! Nicole!" There was an empty silence.

Edna often worried about Nicole. She thought Nicole tried too hard to please and be successful. Drove herself relentlessly. Always pursuing the elusive perfection. Washington D.C. was not the place for her. From what she read in the papers and saw on the six o'clock news, it was a dark place now. War and anger that was palpable. A kind of madness really. And she knew that madness could be contagious.

She remembered that she and Nicole had been talking about Martin. He was still real to her, more real than anything she could see when she glanced about her small room. Photos on a dresser, a few plants, a radio. Material objects were only transitory, but Martin would always be with her. All she had to do was close her eyes and let her mind roll back through the years.

Edna knew Martin even as a child. The farms they lived on were less than three miles apart. She saw him frequently at school and in town, but he was nearly seven years older, so he probably just thought of her as another snot-nosed little kid. And, at first, he was just one of many older neighborhood boys to her. They were all the same—rough, noisy, crude farm boys. Girls stayed their distance, lest they get teased or have their braids pulled.

Edna was pretty, with naturally blond hair and delicate features. She had a quick wit and a ready laugh. When Edna reached fourteen years of age, her body began to blossom, and she showed the beginnings of an ample bust. She couldn't hide that fact no matter what she wore. Sometimes after church the boys and girls would gather in small groups and talk before their parents gathered them up to go home. Edna noticed that the boys began to pay more attention to her. The bold ones stood close to her and tried to say clever things. She noticed Martin often looked her way furtively, but he was too shy to talk to her directly. When she would catch him glancing at her, he would look to the ground and kick the dirt with his feet. She thought he was good-looking. He was somewhat small, but she noticed that he stood straight and he had a nice smile when it came.

In April of 1921, Edna attended a youth luncheon at the church. Martin was there. It was a rare warm and sunny spring day on the prairie. Some kids were playing pom-pom pull-away. Edna didn't want to play because she wore her only pair of good shoes and she didn't want to get them dirty. She was standing off to the side watching. Martin came over and stood next to her. He didn't say anything. Edna didn't even turn her head in his direction, but she could feel his presence. A flock of snow geese flew overhead, their chorus of voices filling the air.

"Oh, I just love the sound of geese," she said.

"Oh, gosh, I do too," Martin replied.

"And cranes."

"Me too."

"Not ducks so much."

"No."

"Not stinky coots at all."

"No, me neither." They both laughed.

"How do birds fly so far and never get lost, I wonder?" Edna asked.

"They have instincts that tell them the way to go."

"I suppose. But still, they fly so far. All the way down south. Their instincts must be strong. Do you think people have instincts too?"

"Oh, yes."

"Do they tell us the way to go?"

"Most of the time . . . but maybe they lead us astray sometimes, too."

Edna thought about this for a moment. "How do we know then?"

"I don't know. I haven't figured that out yet."

Edna heard her mother calling her. "I have to go. It was nice talking to you. Don't be so shy next time. I don't bite, you know."

"Okay, I'll remember that."

Edna didn't see Martin again until a Saturday some weeks later. It was about nine in the morning. Edna had already been up helping her mother with household chores for two hours when there was a knock on the door.

Her father went to answer it. Edna peeked around the corner from the kitchen. Martin was standing on the steps, holding his hat in his hands.

"Is Edna home?" he asked.

"What do you want?" her father asked. There was a tone of suspicion in his voice.

"I want to show her something outside."

"What?"

"Cranes. They're down by the big slough, west of here."

"Are you going to shoot them?"

"No."

"I hear they're not bad eating."

"I just want to show them to Edna. They're whooping cranes."

"Are you sure they're whooping cranes? They're probably sandhill cranes. We've had them here before in the spring."

"No, these are bigger and whiter and I heard them making a deep whooping sound coming in last night. They're whooping cranes. I read about them in a book from the library."

"Well, if you read it in a book." He turned and yelled towards the kitchen. "Edna, you have a caller."

Edna ran to the door. She talked to Martin for a few minutes and then asked her father if she could go with him. "Please, Father, we'll just walk down to see the cranes and then Martin will walk me back. It will only be an hour or so."

Her father said it was fine. Martin Tabert's family was well thought of in the community. Perhaps they should have a chaperone, but he felt the boy could be trusted for a short time on a Saturday morning.

It was foggy and windless as they walked down to the slough, which was about a half mile away. The cool fog tingled their noses and burnished their cheeks a bright pink. Edna was excited. Excited to see these rare and beautiful birds she'd heard about and excited because she was with a young man. Alone. That was a rarity and special. As they got closer, Martin told her to be quiet, and they crept along trying to see through the fog. Martin stopped. He couldn't see them yet, but he could sense they were near. He and Edna stood silently peering into the dimness, and the fog lifted slightly. There the cranes stood. Seven of them. Edna was unprepared for how large they were. Five feet tall, with a wingspan of nearly eight feet. "Oooh," she cried.

"Quiet," Martin whispered.

She leaned in toward his ear. "Sorry."

He turned his head and his gaze fell on her eyes and red lips, so very close. He froze for a moment before turning back to the cranes. They were stalking around in a low-lying area next to the slough now. Signaling each other, "Ker-loo, ker-loo." The sun broke through, casting its morning light on their satiny white bodies, highlighted by black-fingered wings and elegant white-and-black heads, painted with a slash of red. Occasionally they would peck at something on the ground with their javelin beaks or stretch and preen their wings, forming huge fans that Edna thought looked like the wings of angels. She'd never seen anything so exquisite.

Two of the cranes on the closest side began a courtship dance. First bobbing and bowing, hopping forward and back, cupping and flapping their graceful wings. Facing each other, posturing and turning pirouettes. Tipping their heads heavenly, then arching their necks backward, chins pointing to the sky. Then, leaping into the air, wings flapping, hanging aloft like puppets, softly alighting. They circled each other as they danced, aware only of each other and the pull to mate.

Edna whispered, "It's like a waltz." They watched the cranes for nearly an hour, not saying another word. Every few minutes they would steal a glance at each other, both marveling at the beauty and wonder and joy in each other's eyes.

"We have to go," Martin said. He knew his pa would be angry if he was gone too long. There were chores to do.

Edna knew the same thing. Saturdays meant baking bread and washing clothes and cleaning barns. She didn't want her father to be angry they were gone so long after he was kind enough to let her leave with a young man.

They turned, and ducking their heads so as not to be seen by the cranes, they began walking back.

Once they were far enough away, they began to talk. "Will they nest here?" Edna asked.

"I don't think so. The book I read said they nest in northern Canada. They're just migrating through from Florida or Texas."

"That's so far. I can't even imagine it. I've never been farther than fifty miles from here."

"Me neither," Martin said, "but I'm going to, soon." He told Edna about his plans to take a trip in the fall, after the harvest, to see the country's sights. "And now I have something else I want to see, too."

"What?"

"I want to see where the whooping cranes winter in Florida."

Edna didn't respond. She felt a cold chill of trepidation course through her body. For someone growing up in North Dakota, Florida seemed like a far-away exotic and dangerous land. Sunshine and oranges to be sure, but also swamps and snakes and alligators.

Martin noticed her silence and for a second he had a strong feeling that he didn't want to leave North Dakota at all. He liked this little girl who'd suddenly sprouted up and become a woman in his eyes.

"I'll write to you when I'm gone if you like," he said.

"Yes, I'd like that."

After the morning they saw the whooping cranes, Edna and Martin began talking to each other after every church service, but there were always fellow parishioners with snoopy ears around and anything more than simple polite conversation was difficult. Martin and Edna wanted to be alone together, so they started seeing each other on the sly, meeting at a small grove of trees west of Edna's house. It was only a mile for Edna and two miles for Martin. They could run there in a short time and they met every Sunday afternoon. That was the only time they could both be sure to get away.

Eighty-two years later, Edna could still remember those meetings at the grove. She would go outside, pretending to play with the cats in the barn, then sneak out the back barn door, out of sight of the house, and run as fast as she could. Martin would always be waiting, standing expectantly by the biggest cottonwood tree. At first they were too shy to kiss, but she would run up and stop only inches from him and they would look at each other, smiling, their eyes studying each other's countenances. She loved his dark, deep-set eyes. He loved her light blue, fiery eyes. He had a serious face that changed when his smile snuck through. She had a smile that came naturally from a playful, child-like nature. They were content to sit in the grass and look at each other and talk, or sometimes they would walk around the small grove hand-in-hand.

Martin and Edna both loved nature and they talked about animals they'd seen during the week. There are not many animals that can survive the winters of northern North Dakota, so their wildlife sightings were infrequent. Occasional badgers, foxes, gophers, deer, weasels, raccoons, and skunks. They could count the kinds of wild animals they'd seen in their lives on their fingers. Their world was a small one, but it seemed big to them, each small living thing more precious because it was so rare.

Later in the summer, as they became closer, they could no longer help themselves and they began kissing at these encounters. Kisses that left Edna hot and feverish. They always stopped short of fulfilling their carnal desires, however. They had their whole lives ahead of them and they could wait. They made plans for what they would do when Martin came back from his travels. Edna would be sixteen then, and they could date, and they would go to neighborhood dances and the new movie theater in Devils Lake.

On the last day before Martin left for his travels, they met at the grove. It was late September and an early autumn frost coated the trees. "I've been looking forward to this trip for so long," Martin said. "Every day for the last year when I was shoveling grain or cleaning the barn, I would count the days. But now that the time is here, I feel like I am being torn apart. Part of me wants to stay here."

"I want you to stay too, but I want you to be happy, and I know you can't be happy until you see the world."

"There is so much to see. Someday we'll travel the world together."

"Oh, I would like that more than anything."

He kissed her on the lips. Edna shivered with the touch, and at that moment she wanted him so badly that it took every bit of her will to keep from pulling him down to the frosted ground. She took a small package out of her pocket and gave it to Martin. "This is a gift for you. For your travels. So you don't forget me. I had the jeweler in town make it."

Martin opened the package. It was a silver watch fob. Martin looked closely at it. It was etched with two dancing cranes.

"Cranes!"

"Yes."

"I could never forget you."

"And I could never forget you, Martin. As long as I live."

When Edna was older, she read everything she could get her hands on about whooping cranes. She found out that there may have been only about thirty in the whole world at the time that she and Martin saw them. *What are the chances of that?* she would think. Thirty in the whole world, flying from Florida or Texas to northern Canada. What told them to land in that field between her home and Martin's? They would always remain to her a symbol of the fragility of purity in the midst of a dark gray world.

Chapter 4
NICOLE

We also have to work, though, sort of the dark side, if you will.
    —Dick Cheney, September 16, 2001

Nicole drove fast. The highway was smooth and the land was level. She turned west on Highway 200 and set the cruise control at eighty. She made a plan as she drove. She would get to Bismarck in the late evening. She would find someplace decent to eat—if there was such a place. Get up early. Work out. She would be at the North Dakota Heritage Center when it opened. Edna had shown her a newspaper clipping about Martin's death. She said it had been in all the North Dakota newspapers at the time. Nicole thought there could be a clue as to the place of his grave in one of the newspaper articles. If so, the Heritage Center might have them on microfilm.

Nicole was driving through the small town of Carrington when she saw the patrol car. She touched the brake. It was too late. The flashing red lights and siren came on behind her. She pulled over and craned her neck to look in the rearview mirror. She waited, moistening her lips with her tongue. She knew he was checking her car license plate on his computer. It was a rental car, so that wouldn't tell him much. She rolled down her window slowly when he approached.

"Is there something wrong, officer?"

"May I see your driver's license, please?"

Nicole pulled out her license. She placed her U.S. Department of Justice I.D. conspicuously on top and handed them to him. He studied them for a minute.

"Are you on official business here?" he asked.

"Uh, I'm not supposed to tell anyone that," Nicole said. "It's confidential. I'm sure you understand." She looked him right in the eyes. "I'm sorry if I was speeding. I guess I was in a little bit of a hurry. I have to drive all the way to Bismarck tonight and then fly back to Washington, D.C., tomorrow." She smiled her most warming smile. "I wish I had more time to see the pretty little towns around here."

Nicole saw his eyes wander downward over her body for a second before he looked at her license and I.D. again. "People don't care too much for the feds around here. Just take it easy."

Nicole drove on, feeling vaguely upset with herself, but not knowing why. Soon the night closed in, dark except the dim stars and moon pulsing above. She drove more slowly, her headlights fuzzy in the foreground. It would take a few more hours of driving. She felt exhausted. It had been a very long day. The wind buffeted the car and she sometimes found herself straddling the middle of the two-lane highway or swerving from the edges. *Concentrate. Concentrate.* She saw another car, its headlights visible for miles as it approached. She clutched the steering wheel, trying to drive straight in her lane. The lights seemed to mesmerize her. She imagined herself losing control of the car and swerving into it. The car dimmed its lights at the last minute and sped by.

Nicole counted the small towns as she passed by them: Sykeston, Heaton, Bowden, Hurdsfield, Goodrich, Denhoff, McClusky, Underwood. Absolutely nothing moving in these towns at night. Sometimes not even a stop sign on the main street and only a few scattered lights. Her thoughts tumbled as she drove. Things had gotten tense at work. She was working long hours. She'd been pressured to do things that disturbed her. She tried to shut those things out of her mind as she drove. She tapped the steering wheel, she wriggled her legs, she turned on the radio. She repeatedly hit the scan button but could only pick up three country western stations. She sang along to Toby Keith, Tim McGraw, and the Dixie Chicks at the top of her voice. She saw herself from above, hurtling down that highway in the flat straightness.

Nicole checked in at the Holiday Inn only because she recognized the sign. When she arrived at her room, she was disappointed to find that it faced the big, noisy indoor pool. Nicole thought about requesting another room, but she was too tired. She found the Space Aliens Grill and Bar nearby and ordered a "Spaceship Salad" and two extra dry martinis. She thought the food was disgusting, the martinis so-so. When she got back to her room, her stomach was queasy. She wasn't sure if it was the food or something else. She found the Tums in her purse, fumbled with the lid, and tossed several in her mouth. She slept fitfully, thrashing about. It seemed very hot in the room for the winter. She got up to turn on the fan. She went to the bathroom. She threw the cover off the bed and and lay back down under the cooler sheets. Nicole had never had insomnia in her life before the past year. Now it was a common occurrence. Thoughts of work rose in her head. She felt trapped there, doing what was expected, but not exercising her own judgment. Trying to please her boss, Mr. Lee. He was so forceful, so sure of himself, and she didn't have the self-confidence to stand up to him. Her life had been like that for a long time. Striving for the pat on the back. What was the point? Was that just the way life was?

When her 6:30 a.m. wake-up call came, Nicole was too tired for her planned workout in the fitness center. She fell back asleep and when she awoke a second time, she was surprised it was nearly ten. She didn't have time for a shower. She brushed her hair in the mirror. The blond highlights in her long brown hair needed to be re-colored. And she needed a cut. She applied some lip gloss, pressing her lips together.

The Heritage Center was located next to the State Capitol building — nineteen stories tall and the highest building in North Dakota. She couldn't miss it. She parked right in front. It seemed strange how few cars were parked outside, so unlike the nation's capital where people would fight over the rare public parking space. She walked straight to the front desk at the Center and told the receptionist what she was looking for. The receptionist called the reference librarian, Mr. Davison, over. He was friendly and quick to help her. He knew something about the Martin Tabert case. There was a file collection, quite a large one, he said. It was on microfilm, and as he described the contents, she realized that it would take some time to look at it. *I'll get a quick coffee and work through the lunch hour and I can still catch a flight this afternoon.* She gulped a coffee and Danish at the capitol coffee shop and settled in at a small table with the microfilm projector.

The historical record was intriguing. There had been an investigation by a lawyer, Gudmunder Grimson, whom the family had hired after Martin's disappearance in 1922. Martin's death had sparked interest in the Eastern press. The *New York World* had put a reporter on it, Samuel "Duff" McCoy. There were numerous newspaper clippings the lawyer and family had collected. Martin had died at a convict work camp run by the Putnam Lumber Company.

There was some information about the convict camps they ran and also statements and affidavits the lawyer had collected regarding Martin's death. Many of the details were gruesome. She worked quickly, perusing the articles and statements, trying not to think too much about them. She had to focus on the grave issue. Where was he buried? A couple hours later she'd found what she was looking for.

Unfortunately, the newspaper stories and statements were conflicting. Arthur Johnson, a former inmate at the convict camp, related that Captain Higginbotham ordered him and another inmate by the name of South Carolina Eddy to prepare Tabert for burial. "The sheets and even the mattress on his bunk were covered with blood and the sheets stuck to the body." He said that Martin was buried in a ten-dollar coffin wearing a white shirt, a coat, and a pair of convict pants belonging to a Negro who'd escaped. Another account said Martin was buried in a five-foot hole dug in the ground of a Dixie County swamp by two old Negroes, "dropped in a hole half-full of water." Convict Glen Thompson said Martin was buried at Perry, Florida. A fourth account by a Putnam Lumber Company employee said he was buried in a thirty-dollar coffin in the community cemetery at Clara, Florida. The employee said it was a respectful funeral, including "a small group of kind-hearted township people singing hymns, wide-eyed school children looking on, and an itinerant pastor officiating." Another account by a guard, J.W. Jackson, said he was buried at Clara without any services. Yet another, that he'd been buried in the Mingo cemetery.

Other stories and sworn statements reported on efforts to find the body in 1922. They related how Attorney Grimson and members of a legislative committee investigating the death went to Clara, Florida, to talk with witnesses. They located a "darkie" who said he'd helped bury Martin. They drove out to the area, but they were surrounded by a Captain Bill Fisher and twenty to twenty-five men who worked for Putnam Lumber, most of them carrying guns. Captain Fisher talked to the darkie and "intimidated him." A statement by a member of the legislative committee further related:

> They ran the cars out north to the end of the hard road and it [was] afterward determined that it was a mile north of where the darkie wanted to go when they stopped the car and asked if this was the place and he said "NO." After some talk we persuaded him to go back. We went back to the place and asked him to find where he first buried Tabert . . . he said he was afraid.

The group then went to the cemetery where Putnam Lumber employees said Tabert was buried to exhume the body. There, another man said, "[T]here was a certitude . . . that this man Tabert was buried where the darkie said he was buried." Therefore, they did not exhume the body, as they did not know if the body buried in the cemetary was the right one, and the darkie was too scared to properly identify the burial site.

Nicole took careful notes, but she found it all very confusing. Many of the accounts and newspaper articles were contradictory, but the bottom line seemed clear. No one knew for sure where he was buried, even back in 1922. Now it was eighty-plus years later. There was no use going on a wild goose chase. She would tell Edna that it was hopeless.

When she pushed open the door of the Heritage Center, the wind nearly pushed it back in her face. The snow had already started swirling, creating small drifts. *Uh, oh*, she thought. She ducked back into the foyer and looked up the afternoon flight on her computer. *Cancelled.* "Shit, shit, shit," she said. The last thing she wanted to do was spend another night in the Bismarck Holiday Inn. She Googled "best hotel bar in Bismarck" and found the Kelly Inn.

An hour later she had checked in at the Kelly Inn and was sitting on a stool at the bar. She ordered a martini and studied the menu. She almost ordered a salad but decided to order a T-bone steak at the last second. There had to be some compensation for staying in this dump of a town. She was about halfway through her steak and working on her third martini when three men walked into the bar. They stopped at the door, kicked the snow off their boots, and took off their coats. They left their hats on. Cowboy hats, cowboy boots, big silver belt buckles. Nicole had been fascinated by cowboys ever since she was a little girl. Still, she knew that anyone could dress the part. They were probably politicians or appliance salesmen at Sears. All hat and no cattle.

They sat close to her, leaving only one barstool between, and they ordered whiskeys. They talked loudly and she couldn't help overhear their conversation. Something about pickup trucks and stock trailers. Maybe they are real cowboys, she thought. She took a bite of steak. It was juicy, and she savored it as she chewed. The loudest of the three moved his stool closer to her. A minute later he tipped his hat back and turned to her. "Have I seen you someplace before darlin'?" He had a big wide smile under a picture-perfect mustache, like a cowboy in an old Marlboro advertisement.

"I'm pretty sure you haven't," she said. She smiled slightly, despite herself.

"No, you're not from around here. I can tell by your accent. Where you from?"

"East coast mostly. I live in D.C. now"

"D.C.? D.C.? Oh . . . you mean Washington, D.C."

"Right."

"Never been there. I been to Texas once though."

She didn't respond; he downed his whiskey and motioned the bartender for another.

He turned to her again. "You must be a lawyer," he said.

"Good guess."

"Oh yeah. I'm not as dumb as I look. This is the state capital. We get lots of lawyers."

"I bet you do," she said. She noticed he had deep blue eyes. She was almost interested, but she didn't have the time or energy. She cut her steak.

Now, another one of the cowboys moved in. "Ma'am, ever ridden a horse before?"

"No . . . well ponies when I was young, but it's not my thing."

"Oh, we could take you horseback ridin'. It's a whole different thing to ride a cowboy horse."

"I bet it is, but it's a little cold for horseback riding, isn't it?"

"Hell, if you want to stay indoors you could skip the horse and just ride a cowboy," he said. They all hooted and slapped themselves on the back. She excused herself to the ladies' room to escape. As she did so, she realized immediately that it was a mistake. She felt a little tipsy climbing off the stool. They would all be watching her. She had to focus to walk steady.

In the restroom she peed and then took her time at the mirror. She applied some lip gloss and studied her face. She saw the beginnings of a small pimple on her chin and wondered how her skin could break out at thirty-three years of age. When she returned, the men were still at the bar, and they smiled.

The mustache cowboy tried to make conversation. "Darrel is goin' off to the army next week," he said, pointing to the guy on his right.

"Oh, really," she said and looked at him. *Poor schmuck, doesn't know what he's in for.* "Good luck," she said.

"Yeah, I'm going in for three years," he said. "After 9/11, I knew I couldn't stand by and watch them take us over."

"He's gonna kick ass on those A-rabs," the third one said.

The way he said that word, "A-rabs," stringing out the "A" jolted her. Wasn't that the derogatory way her boss, Mr. Lee, said it?

"Can we buy you a drink?" Darrel asked.

"What?"

He yelled to the bartender. "Whiskeys all around. And one of those." He pointed to Nicole's empty martini glass, but she'd already gotten off her stool and headed toward the door.

Nicole's flight the next morning was delayed in Bismarck. Then she missed her connecting flight in Minneapolis to Reagan National Airport. She had to fly into BWI near Baltimore and take a long taxi ride to her rented brownstone near Dupont Circle. She'd lived there ever since she'd moved to Washington, rooming with her friend Paige. She'd known Paige at Brown when they'd lived in the same dorm. Paige could be a little wild at times, but she was tidy and not the type who would eat the yogurt in the fridge that wasn't hers. Nicole could never have been able to afford a place so nice on her own. Housing was crazy expensive in the upscale neighborhoods close to the capitol. As a House staffer, Paige made even less money than Nicole, but she had some trust fund money her grandfather had left her, so she could do what she wanted. Mostly she spent money on clothes. Three hundred dollars for a pair of shoes at Neiman Marcus was nothing for her. The only complaint Nicole had about Paige was that she had male overnight guests too often. She hated being disturbed when she was drinking her morning coffee and some strange guy wandered out of Paige's bedroom in his briefs, scratching himself, and looking in the fridge for something to eat.

Paige was watching television when Nicole entered the apartment, but joined her in the kitchen. "You look terrible, girl," she said. Paige was tall and thin with thick hair to die for, and she always looked fabulous, so she could get away with saying that kind of thing. Nicole was beautiful in her own right, but not model thin, and she was bustier, with actual real-life hips.

"Thanks. I happen to be exhausted. Missed my flight. Sat in the airport. The usual traveling bullshit."

"Oh, too bad. You missed a great reception last night. A banking industry affair. Catered by Mancini's. Awesome cannoli."

"There'll be another next week. I'm getting kind of sick of them anyhow."

"Don't say that. You never know who you could meet. Someone who could help your career. And there were a dozen congressmen there last night."

"I need a glass of wine. Do you want one?" Nicole asked.

"Sure. Why not?"

Nicole poured two glasses of pinot. Paige launched into a long account about some lobbyist she met at the reception who she considered a hunk, and what the women were wearing, and the congressional hearing she would attend next week that would be on C-Span, and how she had to have a new suit to wear because she would be sitting behind the committee members where the television camera might catch her. Nicole's mind was elsewhere and she added an occasional "Uh huh." She drained her glass of pinot and poured herself another. Finally, she interrupted, "Don't you even want to know about my Grandma Edna?"

"Oh sure, sorry. How's she doing?"

Nicole told her about the medical reports. It was a minor heart attack. Still, as the doctor had explained to Nicole, when you're ninety-eight, any heart attack was serious. And she was very weak now. A bout of flu or other illness could spell trouble. Her body was losing its ability to fight things off. Then she explained everything Edna had told her about the Martin Tabert case and the strange request to find his grave. She told Paige about her research through the files at the historical center. She pulled Martin's photograph from her purse.

Paige studied it for a moment. "Nice looking guy," she said. "Too bad what happened to him. Funny she even remembers him after so many years."

"Well her mind ebbs and flows, but she can be sharp as a tack at times. Remembers every detail of the past."

"Old people are like that. My grandma was the same way. She talked about the Great Depression like it was yesterday, but she couldn't remember where she parked her car at the mall."

"Yeah . . . that makes me think . . . if Edna can remember every detail about something that happened so long ago, maybe there is still someone alive in Florida who can remember something about Martin's burial."

"Don't even think about it."

"What?"

"Finding his grave. It would be impossible."

"I suppose."

"No, it really would. Have you ever been to rural Florida? Once you get away from the beaches, there's nothing there. Miles of forests and swamps. Ugh."

"I guess you're right." Nicole gulped down the rest of her wine and looked at the bottom of her glass. "Ahh . . . crap . . . why did she have to ask me? Maybe I should at least make some effort. She is my grandmother, and I know she'd do anything in the world for me."

"You did look into it. You spent a day in Bismarck at the Heritage Center. That's going above and beyond already. Tell her you couldn't find anything. I'm sure that'll be the end of it."

"Okay, okay. I'm tired. I can't think more about it now. I have to get up early in the morning."

Nicole stopped at Starbucks as she did every morning before she went to her office. She liked to get there before the rush and order her venti skinny vanilla latte with extra foam. Then, carrying her coffee, with her soft briefcase and purse slung over the shoulder of her gray business suit, she walked down the street and through the heavy doors of the Department of Justice. Even after working there for three years, she still felt a little bit of a thrill as she entered. It was the culmination of her dream and the long road to get there — Brown University, Yale Law School, clerking for a Federal District Judge, then four years with the U.S. Attorney's Office in Chicago. It had been difficult at times, but she'd worked hard to get ahead and she felt she deserved it. When she landed the job with the Office of Legal Counsel at Justice, she thought she'd reached the pinnacle of the legal profession. The Office of Legal Counsel gave advice to the highest levels of government — cabinet heads and the White House. Its decision on a matter was final. Only the U.S. Attorney General could overrule them and that happened very rarely, especially with Ashcroft. And now, after 9/11, OLC was called upon to render legal opinions on the most sensitive and important issues facing the nation including war, detainees, and interrogations.

She walked to the elevator. She liked the sound of her high heels clicking on the marble floors when it was quiet in the early morning. She took the elevator to the fourth floor. As she walked to her office she glanced at the clock. It was only 6:40 a.m., but she could tell by the lights on in the offices that already half the lawyers were there. The rest would be arriving soon. This was a place where everyone worked as hard as she did—you had to if you wanted to keep up. Many of them would still be there at 10:00 p.m. They took pride in working fourteen-hour days. Plus, everyone knew that the real action only started in the evening, after the federal career bureaucrats had long since gone home. That's when the head of OLC might get a call from the White House or a cabinet secretary. Decision time!

Nicole was just settling in her seat when David Stillman poked his head in the door. "You got a minute?"

She forced a smile. She hated talking to anyone in the morning before she had time to drink her coffee and go through her emails. She hesitated a second, hoping he would respond to her pause. He didn't. "Sure, come in," she said.

He closed the door behind him. *Uh, oh. What now?* They were friends, but they didn't have the type of relationship that called for closing the door, unless it was something he didn't want others in the office to hear. She felt uncomfortable already. David was probably the least-liked attorney in the office. There were only twenty-two of them, and they were like a small club, but he'd been on the outs since Mr. Lee had arrived. Mr. Lee thought David raised too many objections and asked too many questions of those with higher authority. David had lost sight of the fact that they were at war since 9/11. In Lee's vernacular, "He doesn't have the balls it takes to make the tough decisions." The rumor was that he would soon be out. Nicole felt bad about that. He was a decent guy, maybe the most decent guy in the office. When she first moved to Washington, D.C., David had asked her to play on his co-ed softball team. Nicole had been somewhat of a tennis star in high school, she had biceps, and she surprised everyone by how far she could hit the ball. David always let her bat clean-up.

She took a sip of her coffee. He paused for a minute before saying anything. Nicole thought he looked rather pale and sickly.

"The shit hit the fan while you were gone," he said.

"What shit?"

"It's bad." He stopped and looked at her sympathetically.

"Okay, just tell me."

"Remember the Abbu Al-Nasser case?"

"Of course. We allowed him to be deported from Afghanistan to Syria. You know my role in that."

"Yeah . . . I hate to even tell you this."

"What, for God's sake? Something bad happened?"

"Yeah. As bad as it gets. He's dead."

"He probably deserved it."

David looked at her and shook his head in disgust.

"I'm sorry," she said. "I shouldn't have said that. Tell me what happened exactly."

"He was being transferred back from Syria to Kabul. The CIA has a facility there, near the airport, where prisoners are held in complete darkness and isolation. They call it 'the Dark Prison.' A regular hell on earth. He died while being transported."

"Shit . . . stupid. How could they let that happen?"

"He was in pretty bad shape when he left Syria." David looked down like he didn't want to meet her eyes. "I mean in really bad shape. The Syrians put him through the works. Hanging him up for days. Beatings. Broken ribs. Electrodes to his testicles. Still couldn't get anything useful out of him. I guess they must have thought they would try something else, someplace else. Water-board him, probably. We're the experts, and they claim some guys crack under that even when 120 volts have failed. Anyhow, they picked him up in Syria and duct-taped him to a stretcher with a canvas bag over his head. They transported him like that in a steel shipping container."

"Our guys did that?"

"Yeah, apparently they do that to disorient prisoners. He was lying in that container, duct-taped like that, for ten or twelve hours. Probably hotter than shit in there. They swear he wasn't touched otherwise. Who knows? But when they finally took him out they noticed he wasn't breathing."

Nicole hated hearing the details. That was what they all hated, except Lee maybe, and a few others in the White House. "Shit. Assholes. That's sickening," she said. She shook her head. She didn't know what else to say.

"That's not the end of it either," David said.

"What? You might as well tell me everything."

"There are photos."

"Oh, shit." She looked at David. She couldn't believe how shaken he looked. "Does Lee know?" she asked.

"Oh yeah. He knows. He's already sweeping it under the rug. Claims it was all the Syrians' doing."

"Where did the photos come from?"

"Some military guard. A woman. Apparently she wanted a souvenir photo playing tough. She's crouching over the corpse with a big grin, giving a thumbs up."

"Fuck."

They sat there silently for a minute. Nicole felt she was about to retch and she couldn't look David in the eye.

"I can't take this bullshit anymore," David finally said. "This isn't what I signed on for. This isn't what lawyers should be doing."

"I know. You're right." Nicole felt bad for him. Worse for him than for herself. He was such an honest guy. He didn't hide his emotions under a veneer like the rest of them. He really wasn't cut out for this job.

"You're out of it anyhow," she said. "Aren't you doing domestic issues now? I'm the one who was involved."

He hesitated like he didn't know if he should tell her something. He swallowed and then continued. "I pulled the Al-Nasser file last night. There's a good reason why the Syrians couldn't get anything out of him. It's almost certain that he was just a taxi driver like he claimed. Came from a family of goat herders. Just happened to drive a low ranking Al Qaeda official one day because the regular driver was sick. Got turned over by a warlord for a shitload of CIA cash. There is zero evidence to suggest he was a member of Al Qaeda."

Nicole's breath quickened. "Where are the photos?" she asked.

"You don't want to see them."

"I need to."

"That's not going to change anything. Forget it. They're locked up in storage anyhow."

"I have clearance."

"You would have to sign in, and someone might bring it up with Lee. Don't ruin your career like I did. Forget it happened. Isn't that the way to get along? Go with the flow, right? 'Be tough! Be tough!'"

He looked at his feet for a long time. "I'm sorry to have been the one to tell you. You have a conscience. I know that. I always liked you." He walked out the door.

Nicole sat there. She couldn't drink her coffee. She tried, but her hand was shaking too much. She didn't want to spill it on her suit. After two hours, she wiped a tear from her eye, took a small mirror and tissue out of her purse, and dabbed under her eye where her mascara had smeared. Then she rose quickly and walked to the records storage room. She signed in and pulled the Al-Nasser file. She sat at a table and slowly opened it. There were classified reports an inch thick, and at the very bottom of the file were three photos. She could barely focus on them. Abbu's face was black-and-blue and terribly swollen. One eye was puffed up like a softball. His nose was smashed and no longer in the center of his face. You couldn't see much of him beyond that because he had duct tape wrapped around his mouth and his entire body. He was taped to a stretcher so he couldn't move. He looked like a mummy, she thought. She stood up and marched out of the storage room with the file.

"Hey, you can't take the file with you without Mr. Lee's approval," the guard said.

"I'm going to see Mr. Lee right now."

She walked right by Lee's assistant. "Do you have an appointment?" she asked. Nicole ignored her and strode through the door.

Lee didn't seem the least disturbed at her sudden appearance. He wasn't a stickler for protocol. "Good morning, Nicole," he said.

She sat down. He grinned. She knew that he knew exactly why she was there. "What the hell happened with the Al-Nasser case?" she asked.

"Yeah, that's a tough one. We'll get to the bottom of it. There weren't supposed to be photos," he said.

She sat there dumbstruck for a moment. All he was worried about was the damn photos. She took a deep breath to steady herself. "Al-Nasser's dead," she said. "He was tortured. He probably suffocated to death in the heat. Doesn't that bother you?"

Lee answered slowly in his soft, sing-song voice, "That was a mistake. We didn't want him to die. That was the last thing we wanted. We needed information out of him."

"He didn't know anything!" she said, too loudly. She could barely control her voice. "He was a taxi driver for God's sake."

Lee maintained his flat expression. "Could have been . . . but we don't know that for certain. We can't make any mistakes on our watch. We have to make certain."

"What about the Geneva Convention!"

Now he looked sharply at her, and she knew she'd finally reached him. He was put on the defensive. "It doesn't apply in this case. You know that. Terrorists aren't covered by the Convention."

"But it turns out he wasn't a terrorist."

"We didn't know that at the time." He looked sternly at her. "Look, like I've said many times, we're at war. We have no margin for error. The next 9/11 could happen at any time. I wish you could see the CIA memos the vice president gets. Al Qaeda could strike again at any minute. They probably will. Cheney is on our ass every day. And he rightly should be."

"The legal rationale is weak."

"The rationale is not weak! When we're at war the commander in chief's power is absolute. Everything we've done is defensible as a matter of law."

She slammed the file down on his desk and opened it and pointed to the top photo. "Look at this and tell me what we did was right. Just look at it."

He glanced down just for a second and then looked out the window like he was studying the sky. "I've already seen it. I try not to let it bother me. I think about those two planes flying into the World Trade Center."

Nicole sat there. A thought flashed in her head. *I should resign.* But then she thought about how hard it had been to get to where she was in her career.

"Maybe you should reassign me to domestic work," she said. "I don't think I'm cut out for this. I've been feeling really stressed lately."

He looked at her. "Listen, I know this work is tough. But I wouldn't have you here if I didn't think you could handle it. You're a top-notch lawyer, and you've done a great job so far. Besides, I already reassigned David and I can't afford to lose you right now." He paused for a moment, thinking. "Why don't you just take a few days off to relax? You're upset, I can see that, but I'm sure that once you've had a chance to think about it, you'll realize I'm right."

She sighed. She felt she should say or do something more to change his mind, but she didn't know what. "Maybe I should take some time off," she finally said.

"Sure, do that. We can spare you for a weekend. Even a few days, if you need it. Go to Florida or someplace. Sit in the sun. It's nice down south this time of year."

Florida. Nicole thought about Edna and her request. "You think I should take a break and go to Florida?"

"Sure. Go ahead. Sunshine. Beaches. Palm trees. It would do you good."

"Okay, I guess I'm going to Florida."

She got up and began to leave. As she got to the door his voice barked out, startling her. "Nicole!"

She turned around. He was holding the folder out to her. "Put this back in the storage room and don't take it out again."

She took the file and left. On the way back to the storage room, she ducked into her office. She shut the door. She took out the photos and placed them in a manila envelope and stashed them in her purse.

Beware O wanderer, the road is walking too.
—Jim Harrison

In 1921, Martin was twenty-two years old, and he'd spent nearly his entire life on his family's 560-acre farm near Munich, North Dakota. His parents, Benjamin and Katherine Tabert, were hardworking, hardscrabble farmers of German-Austrian heritage. Benjamin Tabert was born in 1857 in Germany and immigrated to the United States in 1874, originally settling in Cottonwood County, Minnesota. Katherine was born in Austria in 1863 and immigrated to the United States in 1881, also settling in Cottonwood County. Benjamin and Katherine were married in 1882 and homesteaded near Munich, North Dakota, in 1901. The Homestead Act provided that anyone could claim 160 acres free if they lived on the land for five years and made improvements. That was not much land in North Dakota, and it was a rough start, but they kept their nose to the grindstone and were proud of making it. They slowly built up their farm over the years, buying adjacent land, adding a large barn in 1908; raising cattle, hogs, and chickens; and planting large fields of spring wheat. The children came thick and fast, and Katherine bore four daughters—Tillie, Helen, Alma, and Edith, and eight sons— John, Edward, Henry, Otto, Rudolph, Walter, Albert, and Martin.

Katherine's life was one of washing clothes, cleaning, and cooking. Two things were certain: the boys would come in dirty from working in the barn and fields every day, and they ate an astonishing amount of food. Although she loved them fiercely, she found it a relief when they began to go off into the world on their own.

By the time World War I ended, most of the Tabert brothers had started farming for themselves; one became a salesman, one a student at the University of North Dakota, and Otto was in the military service. Only Martin was left at home to help Benjamin with the family farm. Martin was a trustworthy young man and not one to grouse about hard work. Benjamin hoped he would stay put. It was difficult to farm that many acres without help, and although most of the grown sons lived nearby and still helped with threshing, they had their own farms to tend. Hired hands were tried from time to time, but good ones were hard to find. Not everyone had the grit to work twelve- to fourteen-hour days in the summer heat on the Dakota plains, and then endure the long cold winters, where there would be nothing to do for weeks at a time, and one only went outside to feed the livestock. Only a son could be depended upon.

In 1920, Otto Tabert came back from the service. He'd served in France and saw some real action in battle south of Verdun. After his discharge, he'd spent several months traveling around the United States to see the country. He had many lively yarns, and Martin would sit for hours as Otto told of the skyscrapers of New York City, the Washington Monument in the nation's capital, the Boardwalks of Atlantic City, the tree-lined streets of Savannah, and the oranges and alligators of Florida. He had traveled through New Orleans during Mardi Gras. He talked of the pageantry of Carnival on Canal Street, the marching bands, the floats, the bizarre and colorful masks, and the beautiful dark-haired beauties with big swinging hips. He talked of the Southern architectural charm, the balconies, the cemeteries with graves high in the air, and flowers everywhere. He described the food: crayfish—which Martin couldn't even imagine—gumbo, shrimp, oysters, fowl covered in sauces, and beignets fresh out of the frying grease. He talked too of moonlit nights, huge paddle boats, and "darkies" dancing on the edge of the mighty Mississippi.

Martin wanted to farm eventually, but after listening to Otto's stories he knew he would never be happy until he had seen a bit of the world first. He'd never traveled farther than the town of Devils Lake, forty-five miles from Munich, in his entire life. His parents could see the wanderlust in his eyes, too, and they were not completely opposed to him getting out and about a bit, but they wondered who would help Benjamin with the farm work. That was worrisome. They suggested that Martin should take a shorter trip during the winter. Perhaps he could take the train to Fargo or St. Paul and stay in a respectable hotel for a week or two. Why, their neighbor, Knute Flugekvam, had taken the train to St. Paul in 1915 to see the movie *Birth of a Nation*. He still talked about it, too. Couldn't he do something like that?

Otto disagreed with their parents. Otto told him, "Martin, you must get out of here! If you don't, you will slowly rot away from the inside. There is so much to see in the world."

Martin was hesitant for one reason: "I can't go, for who will help Pa? He will surely die of a heart attack trying to work the farm by himself."

Otto had planned to stay home for only a few months before seeking his fortune in Chicago. He wanted to obtain a construction job and work on skyscrapers. But when he saw how excited Martin became when he heard about the sights and how keen he was to travel, he felt for his brother. Otto said he would agree to temporarily take Martin's place and help his father on the farm while Martin traveled. So, plans were set. Martin would leave in late September, after the harvest. He would travel across the country for six months. He had a little money saved up; it was not enough to last six months, but he was a strong healthy young man and could stop and work pickup jobs along the way.

Of course, when Martin first made his travel plans, it was before he fell in love with Edna. That was an unexpected event, and it made it difficult to leave when the time came. However, she promised to wait for him. Since she was seven years younger and her parents were opposed to their dating yet, he thought it wouldn't hurt to wait for her as well. They would have their whole lives together.

When the time came, Martin carefully prepared to leave. He wore a black sateen-shirt, pants, coat, and hat, and he packed a small valise with a change of clothes, a razor, bar of soap, pocket mirror, handkerchief, pencil and paper, small Bible, and a pocketknife. He said his heartfelt goodbyes to Edna, and then on the appointed day kissed his dear mother goodbye. She had tears in her eyes and she gave him a box of sandwiches and hard-boiled eggs as he headed out the door.

Martin boarded the train in Devils Lake, bounding up the steps to the passenger car. He liked riding the train. The powerful sound of it. The locomotive hissing and the train lurching and bumping until it finally gathered speed, then the clickety-clack, clickety-clack, as it rolled along. The smell of iron and steam. He watched the countryside fly by and the telegraph wires outside the car dipping and rising with each pole. He'd never been so happy.

Martin's first stop was Chicago. He intended to stay only three days but became so enamored by the city—there was so much to see—that he spent two weeks there, staying in a cheap downtown hotel for a dollar a night. He had passed through Fargo, St. Paul, and Milwaukee on the train, but Chicago, by its sheer size was something else entirely. The city dazzled his mind, and he made mental notes to tell it all to Edna when he returned. He walked the streets gawking at the tall buildings, the lights, the store fronts. He wandered into the department stores where there were more goods than he could ever imagine. Clothes for the men on the right and clothes for the women on the left. Furniture—beds, dressers, iceboxes, washing machines. Toys of every variety—oh, how he wished he was a child again. He visited the stockyards, Navy Pier, and Wrigley Field. If he came back through in the spring perhaps he could see the Chicago Cubs play!

Martin heard about speakeasies from fellow lodgers at the hotel, and he would walk by and hear the music from the sidewalk. The men walking in wore jaunty hats and had a cool confidence. The women laughed loudly and wore dresses that showed their ankles. He was afraid to enter, however. He didn't think that it was a place for farm boys from North Dakota. He ate hot frankfurters, coated with thick mustard and chopped onions, on the street, and occasionally dined at restaurants where he tried exotic food he'd never eaten before—oysters, spaghetti, Waldorf salad, shrimp cocktails, and pineapple upside-down cake.

One day Martin went to the Central Library on Michigan Avenue between Washington and Randolph streets. He'd heard about the dome there, decorated with Tiffany glass, which he badly wanted to see, and he also wanted to study some maps for his further travels. There he met a young man by the name of Eddy who was spending the afternoon reading. He was traveling too, and they got to talking breezily along until they were shushed by a librarian. Martin offered to buy Eddy a soda at a nearby soda fountain. While sipping seltzers, Eddy told him his story. He said he was eighteen years of age and he was born in St. Paul, Minnesota. His mother passed away when he was six and his father was a hapless alcoholic and couldn't care for him and his four siblings. He was confined to an orphanage, the State Public School for Dependent and Neglected Children, in Owatonna, Minnesota. At the age of ten he was placed in the private home of a German farmer by means of a Minnesota Indenture Contract. He spoke bitterly of it and said he was treated like a farm animal and forced to work seven days a week every day of the year. He had to sleep in a windowless attic room, which was cold in the winter and oppressively hot in the summer. He attended school only irregularly, and only from late fall to early spring. Every morning he was forced to kneel and say what he was told was the German Orphan's Prayer:

> Thanks to God, I will never forget I am a poor orphan.
> The trials and tribulations of life will better my state
> here on earth and after death, so I must be faithful
> and humble in serving my master and those who
> feed me and keep me clothed and fed.

Nearly every evening he would face a bare-assed paddling for some minor transgression or not working hard enough. During the day the farmer would frequently cuff him with a stiff slap to his ear. He pulled off his cap to show Martin his ear, which was badly misshapen, like a cauliflower, with a penny-sized hole in it.

The farmer's wife backed up her husband in everything and treated Eddy just as bad. She fed him separately from the rest of the family in a corner of the kitchen and only leftovers. He was never once given a present on Christmas or his birthday. He said one day last summer the farmer had given him an especially vicious thump on the ear for failing to cover the butter crock in the root cellar, allowing rats to eat some of the butter. He'd been hit so hard that he fell to the ground and his head spun. Eddy couldn't take the abuse anymore, and a short time later he knocked the farmer on the back of the head with a two-by-four. As the farmer lay unconscious,

Eddy went to the house and took the farmer's savings from a jar, nearly fifty dollars, while the wife screamed and beat him about the head with a broom. He said he thought he'd earned it and then some for all his work. He fled and he'd been traveling ever since, living on a dollar or two a day, and earning money by doing odd jobs as he traveled. He'd just finished work on a road work crew in Indiana and said he was paid well there. He was currently spending his nights on a fifty-cent cot at the YMCA, where he slept in a room with forty other snoring men. He spent his days in the library where he could study, write, and memorize passages of books.

The two boys agreed to meet up later that evening and see some sights. They had a fine time, strolling the streets, eating hamburgers, and drinking bottles of soda. It wasn't until late in the night that they got in a little trouble. They were sauntering down Division Street when a doorman of an unmarked speakeasy accosted them. After asking where they were from, he said that farm boys from the Midwest were welcome in their establishment anytime. In fact, because he could see that they were good hardy upright boys, he would give them a free beer if they bought the first one for a dime. They could hear the sound of a Victrola coming through the door and the music sounded cheerful. Eddy had occasionally tapped into the farmer's German homemade beer in the cool milk-house and developed a taste for it. He wanted to check it out. Despite his partial German heritage, Martin's family had never been beer drinkers, so Martin asked if they had sodas, and the man said they did. Martin thought there would be no harm in having a couple more sodas.

As they entered the establishment, Martin wasn't entirely comfortable. It looked surprisingly fancy given the outside of the building, with red velour draping throughout, fifteen-foot mirrors, and brass light fixtures. The maître-de asked Eddy to remove his cap and showed them to a table covered with a black tablecloth.

They sat down and gawked about. Eddy drew Martin's attention to two attractive women sitting at the bar who were looking their way. One was a blond and the other had dark hair cut short. They were painted up in rouge and powder and dressed in shimmering velvet dresses with slits up the thigh. Martin and Eddy paid their dimes and were served their beer and sodas by a waiter in a black jacket, bowtie, creased trousers, well-polished shoes, and white gloves. A few minutes later the two women flounced over and asked if they could join them. Eddy said, "You bet," before Martin could even think. The smell of thick sweet perfume nearly overwhelmed Martin as the two pulled up chairs and sat down, the blond next to Eddy, and the brunette sliding close to Martin. The girls called them "handsome young fellas" and asked them where they were from.

"North Dakota," Martin said.

"Minnesota," Eddy said.

"Are you farm boys?"

They nodded.

"My, I bet you're strong," the blond said to Eddy.

He flexed his muscle and expanded his chest. "I've pitched some hay in my time," he said.

"I'll bet you have!" she exclaimed, and the two women giggled.

As they were chatting, the brunette leaned in close to Martin, holding his eyes, as if growing up on a farm in North Dakota was the most interesting thing in the world. Her low-cut dress showed the heavy curve of her bosom and she rather nonchalantly rested her forearm on Martin's thigh as if they were old chums. Martin looked over and the blond was being just as friendly toward Eddy. They tried to make small talk, but Martin and Eddy found they didn't have much to say to such elegant city gals. After chatting for a few minutes, the women asked the boys if they would buy them a drink.

Eddy looked at Martin, Martin shrugged his shoulders, and Eddy said yes. They weren't paying a lot of attention when the waiter served the two women each a fancy miniature bottle. "We always drink champagne," the blond explained. The waiter poured a little of the bubbling champagne into each of their glasses. Martin was about to inquire about the cost when he was distracted by the brunette shifting in her seat so that her garter, a ruffled band of silk and rosettes, peeked through the slit of her dress. He tried not to stare. Part of him was attracted to this woman, while another part of him wanted to flee.

The girls each had a single sip of their champagne when they asked to be excused because they saw someone "we just have to say hi to." Martin and Eddy were left alone and wondering when the girls would come back. Later they saw the two women sitting and laughing gaily at another table with a group of men. "I bet they're laughing at my ear," Eddy lamented. Martin assured him that they weren't.

The two boys were about to leave when the waiter came over with a bill for six dollars for the two miniature bottles of champagne. Eddy protested vehemently, arguing with the waiter about the cost. "That's more than two days' wages!"

"Didn't you agree to buy the girls a drink?" the waiter asked.

They had to admit they did. The waiter raised his hand as a signal. Two big, beefy men with tight suits suddenly appeared at the table. The waiter explained that the boys were refusing to pay for drinks they'd ordered for the women. The two men called them "dumb farm hicks" and threatened to take them in the back alley and beat the holy crap out of them if they didn't pay up. Eddy threatened to call the cops. The two men laughed, "We own the cops. They'll beat the hell out of you and throw you in jail to boot."

Eddy was still arguing with the men, and Martin was thinking that they shouldn't have come in there to begin with, so he said, "We don't want any trouble," and he paid.

As they were leaving, the waiter gave them the two miniature bottles, still half full, and told them they might as well drink it. "Don't feel bad," he said. "This happens to all the farm boys who come to town."

Eddy later reimbursed Martin three dollars and after a breakfast of eggs and fried ham at a lunchroom the next morning, the two boys split up. Martin was heading south, and Eddy said he would stick around a few days until his money was gone and then he was thinking of joining the navy.

Martin was happy that he'd seen so much in Chicago, but he'd also spent nearly half of his money and knew he would have to find ways to live cheaper and earn some money as he traveled. From Chicago, Martin traveled south on the train again, stopping in Jefferson City, Missouri, and then Springfield. On the way he talked to his first colored man on the trip. He was a porter, dressed in a perfectly pressed uniform and sharp cap, and he introduced himself and said to call him "J.P." Martin was wary at first. He'd met only one colored man in his life before J.P. That man had been on a threshing crew that came through North Dakota in 1919. Martin remembered that he was a big, strapping guy who could pitch as many bundles as three ordinary men. Martin sided up to him one day as the men took a water break and asked him where he was from. He said he was from Alabama, and he thought that North Dakota was grand country in comparison. Of course, it was summer then, so he had not experienced the terrible winters. They only had a brief conversation, but one of the farmhands pulled Martin aside a little later and told him that he best not be conversing with "the nigger."

"Niggers carry knives or razors and they will cut you from asshole to appetite if they get their chance," he said.

J.P. didn't look like a man who would be carrying a knife or razor, at least not on the train, so once Martin got over his initial fear, he thought J.P. was a fine fellow. He knew all the best stops, best hotels, and best restaurants from Texas to Canada. They got to talking right along, and Martin told him about his brother Otto's service in World War I. It turned out that J.P. had been in the war too and served in the all-Negro 93rd Infantry Division and had seen heavy fighting in France. He talked about returning home after the war, expecting a hero's welcome, but the country looked aside. "Before I went they was all tellin' me, 'Go fight for *our* country, fight for *our* country.' When I got back to Alabama it was, 'This is *white man's* country, *white man's* country.'" He said he never wanted to go back to sharecropping, and being a porter was one of the few decent paying jobs a colored man could get.

J.P. spoke too of how the Ku Klux Klan was active from the Gulf of Mexico to Canada, and the colored folks were deathly afraid of running up against them. The porters traded information on their whereabouts and stayed away from areas where the white-robed Klan was night riding. Martin had heard of the Ku Klux Klan, even in North Dakota. There was a chapter in Grand Forks and Martin had read about them in the newspaper. The "Grand Dragon" of the North Dakota Klan, F. Hadley Ambrose, was a senior minister of the First Presbyterian Church of Grand Forks. He warned about "Negroes" coming to North Dakota and the dangers they posed. He had linked Negroes with Jews, Catholics, and other "agitators" who they wanted to keep out of the state.

When J.P. found out that Martin was running low on funds, he talked to the colored servers in the dining car and got him a meal at half price. Martin dined that day on a big breakfast of calf liver, eggs, bacon, hot biscuits, and coffee. Then they packed him a lunch of beef tongue sandwiches and shortcake, and J.P. snuck it to him for free with a wink. Their generosity astounded him, and he began to realize that life was not always as he'd been told.

Outside of Springfield, Martin said goodbye to J.P. and joined up with a group of husky harvest workers heading south. Like many young men of that time, they traveled with the hobos, jumping freight trains to traverse the country. The hobos taught them the ropes — how to ride on the tops of boxcars or on the draw rods below the bodies of the cars. It was dangerous if you didn't know what you were doing. Martin heard stories of men who'd fallen off, their arms and legs severed or their heads crushed. The railroads in the middle of the country would often just let the men ride for free if they weren't too obvious about it, but the hobos told him that down south it was different. "Bulls" were hired by the railroads to throw people off the trains, often busting their heads with clubs in the process. Martin was warned to watch out for them.

Martin no longer had sufficient money for nightly hotels, and he stayed in hobo jungles along the side of the tracks. The hobo jungles were nothing but burlap and tar paper shacks and lean-tos, populated by men huddling around campfires, dressed in dirty overalls, patched trousers, buttonless jackets, and smelly old sheepskin coats. They were looked down upon by higher society, but seemed to Martin to be decent enough people who were quick to share their last bit of food or drink. He ate delicious hobo stew made from a stolen chicken, potatoes, onions, salt, and pepper boiled up in a large metal can over a fire. He met all types — people out of work, teachers, mechanics, labor men, anyone who didn't have the fare to ride the trains legally. He sat around the campfires with them and listened to their yarns, learned to drink beer for the first time and play cheap hands of poker.

He met a Wobbly—a member of the International Workers of the World—at one of the hobo camps. He was an old fellow, held his head bent to one side and was given to a strange tic on his lower lip. Occasionally a small stream of drool ran down his chin, which he wiped off with a dirty red handkerchief. He said his name was Tom Yates, and Martin sat with him and a few other harvest hands around a fire near the tracks one night. Tom was a quiet fellow at first, but once he got to trust them, he opened up and talked like he couldn't turn off the spigot. He admitted to being wary of strangers because most of his fellow Wobblies had been put in prison or run out of the country by anti-union thugs, Pinkerton detectives, and federal agents. The ones who were left were forced underground and were always on the look-out for spies and detectives. Tom told how he'd worked as a migrant worker and then a union recruiter for over twenty-five years, moving from the hop fields of California, to the mines of Utah, Colorado, and Montana, on to the wheat fields of the Great Plains running from Oklahoma to North Dakota, and as far east as the lumber camps of Minnesota and Wisconsin. He'd spent nearly two years of that time in various jails and had been bloodied, busted, and beaten by clubs more times than he could count. He barely escaped a lynching in Butte, Montana, in 1917, diving down a railroad embankment and nearly breaking his neck fleeing vigilantes.

Martin had heard of Wobblies before. Occasionally, Wobblies came through the farm country near Munich and tried to organize the harvest workers. His father had spoken about them, saying that he thought their fight was just, given the conditions he'd heard about in the mines out west and the lumber camps in Minnesota. He simply didn't want them on his farm. "They want an eight-hour workday, and if we had that here we would never get our crops harvested."

When Martin heard Tom's stories, it was hard for him not to be sympathetic to the man's plea for justice for the working man. He told of men recruited to travel across the country for temporary work and promised one wage and then found that the wages were much lower when they arrived. He told of men dying in mine shaft cave-ins because the bosses refused to pay for basic safety equipment. He talked of mothers and children sick and dying in tents and lean-tos in the work camps in the fields of California for lack of decent food and sanitation. "The bosses is in it for themselves. No one is lookin' out for the working man. If the working man complains or strikes for better wages, the powers that be weigh in and start busting heads with a vengeance. They got the power," he said, "and power determines who has the biggest club. The biggest club rules the world. Why, this land was built on the corpses of men who were worked to death so that a very few could enjoy their champagne and caviar and fine cigars."

Martin asked, "Are Wobblies communists?"

"Hell no," Tom said. "That's what the powers would like folks to believe, but we're as different as bread and water. Communists believe in the power and control of the state. We believe in the power of the working man and industrial democracy. One union. One union is what we stand for!"

Tom was a good talker and offered to sign the men up right then and there for an initiation fee and give them a red membership card. Immediately after saying it, he looked around at the men — all dirty, down-beaten, and poor — and said, "On second thought, you men best keep your coins in your pocket for your next meal. The union's probably dying anyhow. We're beat up and there are few of us left anymore . . . but . . ." He jumped up in a snap shouting, "We shall rise up again before the end of time and free the working man!" He began to sing a Wobbly song.

Workers of the world, awaken!
Break your chains, demand your rights.
All the wealth you make is taken
By exploiting parasites.
Shall you kneel in deep submission
From your cradles to your graves?
Is the height of your ambition
To be good and willing slaves?

Arise, ye prisoners of starvation!
Fight for your own emancipation;
Arise, ye slaves of every nation.
In One Union grand.
Our little ones for bread are crying
And millions are from hunger dying;
The end the means is justifying,
'Tis the final stand.

It was a defiant, triumphant song that gushed forth with fervor and echoed across the land. At first, the men watched him as if he was a mad man, but before long one man joined in, then Martin and the other men, and they were soon shouting the song out too, and stomping around the fire in a circle. The fire threw immense shadows of the men onto the surrounding trees, making them appear to be giants, and for a moment in time, Martin felt a deep happiness from the comradeship of these men.

Martin and the men left Tom the next morning. He was headed west, and they were all headed south, but they gave Tom a pat on the back and wished him well. Tom handed all of them pamphlets and leaflets about the IWW, but once he was out of sight, one of the men advised them to throw them away. "If the authorities catch you with this literature down south, you'll disappear and never be seen again."

Martin was glad he didn't pay an initiation fee, because he was now very short on funds and work was harder to find than he expected. He would stop at farms alongside the railroad track, hoping there wasn't a bone polisher, the hobo term for a mean dog. He would clean the soot off his face with a little spit, dust off his clothes, comb his hair, and knock on the farmhouse door asking for work. Often he would be greeted by a mistrustful face and a "git outta here," but other times they would give him some work, especially if he had a chance to explain that he'd grown up on a farm and knew farm work. Sometimes he would earn a dollar or two, but more often it was simply a meal and a place to sleep in the barn for a day's labor. He chopped firewood, put up fencing, and stacked hay bales. He got a job east of St. Louis shelling corn for four days. The farmer gave him scant meals—only chitlins and greens—and three dollars for four long days' work.

He had an unsettling experience northwest of Nashville, near the Missouri border, where he got a job cleaning a hog barn. He walked up to the door of a small weathered farmhouse and was greeted at the screen by a fat lady who must have tipped the scales at two-hundred fifty pounds or more. She called to her husband inside the house. "You got some work for a bindlestiff, Donald?"

He heard the man yell back, "Give him the boot."

"Ain't you been sayin' you lookin' for someone to clean the hog barn?"

The husband came to the door and looked Martin up and down. He was a smaller man, about Martin's size, except scrawny looking. "You ever swung a pitchfork at a manure pile before?" he asked.

"Yes sir, many times."

"Twenty-five cents a wagon load. Grub and a place to sleep."

Martin took the job. It wasn't until he started that Martin realized he would only be able to do a few loads per day. The barn hadn't been cleaned in a decade or more and was three feet high with hog manure. Packed solid like turf. Every pitchfork-full had to be worked back-and-forth and back-and-forth before it could be dislodged from the compressed heap of manure. It was the toughest barn cleaning he'd ever done. Every once in a while he would come across the remains of a baby piglet in the manure, the mother sow having rolled over and crushed the life out of it, and the farmer not bothering to pick it up. The food was plain but edible. He slept in the hay loft.

Problems started on the second day when the farmer's daughter began to hang around watching him work. She was a plump fifteen-year-old—plump cheeks, plump breasts, and a plump rear end that moved north, south, east, and west with every step. She wore a torn and soiled blue cotton smock that was much too short for a fifteen-year-old and showed plenty of her chubby white legs. Even at twenty-two, Martin could see that she was the type whose ripe sweetness would quickly fade the first time her belly swelled.

On the second day, her daddy saw her at the door of the hog barn watching Martin and hollered at her, "Git back to the house." She ran off, and he came over and warned Martin to stay away from her. "Best keep your eyes on the shit pile. She's got the devil in her. I think she's come in heat and she likes to tease men and get them all bothered up. Can't knock it out of her. She's going to hellfire, sure as can be. You're warned to stay away from her unless you is set to marry her. Her mother was about the same age when she be-witched me, and I was shotgun-wedded nine months later."

Martin heeded the warning. He thought she was nothing in comparison to his Edna. Later in the afternoon, Martin saw the farmer leave for the field with a team of horses, and he noticed that the girl was back at the barn door watching him. He told her, "You best get outta here. I don't need any trouble." She just giggled and rocked back and forth on her heels, and Martin began to think she was only half sane.

That evening when he was getting ready for sleep and washing his face at the pump, he noticed the girl watching him again. The rays of the setting sun shone through her smock outlining her curvaceous figure. She had one hand on her hip, and she was staring at him like he was the last chunk of pork in a big pot of beans. "You're the man I want," she said. He splashed the cool water on his face, and when he next looked up, he could see that she had her hand under her dress and was rubbing herself indecently. Martin turned his head but couldn't help stealing a look now and again, just to see if she was still doing it. It was enough to bewitch anyone, and Martin had to restrain himself as his pecker hardened like a steel rod.

He was drying his face on the dirty towel when he heard a roar. It was the farmer, red in the face and mad as all get out. "I told you to stay away from that boy," he yelled at the girl. He grabbed her by the hair and pulled her toward the house, yelling back to Martin as he went, "You're going to get yours too, boy." He heard the girl's screams from the house and knew she was getting a good thrashing. Martin took off running without waiting for his two days' wages.

Martin rode the rails to Memphis and jumped off with two other men outside of town. He was hungry and started to make his way alone towards some gray, unpainted shacks and lean-tos on dirt alleys across the railroad tracks, hoping to find some work or food. One of the other men ran after him and grabbed him by the shoulder and insisted he come with them. "That way is jigtown," he said.

"What's jigtown?"

"You know. Niggertown. You don't want to go there."

"Why not?" he asked.

"Well . . . you just don't, that's all. They're niggers. Don't you know nothin'?"

Martin stayed two nights in Memphis, but it was a rough city with no work to be had, so he hopped another train heading south.

Martin rode in a box car looking out the door. He saw the country rolling by, and he could see it was changing. Cotton field after cotton field. The brown smudges of smoke drifting up as straw-hatted tenants burned the fields of broom sedge and blackjack. Black sharecroppers plowing around old stumps. Spanish moss now hanging from cypress trees. Faded white plantation houses covered in dead vines. Small towns with general stores, mule markets, cotton gins, and tin-roofed houses.

He got a two-day job in northern Mississippi, beating cotton stalks down. He'd never done that type of work before, but he picked it up quickly. The farmer gave him a hickory club about the length of a good walking stick. Then he sent him out in the field where he walked down the rows, beating down the stalks on either side. The stalks were about ankle high and dry and brittle in the winter and they beat down easily. Martin walked steady, got paid by the row, but only made five dollars and sixty cents in three days. The man charged him two dollars for his food, leaving him with three dollars and sixty cents.

Martin spent Thanksgiving in Jackson, Mississippi. He stayed in a hotel near the river for fifty cents a night, hordes of bedbugs biting him as he tried to sleep. He had a room at the end of the corridor on the third floor, and he could hear the din of laughter as men and women opened and shut doors all night. It was a lonely Thanksgiving, no turkey and fixings like his mother cooked, and he was sorely missing Edna. He was committed to traveling for six months as he'd planned, and winter was setting in, so there was no need to go home yet, but oh, how he thought about her at night. He could remember every detail of her sweet face and her bright eyes as she ran up to him at the grove under the tallest cottonwood tree. He wrote Edna a letter:

Dearest Edna,

I hope this letter finds you well and enjoying the season with your beloved family. I miss my folks and home and the prairie. Most of all I miss you. How fondly I remember our last meeting at the grove and your fine gift. Every day I pull the watch fob out of my pocket and look at it and remember the cranes and the beauty and wonder on your face that day. I have experienced so much on my travels. The world is a wonderful but strange place. Oh, the things I have seen! Cities so big that you could walk for days and never see all the sights. Hills and trees in the countryside stretching as far as a man can see. Nowhere is it as flat as where we live. I have met many kind people and a few mean ones. We will have so much to talk about. It is my fondest wish that we can travel together someday.

We will be together again soon.

Faithfully and forever yours,
Martin

He walked the streets in Jackson for three days, knocking on doors and asking for work. "No, no, no," was all he heard. He was getting mightily discouraged when he walked up to a two-story brick house on North Congress Street—white columns in front, a spacious veranda, and two paired chimneys giving it an elegant style—although the home did not appear particularly well maintained. A woman came to the door, dressed in a long black dress. Her face was chalk-white, and she looked to be in her late sixties or early seventies. She greeted him with a stern look. He smiled, clutching his hat to his chest, and asked about any yardwork she might need done.

"No, can't say as I do."

He thanked her and was about halfway down the walk when she called out, "Wait, young man. Come back here."

Martin turned around. "Where you from?" she asked.

"North Dakota."

"Oh my, honey-child, you shore are a long way from home . . . come to think of it, I could use someone to do some garden work on the east side. I've been putting it off, but I might as well have you do it, seeing as how you're here right now and eager to work." Martin wanted her to keep talking just to hear the sound of her cordial Mississippi voice.

She introduced herself as Mrs. Clifford Phillips and showed him around the side of the house. He could see that bushes had grown up without recent pruning, now nearly covering the window. She called the bushes "English Yew," and she wanted them hacked out to plant irises in the spring. "I'll pay you two dollars for the job," she said.

That was good money and Martin quickly set to work with a pick and shovel. He soon discovered, however, that the roots were tough and gnarly and ran deep. By mid-afternoon he had the bush out, but he thought the remaining soil too sandy and rocky to support flowers. He went to the door and explained that he was taking the wheelbarrow down near the river to bring back some good black dirt. "That's a fine idea," she said, "but I can't pay you more than two dollars, if that's what you're thinking."

"No, ma'am. No extra charge. I'm just thinking that would be best for your flowers come spring."

The sun was going down when he finished and walked up to the door.

"I've been watching you out the window," she said. "I can see it was harder work than either you or I expected. You wash yourself up in the sink now and stay for supper."

Once Martin entered the dining room, he was surprised to see the table set with a white tablecloth, china plates, and fancy sterling silverware. Two candles were lit on each end of the table in heavy wrought-iron holders. He didn't think the table was for him, but there were only two places set and no one else about. Mrs. Phillips introduced him to her help, Josie, a Negress, appearing even older than Mrs. Phillips, who was dressed in a gray dress and a starched white apron. Mrs. Phillips explained that her Josie had been with her for over forty years. Martin was taken aback as Josie began to bring food out from the kitchen: buttermilk biscuits, greens with ham hocks, chicken and dumplings, mashed potatoes, fried tomatoes and okra, several types of pickles and relishes, applesauce, and finally, coffee and a chocolate meringue pie for him, and a small dry sherry for Mrs. Phillips. Mrs. Phillips was exceedingly gracious and talkative, and Martin stayed several hours as she told him about her family history going back many generations to her ancestors who'd come from Scotland as indentured servants. She spoke too of her dear late husband who'd passed away three years ago of a sudden heart attack and what a fine gentleman he was. She confessed that she sometimes still talked to him during the day, until the realization struck that he wouldn't answer. She asked Martin about his family and his travels as Josie put piece after piece of pie on his plate. "Do you have someone special?" she asked.

"Yes, I do. Her name is Edna. She's sweet as can be and smart as a whip. I never told anyone this before, but when she gets old enough I intend to marry her."

"How old is she now?"

"She just turned sixteen."

Mrs. Phillips laughed. "That would be considered plenty old enough in Mississippi. Why, they say it's best to marry as soon as the sap starts flowing. I was married when I was seventeen, and truth be told, my momma had to let out my dress two times before the wedding day. Ah-hem. Well, enough of that. You're old enough to know what I'm talking about."

Martin suspected he did.

"You need to see a bit of the world, I can see that," she said. "All young men like to do some rambling and roving and see what's over the hill. But once you get home, you hold your Edna close and don't ever let her go. Life is too short not to."

"I will, ma'am," Martin said, and at that moment he felt nothing was truer in all existence.

When it came time to leave, Mrs. Phillips gave Martin his two dollars, added a silver dollar "to buy something special for your gal," and asked Josie to pack him a wooden apple crate loaded with extra food.

Martin ate well for several days, but once the food was gone his prospects soon looked discouraging once again. He found out that the other men at the hotel were a group of yokels. They were mostly hardened men who drank hooch, played a gambling game called "skin" during the day, whored around at night, and worked as little as possible. They were not his type, and after he learned their ways he did not associate with them. He found a cheap cafe that had decent prices, and he went there often. He could get a two-eggs-toast-bacon-piece-of-pie-and-coffee breakfast for twenty-five cents.

One day he was sitting at the counter pondering his travel possibilities when he met a young man about his age and struck up a conversation. The man said his name was Nathan. By the looks of him, he was a sharp-dressed fellow on the rise. He wore a straw hat with a broad band of flowered cloth, a white shirt, black vest, and flared striped trousers. Spotless peg-topped, white-and-black shoes lent an unmistakable jauntiness to his appearance. He'd already traveled down the east coast from his home in Queens and been all the way to New Orleans. He left home with a suitcase full of Bibles to sell and thereby make his traveling money. Now he was plum out of Bibles and looking for work like Martin. He was a quite a raconteur, and Martin spent hours at the café drinking coffee and listening to his stories of how he'd fast-talked some rube out of a dollar with his sales pitches. According to Nathan, it was the poorest folks who would most often buy a Bible—often with their last dollar—believing that God would reward them for their righteousness. The wealthy were already well rewarded, so they didn't have to worry so much about righteousness. Nathan pitched them the expensive gilt-edged Bibles that could be proudly displayed about their homes.

Next Nathan got to talking about women he'd known. You'd have thought that there was no man in the world more desirable than a Bible salesman. He said he'd gotten the go-ahead eye more times than he'd been slapped. He told a story of a woman he met in South Carolina in some backwoods town. He had knocked on the door and she came up to the screen in a white gingham dress that clung damply to her body like skin to a peach. Three young'uns hung on the back of her dress. He was just a few minutes into his sales pitch when she shooed the children out to play and invited him in for a Coca-Cola. He watched as she sashayed across the room and leaned over to get the cola from the ice box, and he knew from the dilatory time she took that she already had her own ideas. He looked around the house and inquired as to her husband's whereabouts. She said he went to the general store, and he would right now be lounging on the front porch with his buddies sipping whiskey, and he couldn't be expected back for hours, if he came back that day at all. Not five minutes later, she threw the Bible he was showing her against the far wall and pulled him into the bedroom. He didn't even have his trousers down and she was naked on the bed, lifting her vulva up and out at him. "Take me, take me, sweet beets," she cried. He said he dove right in and she wrapped her legs around him like a two-bit slut and screamed in his ear for him to give her everything he had. No sooner than he'd done that, she begged him, "Do it to me again." He told her he had to rest up a minute, but she kept her ankles locked around him and wouldn't let him roll off.

He was still on top of her and starting to notice that her hair was matted and stringy and she had a canker sore on her lip and she wasn't quite as pretty as she'd seemed when he'd first seen her at the door, when he heard footsteps and the door was flung open. It was her husband, and he was holding a gun in his hand. She tightened her legs around him, holding him as if he was a shield, which he suspected he was. He heard the husband cock the hammer and he bit her on her shoulder and she released him and he rolled off. He looked up and was relieved when he saw the husband was aiming at his wife and not him. She said, "Honey, you shoot me with that there gun, you ain't ever gonna git any of this again." Nathan jumped out the window, rolling over in a briar bush. He was up and running from the house buck naked when he heard the shot. He stole a pair of overalls off a clothesline and beat it back to his hotel. After a time, he felt some remorse he said—having gotten a woman killed or maimed when he should have been fixed on selling the Good Book—and he hung around town for a few days, hanging low, trying to learn the scuttlebutt. A few days later, he was in the saloon when he overheard some men telling how the husband had indeed shot his wife, but he only winged her in the leg, and she'd declined to press charges.

Martin and Nathan went down to the hobo village near the rail yard and there met up with a group of other down-and-out men. They were all looking for work and talking about the opportunities. Head west to Texas or California or east to Georgia or Florida. Or maybe head south to Baton Rouge or New Orleans. Most were set on California, a land of dreams to them. Martin knew that if he went to California it might be many extra months before he could work his way back home, and he didn't want to do that. He wanted to visit New Orleans like his brother, but Nathan said one could only obtain the foulest type of work there. There was a tall slick-haired man roaming about the yard, seemingly solicitous of the men's welfare, and telling them that there was plenty of work in Tallahassee. "Easy money," he said. "Why, you can make enough in a day picking oranges to live off for a week. Plus all the sweet oranges you can eat." Nathan liked that idea immediately. Martin was scared of the bulls he'd heard about in the South, but the man said it was safe to ride the rails there. It was also in Martin's mind that he might see whooping cranes in Florida. All things considered, heading to Florida seemed like an attractive proposition. It wasn't until later that the men realized they'd been bamboozled, and the man likely worked for the lumber companies in Florida and was trying to steer labor their way.

Martin, Nathan, and a few other men jumped on a Louisville and Nashville Railroad train as it was leaving Jackson heading for Tallahassee. Nathan and Martin found an empty car with a soft bed of straw in it. They stood at the door looking out as the country rolled by. "We're headed for the promised land," Nathan said. "Ain't life grand."

Later in the fading light of the day, Martin got up to piss out the door. The track bed was poor there, and the swaying of the train made it hard to stand up, but he could anticipate the rhythm after a time. Martin stood there, feet apart, and watched as cypress forests and dark swamps rolled by. It seemed like endless miles of nothingness that could swallow a man up. They crossed a river on a high wooden trestle. It looked like a long, long way down.

Nicole's flight landed in Tallahassee at 4:00 p.m. She walked to the car rental agency and rented a compact. She studied a map. Dixie County was in the armpit of Florida, roughly halfway between Tallahasee and Tampa. Cross City was the closest existing town to the area where Martin was supposedly buried. It was a small town with a population of about 1,700, but she would have to stay

The Taste of Dixie Diner in Cross City, Florida.
Photo by Paul Legler.

there. Online she found the Sun Shade Motel. A review of the motel said, "Good enough. Clean rooms and friendly staff." She called and asked if they had a vacancy. They did, so she booked a room.

With traffic it was about a three-hour drive on two-laned highways riddled with potholes. She'd never seen this part of the South before. Many of the small towns looked run-down, with the well-built brick buildings of the past boarded up and replaced by half-empty strip malls featuring The Dollar Store, Dollar General, Dollar Tree, or Family Dollar. Between the towns there were miles of endless pine trees punctuated by the odd house set back in the woods. They could be modern suburban homes, trailer houses, or shacks. There didn't seem to be any particular order. She passed dozens of dismal yard sales, old household goods displayed on tables and used clothing hung on wires between trees. Every few miles there was a fruit stand, now shut down for the season. She watched as the billboards sped by—Waffle House, Shell City, Guns & Pawn, XXX Adult Superstore, Pregnancy Help. Another Waffle House. People in D.C. would make fun of that kind of place, but she loved waffles, and the thought of them made her hungry. Her grandmother, Edna, had often made waffles when she stayed with her in the summer. She remembered how she would eat them one after another, smothered in butter and maple syrup. She hadn't eaten since breakfast, so she decided to stop. The booths were full so she took a seat at the counter. The waitress poured her coffee without asking and quickly took her order. When the waffles came, she spread on the butter and watched it melt. Then she poured on the syrup. She took a bite. They were good she thought, maybe not as good as her grandma's, but pretty damn delicious.

The waitress was friendly, serving all the folks at the counter and she was waiting some of the table besides. Her name tag said "Raley." She had dyed-black hair, and she must have been in her sixties, and she was bustling about with as many as four plates stacked on her arms. Still, she made time for a little conversation while re-filling Nicole's coffee. "You're not from around here, are you, hon-ey?" She had the deep rasp in her voice of a heavy, lifetime smoker.

"No, I'm from Washington D.C. Born in Chicago originally."

"Oh, I worked in Chicago once. At the Palmer House Restau-rant. It was one of the finest restaurants in the country at the time. I've waitressed all over—New York, Pittsburgh, Denver, Seattle. Moved here twenty years ago. Couldn't take the cold anymore. Dumped my husband about the same time. He was a bum. Got a new one last year, a Florida Cracker. Keeps me young."

Later she stopped back to top off Nicole's coffee and asked, "Where you headed, honey?"

"Dixie County."

"Oh my, what on earth for?"

"I'm doing some historical research."

"Good for you. A historian, huh?"

"Sort of."

"Are you traveling by yourself?"

"Yes."

"You better be careful down there. It's no place for a gal trav-eling alone."

"Oh?" Nicole paused. "I'll be careful."

Nicole hadn't thought about any dangers in Florida. She wondered what Raley might be implying. Alligators on the loose? Redneck hillbillies? Her conception of the South outside of Miami (which she'd visited once) and Orlando (where she'd visited Disney World and Universal Studio with her father) was limited. She left Raley a large tip.

Nicole continued her drive. As she got farther south, she no-ticed that the towns seemed to get smaller and smaller and more dilapidated. When she hit the Dixie County line, there was a large billboard, WELCOME TO DIXIE COUNTY, HOME OF THE CITIZEN'S GRAND JURY. THE TIME FOR ARMED REVOLUTION IS NOW! She almost drove into the ditch reading it. *I'm not in Washington D.C. anymore,* she thought.

It was dark by the time she found the motel and checked in. The woman at the desk spoke with an unidentifiable accent, perhaps Eastern European. She asked how many days Nicole would be spending there. She said she didn't know. "You'll have to pay every day in advance then," she said.

"That's fine."

Nicole took her key and walked to her room, which was on the ground floor facing the parking lot and highway, but all the rooms were like that. There were four cars parked outside the motel besides her own. The room was spartan, but clean, and she was glad to see it contained a small refrigerator. She unpacked a few things, although she'd brought very little—two skirts, two blouses, a pair of shorts, a t-shirt, her make-up case, and a paperback book. She sat on the bed which smelled harshly clean of old cotton and bleach. She didn't feel like watching television or reading. The coffee refills at the Waffle House had made her jittery and she didn't feel like crawling in between the sheets either.

Nicole walked outside and sat on a white plastic chair outside her room under the small door light. She tried to ignore the whirling of the night insects. Other than for the occasional car or truck speeding by on the highway, it was still out there in the cooler evening air. Street lights burned in the town, but no one was walking the streets. A feeling of melancholy fell over her. She decided to call her grandmother. The phone rang a dozen times, but there was no answer. That concerned her, but she figured that Edna might be asleep already. She thought about calling her father, but decided that he would worry too much if he knew she was traveling in that part of Florida by herself.

Her mother, Ginny, came to mind and she suddenly felt a strong desire to talk to her. They'd never been close, but she still loved her despite everything. Nicole's mother had left her father when Nicole was just ten years old. She ran off one day with a drummer for the Rusty Dusty Traveling Band, a semi-famous country-folk-rock group. His name was Devlin Johnson, and her mother met him at the Ramada Inn bar in Evansville, Illinois, the night before a concert. Her mother was with her girlfriend, Janice, and Devlin gave them both free tickets to the concert. The two of them left their husbands at home and went to the concert and never came back. Ginny hooked up with Devlin and Janice hooked up with the sound engineer. Ginny and Devlin had settled in Nashville. When Nicole's parents got divorced, her father, Tim, took custody of Nicole. Her mother was on the road too much with Devlin to take her. Nicole visited her two or three times a year in Nashville for a few years, but after high school the visits became Christmas only, and they petered out when Nicole was in law school. Nicole had only seen her mother every few years since then.

"Hello."

"Hi, Mom, it's me, Nicole."

"Nicole. Oh dear, it's good to hear from you. Is anything wrong?"

"No. Nothing's wrong. I just thought I'd give you a call to see how you're doing."

"I'm fine. How about you?"

"I'm fine too, Mom."

"Where are you calling from?"

"I'm in Florida actually."

"Florida? Oh, you're spring-breaking."

"I'm not 'spring-breaking.' I've been out of college for years, remember?"

"Of course. I know that. But spring-breaking never ends. Wasted away in Margaritaville, right?"

"That's your generation, Mom."

"I guess so. Why are you in Florida then?"

"I needed a break from work . . . and . . ." Nicole hesitated, but she decided to tell her mother about Edna's request to find Martin's grave. As she was explaining it, she noticed a prolonged silence on the other end, and she knew it was a mistake to talk about it.

Her mother finally said, "It sounds like a strange request to me. It's better to let the dead lie in peace. Life is for the living, I always say."

"Well, Edna's still alive. I'd like to help her if I can."

There was a noticeable sigh. "Well, that's nice, dear."

"You say that like you don't approve."

"No, no, whatever makes you happy, I guess."

"It's been so many years; it's probably a waste of time." Nicole slapped at a large flying insect that had landed on her leg.

"Of course it is," Ginny said. "You should go to the beach instead. I don't see any point in looking for some old grave. She shouldn't have even asked you. It's so typical of your father's side of the family. It's that Norwegian heritage. They're always so rigid."

"What do you mean by that?"

"Oh, just that Edna is always so concerned about doing the right thing. That strong sense of morality. And no rest until the work is done. That sort of thing. Life is too short for that in my book."

"I don't know about that. Edna knows how to have fun," she said. "I guess she was quite the square-dancer at one time. You hardly even knew her."

"Oh, that's not true. I saw Edna quite a few times. Your father and I visited the farm once before we were married. And she came to our wedding. She drove all the way to Chicago from North Dakota by herself. I remember she gave us towels and sheets and pillowcases and doilies for a wedding present. Imagine that. Doilies! Like we would use those. Ha! I think I used them to patch some jeans."

"She probably spent a lot of time crocheting those."

"A waste."

Nicole was silent; after a long pause her mother said, "Of course, it was nice of her to make them, but we could have used something else."

"Whatever, Mom."

"Why your dad sent you up there to live with her in the summers, I'll never know."

"You didn't want me, remember?"

Ginny let out a huff. "It's not that I didn't want you, sweetie. It's just that Devlin and I were on the road so much. I took you when I could."

"Yeah, twice a year for a week."

"Oh, it was more than that . . . seemed like it anyhow. I guess we were living the fast life then. We have a slower pace now, with the house in the country and all. Devlin's gone a lot less. Spends a lot of time at home. We have two horses you know. It takes a lot of work to care for them. Then he has his bow hunting, too. I don't like that, but he likes to get out in the woods sometimes. Keeps him happy."

There was a pause and the faint sound of air being drawn in, and Nicole knew her mother had lit her "occasional" cigarette. She'd hated her mother's smoking her entire life. The stink in her house and car nauseated her. Her mother resumed, "Maybe I should have spent more time with you after our divorce, but I tried to be there for you when you needed me."

"Mom, I love you, but you were never there when I needed you. You were always off doing your own thing."

"Well . . . you could have called me anytime. You had my number."

"Right . . . maybe you would answer. Half the time you didn't."

"That was before cell phones, dear. I couldn't exactly sit by the phone waiting for you to call, could I?"

There is no one more self-righteous than an aging hippie, Nicole thought. She remembered the time she was twelve and had her first period. She was struck with cramps rising in spasms. There was no one there to show her what to do, and she had no idea of how to put a tampon in. Nicole remembered how she called her mom, but her mom didn't answer, and how she told her dad she was sick, and she spent two days lying in bed with her knees drawn tight to her chest and crying.

"Can we change the subject?" Nicole said.

"Of course we can." Ginny was silent for a few seconds, and Nicole knew she was trying to think about what to say. "Are you eating organic foods, dear? Stay away from those chickens with the antibiotics. I was just reading about that. You need to buy the chickens that roam free."

"I know, Mom, I try to, but that's not always so easy in D.C. The organic stores are mostly in the suburbs. I go when I can."

"Well, it's worth a trip for your health. You know I'm strictly vegetarian now." Then she launched into a long story about her recent trip to India. She'd traveled with a group of women and they had attended a puja at an ashram. Five thousand people were there from all over the world. The swami had personally blessed her in the Holy of Holies at a temple in Tiruvannamalai. "He changed my life," she said. "He has this amazing energy."

This was about the hundredth time that Nicole had heard her mother say that something or someone had changed her life. She couldn't help but roll her eyes. "He reminded me of a young Ravi Shankar," her mother said. "You know, the guy who played the sitar with the Beatles. I used to have all their albums when I was in college . . ."

Nicole tuned out. She despised hearing about her mother's past. It was like the greatest period of time in human history just happened to fall in the years she was young. Her father had been a hippie when he was young too. But he'd moved on and he didn't talk about the summer of '69 for the rest of his life.

Nicole's parents had met as students at Carleton College in Northfield, Minnesota, in 1967. They drove out to San Francisco in the summer of 1969 in a Volkswagen van, and Nicole had heard the story a dozen times about how she'd been conceived in the back of that van parked on a side street where they spent the summer making beaded necklaces and selling them on the street. Her mother dropped out of college when she became pregnant. Her father stuck with it, working nights at a local bar while he finished school. He wanted to become a poverty lawyer and entered the University of Chicago Law School after graduating from Carleton.

Nicole still had a photo of her parents from that period of time that she found after her mother moved out. It was one of the few photos of her as a child with the two of them. Her father is dressed in bell-bottom blue jeans and a tight red shirt and is holding Nicole up in the air. She must have been about two years old, and she is cute and laughing, reaching out with her little hand to touch her father's beard. Her mother is dressed in cut-off jeans and a peasant blouse with obviously no bra. She is sitting in a lawn chair at what looks like a party because there are other people in the far background standing and drinking beer out of plastic cups. She is smoking a joint on a roach clip and looking up and away as if she is talking to someone outside the frame of the photo.

Nicole's father graduated from law school when Nicole was three years old. He worked at Legal Aid for two years doing housing law, mostly unlawful evictions. He was appalled by the housing rented by some of the city's biggest slumlords. He sued them right and left. But over time he became equally appalled by some of the tenants who threw their garbage in the hallways or tore the fixtures out to sell for drug money. Tim's family was living in a small cramped apartment themselves. It was all they could afford on his salary of $11,000 per year. There were robberies in the area, and he didn't think it was a safe neighborhood for Nicole. He quit his Legal Aid job and obtained a position with a large Chicago law firm, Baker and McKenzie, and they moved to Wilmette, a suburb on the North Shore, so that Nicole could attend better schools. Her mother thought her father was "selling out" and wanted to move to California and join a commune. They argued about this constantly, along with everything else. Nicole remembered trying to stop them, begging, "Don't fight Mommy, don't fight Daddy."

Nicole had always been closer to her father. He was an avid tennis player and had started her at a club when she was four years old and would never miss one of her tennis matches. At Baker and McKenzie he specialized in international law. Two years after the divorce, they moved to Bethesda, Maryland, where he worked in Baker and McKenzie's D.C. branch. He joined the Congressional Country Club so Nicole could take lessons from the club pro.

Nicole had always been the type of child who sat in the front of the class, raised her hand at every question, and went straight to the club after school to practice tennis for three hours. She even skipped her senior class beach weekend at Ocean City so she could get more practice in before the junior tennis championship. She graduated from Whitman High School in Bethesda in the top two percent of her class and went on to college at Brown. Her father accepted a position in Hong Kong after she left home and had lived there ever since. He was now the corporate counsel for a multi-national conglomerate and headed the Asia legal division.

It was during the first years after her parents' divorce that her father would send her to her grandma Edna's for the summer. That lasted until she was fourteen, when she decided that she'd rather spend time with her friends in Bethesda. Plus, she was a pretty good tennis player then, and there were no tennis courts anywhere near Edna's farm.

Her mother interrupted Nicole's thoughts. "Are you listening to me?"

"Sure, Mom. I'm just a little spacey after the long drive. What were you saying?"

"I was telling you about my trip to India. It's like the U.S. was back in 1969. People from all over the world. They wear beads and bangles and smoke ganja. The vibe is beautiful, just beautiful. And the sex. My God, the place is just oozing sex. Of course, I don't experiment like I used to, what with the AIDS and all, but I had to experience it as long as I was in India. They have that Kama Sutra there you know, and the swami twisted me around in positions I never knew existed."

"I thought swamis were supposed to be celibate."

"Well, yes . . . but this one wasn't. He could do it for hours."

"Okay, Mom, TMI."

"Well, I'm not dead yet you know. Your sexual needs don't go away just because you reach fifty."

"I understand that, Mom, but I don't need to hear the details. Plus you're married."

"Oh pooh, I told Devlin all about it when I got home. He thought it was funny. We have an open relationship. You know that. He'd do the same thing if he were there. I know he samples the groupies from time to time. I don't care." There was a moment of silence again. "The toilets are bad in India though. That's one thing they haven't got figured out yet. Just holes in the floor. You have to squat. And no toilet paper. Even the porta-potties at a Grateful Dead concert are cleaner, and that's saying something. Did I ever tell you about the time we saw the Grateful Dead at Redrock . . ."

Blah, blah, blah. Nicole thought about her childhood with Ginny. As long as Nicole could remember, Ginny had played the hippie earth-mama part. She didn't believe in boundaries for children. Whatever Nicole did was fine with her. She could stay up as late as she wanted or eat anything. Count Chocula for dinner. She took Nicole to a clinic to get her birth control pills when she was fifteen years old. "I know what it's like when you get those horny feelings," she said. At the time, Nicole had a tennis poster of Chris Evert on her wall and spent two hours doing homework every evening. Her world was tennis and school. She had little interest in boys. She threw the birth control pills away. She wouldn't need them for several years.

"How is your work going, sweetheart?"

"What?"

"How is your work?"

"Fine." Nicole didn't want to get into a discussion about her troubles at work. Her mother had never been supportive of her working for the Justice Department. In her mind it was caught up with the government and law enforcement and they were never to be trusted. She still called police "the fuzz" like it was the 1960s.

"You sound tired, honey. I hope you're not working too hard."

She lied. "No, I'm not working too hard."

"I suppose things got pretty crazy in D.C. after 9/11."

"You could say that."

"I don't trust that Bush and Cheney," she said.

"I'm a few levels below any of that, Mom."

"Well, you're a smart girl. You can always quit and do something else."

"I'm not thinking about quitting, Mom."

They talked a few minutes more, and Nicole said, "I have to go now. I love you, Mom."

"I love you too, dear. Bye."

Nicole thought she should go visit her mother again soon. Maybe next year. She felt a chill settling in with the night. She looked up. It was clear and the stars were sharp. Somewhere toward the rear of the motel, she could hear two raccoons screaming. They made an awful sound that made her skin creep. She walked inside and bolted the door. She sat on the bed again. She remembered her mother's last words of advice: "You need to follow your bliss." That was her mother's solution to everything. She wondered if she was still trying to follow her bliss with Devlin. Was her mother happy? She acted like it most of the time, but maybe if you pretended that the world hasn't changed since 1969 it was easier to find your little space of happiness.

Nicole didn't know what her bliss was. As she sat there, she asked herself, "What makes me happy?" She had no clue. She liked her legal work as an attorney, but when she thought about it, she knew it was mostly the winning and approval she craved. She'd always been like that. Placing first in the tennis tournament, getting straight A's, being accepted at an Ivy League college and Yale Law School, making the Law Review, getting the job at OLC. The only thing she hadn't been 100 percent successful at was men. There were the few short-term boyfriends in college and law school, but no relationship lasted more than a year. While she'd worked in the U.S. Attorney's Office in Chicago she'd dated only sporadically — a fellow lawyer, an accountant, a software salesman — she'd always seemed too busy working. Sixty- to eighty-hour work weeks were normal for her.

Nicole lay back on the bed and looked at the ceiling. A state of heaviness washed over her. It would be hell when she got back to work. There would be a thousand emails in her inbox and a hundred phone calls to return. Then there was the issue of the photos she'd taken from the Al-Nasser file. Thinking about them started to make her heart pound. She needed to bury that in the back of her head. No, she absolutely couldn't think about that now. One thing at a time. She wished she had a drink.

It was 3:00 a.m. before Nicole finally fell asleep, and she didn't wake up until nearly 10:00. She dressed and walked to the motel office. The woman at the desk looked up. "Hi, do you know where the nearest Starbucks is?" Nicole asked.

"No Starbucks. We have coffee. You take. It is free." She pointed to a Mr. Coffee maker in the lobby.

"Thank you." Nicole took a small white Styrofoam cup, poured herself some coffee, and tasted it. It had that dark oily taste of coffee that has been heated for a long time. She added some sugar and powdered cream from the tiny paper packages. She went back to her room to plan her day. As she sipped the awful coffee, she decided to start by going to the library to see if they had any information on Martin Tabert or the convict camps. Then she would drive around to figure out the lay of the land. Tomorrow she would search cemeteries.

Nicole found the library up Highway 19. It was a small building, part of a regional library system, and there was only one car parked outside. The librarian was a middle-aged woman with glasses and long brown hair with the bangs pulled up and back from her face with a barrette. She wore a beige cashmere sweater, a tweed skirt, and a string of fake pearls. She was very gracious and appeared delighted to provide assistance to someone. She showed Nicole to the small history section. It was in the far rear and had the aged-library smell of dusty, seldom-used books. Most of them were about the Civil War. Nicole found a few books that touched on the history of Florida in the 1920s, and she perused through them. She found out that one of the inventors of air conditioning was Dr. John Gorrie from North Florida, and she found out how turpentine was made, but there was no mention of Martin Tabert or anything about the convict labor. She inquired about other sources of information in the regional system, but the librarian said it would take several days or more to get books from the other libraries, and Nicole hoped to be gone by then. She chatted with the librarian for a few minutes before she left. She found out that the population of the entire county was only about 14,000 and that it was one of the poorest counties in the country. "We're still fighting the old traditions of people trying to survive on forty acres and a mule, rock bottom wages in the forest industry, discrimination, and isolation," she said. "The biggest ambition of many of the folks around here is to get on disability so they can sit home and do nothing. People come into the library every week looking for information on how to get those disability payments. Of course, there are some that need it. I don't begrudge them that need it." They talked for a few more minutes about the weather and how the magnolias would be blooming soon. Nicole thanked her for her help.

Nicole then drove around the town and up and down the highway for a few miles to get a sense of the community. Most of the poor whites lived southwest of town. The housing was mostly trailer homes or single-story, run-down clapboard houses. Some still had tin roofs, weathered the color of sun tea. Confederate flags hung from front porches, and old, crudely-painted IMPEACH CLINTON signs hung on trees and fence posts. Collapsed wooden outhouses dotted the back yards. Vines of kudzu climbed every living thing.

The Cross City business district was mostly vacant. The courthouse in the center of town, reminiscent of a suburban hardware store, had an imposing black stone monument of the Ten Commandments on the front steps. Rough looking men drove around the city streets in pickup trucks with pit bulls peering out iron-barred cages in the rear. The men turned their heads and stared at her as she passed. To the southeast of town, the spindly pine forest gave way to pastures and horse ranches. The wealthier whites apparently resided there, and the homes were more substantial, many of them large brick houses in the Southern architectural style, with large yards and horse pastures with white-painted fences. The men drove large SUVs and wore cowboy hats.

The east side of town, and especially the northeast, was dominated by African-Americans. Clusters of noisy children played in the streets. Cannibalized automobiles with broken windows dotted the yards. Much of the housing was dilapidated, just shacks really, providing only minimal shelter from the sun and rain. Nicole could hardly believe that people still lived like that in twenty-first century America.

Later in the afternoon Nicole decided to head south and west to see the country in that direction and to check out the ocean. She needed a beach bag, towel, and sunscreen, so she stopped at a gas station/convenience store that carried a few tourist trinkets. Nicole found a straw beach bag, marred only by a big bright pink flamingo on the front, and she picked up some Tums and a bottle of water along with the sunscreen. She didn't purchase a towel as the only ones they had were decorated with Teenage Mutant Ninja Turtles, My Little Pony, and Confederate Flags.

Nicole drove back to the motel and put a towel from her bathroom, her sunglasses, and her paperback in the beach bag. She studied her map. The closest beach was Horseshoe Beach down Highway 351. Nicole had driven about twenty miles when she hit a detour due to road construction. The detour took her down a rough gravel forest road. There was nothing to see and no houses. Both sides of the road were thick with seemingly endless miles of raw pine woods. After about six miles she began to question whether she was on the right road. There were no further detour signs and she'd passed only one car coming her way. She saw two buzzards fly up from the road ahead and had to swerve around an unidentifiable dead animal they'd been scavenging. She felt anxious as she drove, and her hands were sweaty on the steering wheel. She was wondering if she should turn around and go back, when a pickup truck came roaring up from behind, filling her rearview mirror and buffeting up dust. The road was narrow, so she pulled as far to the right as possible. As it passed it slowed down, and she saw that it was two men with three dogs in the back. A bumper sticker on the rear said, I BELIEVE IN GOD AND GUNS. Once they were around her, she saw their brake lights flash and they began to slow down. Nicole touched her brakes. *Are they trying to make me stop?* She panicked for a second, but the pickup turned off on a side trail that was marked with a sign for a hunting club. She was unhappy with herself for being so apprehensive. In another mile the detour ended, and she was back on a paved road. She arrived at the beach and parked in the small parking lot.

Nicole took the beach bag with her and walked out onto the beach. She took a deep breath of the saltwater smell. Then another. The smell reminded her of when her father took her to the Maryland shore after her parents' divorce. He liked to go to Asateague Island and walk south on the beach to get away from the crowds. There were miles and miles of pristine white beaches with hardly a soul in sight. Her father would join her on the sand, building fantastic castles with moats and towers and gatehouses. Then he would pick her up and carry her into the ocean. She remembered clinging to his neck until she got used to the temperature of the water. Then he would throw her into the air and she came splashing down, giggling and laughing. She wanted the beach to be like that again.

This was not the beach of her memories. It was littered with plastic bottles and items of trash washed up by the ocean. The sand was gray and scuzzy looking, the water foamy like dirty dishwater. There were only a dozen or so people there. She arranged her towel on the gray sand. The tropical air felt stale and clouds blocked out the sun, but she slathered on some sunscreen anyhow, just in case. There was a light Gulf wind. She sat there staring out to sea, her mind unfocused. *I wonder how Edna is doing.* She called the nursing home. Edna was asleep, but she talked to the nurse and was told that there was "no change."

Nicole decided to take a walk along the beach. As she was walking, she was overcome by a feeling like she was in a movie and she was watching herself. The people on the beach were actors only pretending this was real life. She had a part too, but she had no lines that she could think of. She had only walked a few hundred yards when the beach petered out and there was a marshy, mucky area with scattered rushes bending in the wind. For a moment she watched a Great Blue Heron stalking fish in the reeds until her presence made it nervous and it flapped off, slow and low over the water.

She walked back up the beach and back to her car and returned to Cross City. Once in her room she drew the blinds and flopped on her bed. She tried not to think. She had developed a trick for this where she would close her eyes and imagine she was painting the flickering lights and patterns she saw beneath her closed eyelids.

That evening she walked to the nearby Taste of Dixie Diner. A warm waft of deep-fried foods greeted her. There were few people in the restaurant. She sat at a table facing the highway, feeling lonely, and watched the cars on the highway speed past. When the waitress came, Nicole ordered the catfish special. Her father had always advised her to order the special. She ate what she could of the catfish, although she didn't have much of an appetite, and the hush puppies were greasy and overcooked. Her cell phone rang as she was finishing her meal. She looked to see who was calling. It was Lee. She didn't answer. *What does he want?* She found herself gripping the table with both hands. Five minutes later her phone rang again. Knowing she would have to answer it eventually, she picked it up.

"Nicole."

"Hello, Mr. Lee."

"How is your vacation?"

"Vacation?"

"Your time off or whatever?"

"Fine."

"Where are you?"

"I'm in Florida."

"I know, but where in Florida?"

"South of Tallahassee. At the beach."

"In hindsight, maybe it wasn't a good idea for you to go to Florida. I'm hoping you can come back to work soon. We miss you here, Nicole."

"I still need some more time."

He was quiet for a moment. Too long. She wondered what was up. Finally, he said, "Nicole, I always liked you. I thought you were on the team."

"I am."

"Are you?"

"Yes, why would you ask that?"

"Well, we've had a serious breach of security."

Nicole's chest tightened. She took a deep breath. "I don't know what you're talking about."

"I think you do."

"No. What breach of security?"

"The Al-Nasser file. There are three photos missing. I don't have to tell you what would happen if they fell into the wrong hands."

"That's news to me."

"Are you sure?" he asked. "You had the file last. The only other person who accessed it was Stillman."

"David wouldn't take them."

"Well, we'll find out. I'm having his office and apartment searched."

Nicole's chest tightened again. "What? You're kidding."

"No, they're searching it right now."

"You can't do that without a warrant."

"We don't need one when it involves national security."

Nicole's thoughts seemed to travel from her head to her gut. David was taking the heat for something she'd done. She knew she should keep her mouth shut, but she couldn't help herself. "Is that your legal opinion? Because the last time I checked the Constitution, it didn't provide for that."

"Don't lecture me on the law," he responded loudly. "We're at war. I'm beginning to think that you've forgotten that."

"No, I haven't forgotten."

"You better not."

"Is that some kind of threat?"

"Take it any way you want, but you listen to this. Whoever has the photos better have them in a safe place. And they better be back in my hands soon. I won't leave any stones unturned."

"You would have my apartment searched too?"

"Damn right I would."

"Mr. Lee, I have a roommate and I swear the photos are not in my apartment."

"I hope not, but frankly I'm worried about you. You don't seem yourself."

She paused. There was some truth to that statement. "I just need some time. I'm helping my grandmother out right now," she said.

"Does she live down there?"

Nicole lied. "Yes."

"Well, if you need anything, just call. And if you go anyplace else, I need to know."

"Are you worried about me or the photos?"

"Both. I care about you. I want you to come back to work soon. But the photos are a matter of national security. If they get out it could jeopardize our whole enhanced interrogation operation."

"I understand that. First of all, I don't have them. Second, I just need a couple of days or so. I should be back in the office soon. The photos will turn up. They probably just got misfiled somehow. Trust me."

"I can't afford to trust anyone. Not even you. But you do have a good track record up until now. And I think you know that you have as much to lose if those photos get out as anyone. The damn liberal *New York Times* would have a field day. Senate hearings likely. You're linked to what happened. Don't forget that."

"I know. I know. And I'm not happy about it."

"Well, think about it. Think about it carefully. I don't think you want to throw your career away and end up working as some solo practitioner in a strip mall doing divorces and misdemeanor defenses."

Nicole thought about how hard she'd worked to get where she was at the highest echelon of the Justice Department. She had made her choices, and she was far down that road. She couldn't change that now. "No, I don't want to do that," she said. "Just give me a week."

"I'm not entirely comfortable with that. I'll check back with you in a few days."

"I have to go now."

"Okay. One last thing."

"What?"

"I'll have someone keeping tabs on you."

"What do you mean?"

Click. He'd hung up. Nicole looked down at her hands. They were shaking. They didn't look like they belonged to her. She sat on them to stop the shaking.

Nicole badly wanted some calming alcohol, so she drove to the package store down the street and bought a bottle of Pinot Grigio. She drank the entire bottle while watching a late-night movie. She thought it would help her sleep, but she woke up at 3:00 a.m., her pillow wet with sweat. She rose and turned the lights on and poured a drink of water from the sink. She turned the lights back off. She thought about her mother, and she thought about her work, and she thought about her life from her first memories to the present moment. She couldn't sleep and she tossed and turned for hours. Images flashed through her head at lightning speed—her grandmother lying in bed looking so frail, then Martin Tabert's photo and Abbu Al-Nasser's photo. She felt like she was having a difficult time breathing. She wanted desperately to go home.

Two miles outside of Tallahassee in Leon County, Florida, the brakes hissed, the iron wheels screeched, and the train came to a sudden stop. Martin stuck his head out the boxcar door and looked up and down the side of the train and saw it lined by a group of men, all looking rough and armed with axe-handle clubs. Standing farther back, on the small knob of a hill, stood Sheriff Jones, rifle

Guards of a convict labor camp.
Photo courtesy of State Archives of Florida.

in hand. He had a bristly mustache and wore a long duster, about touching the ground, and he was smoking a cigar.

Nathan looked out, too, and said, "Oh shit, we're in a fix now."

"Are they bulls?"

"Worse than that, I expect."

The men with clubs searched every boxcar, rousting the men out, and ordering them to form a line near the tracks. Seeing the clubs put a fright into Martin. He jumped out of the car and lined up, as did Nathan. He counted nine men who'd come out of the boxcars. Seven of the men were white and two were colored. They were surrounded by eleven men with clubs. The men forced off the train were all casting about, trying to get a handle on the state of affairs and their chances. One man made a dash for it. Two of the men with clubs took off after him. He had a good fifty-foot head start, and he ran like a deer. Martin thought he would make it. *Go, go, go.* The man ran parallel to the tracks and then turned and headed for the woods, but he was tripped up by the heavy maypop vines surrounding the track bed. They were on him. He was down on the ground and out of sight, but Martin could hear the thuds and the man's grunts and groans as the clubs hit his body. They dragged him back, a bloody lump on his forehead and his nose gushing blood.

Once the man was thrown into line, Sheriff Jones took the cigar out of his mouth for the first time, and said, "I am J.R. Jones and you men are hereby placed under arrest by the authority duly vested in me as the Sheriff of Leon County. You are charged with the crime of vagrancy for riding this here train without paying your fare. By the looks of you, I can see you're all scoundrels and miscreants. You'll be brought to jail, and tomorrow you will be tried in a court of law. Any other man who makes a run for it, I will not hesitate to use this rifle. I've been known to shoot off a turtle's head from a hundred paces." He stared at the man with the lump on his head, and the man looked down and wiped his bloody red nose with his sleeve.

One man spoke up, "We ain't got no money to pay a fare. That's why we ridin' the rails. Can't you see we're just workin' men tryin' to find jobs?"

"Tell that to the judge," the sheriff said. "Y'all will get a fair trial. We're civilized, law-abiding folk down here. If you're found guilty and you have no money, you can work off your fine." He looked at the line of men, hacked up a spot of smoker's phlegm, and spit on the ground.

The train gave a loud whistle, the couplings clanked, and it pulled away. The men were marched into town and to the jail. The jail was a dilapidated structure made out of rough pine with but one small window. It was lit inside by a single kerosene lantern, casting a dim light on mildew-covered walls. Inside were two cells, empty, except for one drunk sleeping it off, and the white men were put in one cell and the colored men in the other. Martin felt a cold quake strike his body when the cell door clanged shut behind them. The men talked in quiet tones, fearful of the unknown that awaited them. After a few hours, they were fed a mushy cornbread and water. When it got dark, a guard blew out the lantern, and the men lay down the best they could on the bare floor.

Early in the morning, they were marched to the courthouse. The men were forced to stand and told to keep quiet and they waited for forty minutes, shuffling their feet and looking at the plank floor. The bailiff entered and pounded a gavel and said, "All rise."

Leon County Judge B.F. Willis walked in through the back door and sat at his bench. He did not meet the eyes of the men in the room but nodded to the sheriff and shuffled some papers. Judge Willis was a man of medium height, balding, steel-gray eyes, and generally undistinguishable, except when he was unhappy with someone or something. Then the side of his mouth would curl into a snarl. He had a low, calm-sounding voice laced with a haughty, condescending undertone. He was known in Leon County as someone not to be crossed. His power was absolute. Even the sheriff kowtowed to him. It was a power exercised with a casual arrogance, not giving a damn what others thought. Anyone who disagreed with him was dismissed as a fool or worse.

Judge Willis was well-known in the county for having accidentally shot a friend of his in the backside while quail hunting, peppering him good so that he couldn't sit for months. The judge blamed it on the victim, saying that the man should have known better than to get out in front of him when the quail were rising. The man who'd been shot apologized to the judge, saying it was his mistake. Some people thought that the judge should not have been drinking before he went hunting and that the drinking may have contributed to the shooting accident. Indeed, it was no secret that the judge often imbibed on confiscated moonshine. They also thought he should have known where the other hunters in his hunting party were before he pulled the trigger. That was an ironclad hunting safety rule, even in the deep South. But no one in the county would dare express those thoughts until many years later, after the judge had long since passed away from a heart attack.

After he looked at his papers for a minute, Judge Willis turned to the sheriff. "What do we have here today?" The sheriff proceeded to tell the judge how he'd found all of these men riding the rails and not paying a train fare. That made them vagrants in the eyes of the law.

Judge Willis shook his head solemnly. "Do any of you have anything to say in your defense?"

The man who'd spoken up earlier explained again that the men had no money for a fare and were simply looking for work.

Judge Willis spit out his response, "I expect that's a lie. If you were working men you would already have jobs. You'd have money to pay a fare. No, you are men of dissolute habits, hanging loose upon society. Well-disposed citizens cannot tolerate such behavior."

The judge glared at the man, and he didn't dare say anything further. Then Judge Willis said, "I have listened to every particle of evidence in this case, and I hereby render a verdict of guilty."

He fined each of the men twenty-five dollars plus court costs of twenty-five.

One of the men had forty dollars in his shoe and borrowed ten dollars more from a companion and he walked. Some others, including Martin, said they would wire friends or relatives for it. The judge looked contemptuously at them, but shook his head to suggest that such an arrangement could be made. He then ordered each of them to ninety days labor to work off the fine if they couldn't pay it.

Judge Willis turned and addressed the two colored men, standing off in the far corner. "We don't tolerate vagran' niggers here. There was a day when niggers weren't allowed to go riding about the country, laying about, refusing to work, and scaring our women folk. They worked on our plantations, and we provided for them as we would for our own children, and we were all better off. Country has gone to hell since the glory days of the Confederacy, I reckon. But we still have our ways of maintaining order. I don't want to see you niggers before me ever again. I don't ever forget a face, not even a black one. You will rue the day if I do."

The colored men said in unison, "Yas, suh."

Judge Willis said that all the men were to be rendered to the sheriff to work off their fines. The sheriff in turn told them he had a contract with Putnam Lumber Company for their labor. "Putnam Lumber Company has the full authority to use any lawful means to enforce my order. You will obey their employees as you would me or face the consequences. I reckon you'll learn soon enough what those are. Just let me warn you that they don't tolerate shirkers. You will work hard and do as you're told. Do you understand that?"

Every man looked at the ground. The men were then marched back to the jail by the sheriff. They were to wait there until they could be transported to the Putnam Lumber Company convict work camp farther south in Dixie County.

The Putnam Lumber Company had operated in northern Minnesota and Wisconsin for the previous two decades. The president of the company was William O'Brien of St. Paul, Minnesota, who became extremely wealthy from the lumber business and built a mansion on Summit Avenue. After most of the easy lumber in Minnesota and Wisconsin had been cut, the company bought up 300,000 acres in Florida. They began sawmill operations in 1919, exporting lumber to the Caribbean.

Lumbering required hard physical labor, and it was often dangerous work. O'Brien and his partners were used to recruiting Swedes and Finns to immigrate to the northwoods of Minnesota and Wisconsin and work in the lumber camps. The Swedes and Finns were men of few complaints, and they were hardy young immigrants. If the lumber company fed them well and paid them a little, their labor needs were supplied. If the men got injured, which they did in droves, the company cut them loose. There were always more immigrants looking for work. Florida would prove to be something different entirely. Work in the cypress swamps of Florida was too much for most men, even strong Swedes and Finns. It involved working in stifling heat and humidity, often in water up to a man's thighs. Transporting the lumber to the coast, where it could be shipped, was an ornery task. Railways had to be constructed by building up roadbeds over the swamp. The trees were then cut and

A cypress forest in Dixie County, Florida.
Photo courtesy of State Archives of Florida.

logs hauled to the rail line through those swamps where even horses and mules floundered in the treacherous muck.

In addition to the trees cut for lumber, pine trees were slashed to drain the sticky resin, which was used to make turpentine and other naval stores. The process required making V-shaped cuts in the trees and attaching cups to catch the dripping resin, or gum. Then the gum had to be periodically collected in a bucket, which was carried from tree to tree. One man was expected to care for thousands of such trees and it was exhausting work, struggling through the heavy undergrowth, often in mud and water. The men were always getting sick with malaria or cut by sharp palmetto leaves or bitten by snakes. The death rate was extremely high, and they couldn't hire enough men at customary wages. Even colored men couldn't be hired for the work and, indeed, many had fled the area after the Civil War because of the harsh treatment they couldn't endure. So there was always a labor shortage.

Putnam Lumber turned to convict labor as a means to solve their labor shortage problem. For over half a century after the Civil War, thousands of men and women would spend years of their lives, and untold numbers would die, in the convict lease system. Convicts supplied low cost labor and they posed no danger of organizing unions for higher wages. Convicts could also be worked hard—near death—in rain or shine, cold or wet. The state imposed no rules or oversight regarding their treatment. Putnam Lumber considered short-term convicts better than long-term convicts. Men with shorter sentences could be worked to an extreme for their ninety days, but if they worked a long-timer too hard he would likely die before his time was up. Putnam Lumber would lose money on him.

Arresting people for vagrancy was the ideal way to get a steady supply of short-term convicts. Vagrancy covered a wide variety of behavior and could be applied to any man who was not gainfully employed. Leon County, being on the railroad line whereby men came into Florida, was perfectly situated to take advantage of these laws. Later, Martin's surviving relatives would find out that Sheriff Jones had a deal with the Putnam Lumber Company to supply labor for twenty dollars a head. He also had a deal with the brakeman to wire ahead as to the number of men on each train riding without paying their fare. Jones supplied over one-hundred men in the last three months of 1921 alone. The judge also got rich off the deal, scooping up any fines, plus a cut from Putnam Lumber Company as well.

When he got back to the jail, Martin immediately asked to send a telegraph:

> In trouble and need fifty dollars to pay fine for vagrancy.
> Please wire money in care of sheriff. Martin Tabert

Martin sent the telegraph to his brother John at his farm near Munich, knowing that his brother would quickly come to his aid. John received the telegraph late the next day and immediately mailed a bank draft with the money. When the postmaster in Tallahassee received the letter, he notified Sheriff Jones. Sheriff Jones told the postmaster to return it. The Tabert family was surprised when the letter came back several weeks later unopened and marked "Return by Request of Sheriff. Party Gone." Martin had already been transported to the convict camp in the cypress forest in Dixie County, Florida.

Edna woke with a start. She couldn't breathe. She tried yelling for help, but she couldn't get any air. All she could manage was a raspy whisper. "Help me, help me." She thought she was dying. Then something white appeared before her eyes. A blur. She couldn't make it out.

"The tube came out of your nose. Let me fix that."

Edna took a breath, then another.

"Is that better?"

"Yes . . . yes," she whispered. Edna saw a woman wearing a white uniform in front of her. Who was that? Her mind was fuzzy. She tried to rise.

"No Edna, lie still or we'll have to tie your wrists to the bed again. The doctor said you shouldn't get up yet. Maybe tomorrow. You need your rest now."

She quit struggling. It was difficult to discern the present. Too puzzling. The past was clearer.

Edna's grandfather Nils Larson was from Hjardal, Norway. Nils's father didn't have enough tillable land for his children to spread out in this rocky, mountainous country, so when Nils was fourteen years of age his father sent him to sea to learn the trade of a sailor. He spent four years on ships transporting goods to and from Iceland, Scotland, England, and other European ports. It was a harsh life, working sixteen-hour days, sleeping in wet, cramped quarters, and living on hard tack and dried cod. It was not a life he loved, but he felt he had little choice, and he was able to send a small sum of money home every month to his parents.

Nils had been sailing for four years when his ship was hit by a violent storm at sea. The sailors could see it coming, building up in the west in an ugly, dark mass, then churning more and more rapidly as it approached, but despite their pleas, the captain would not run from the storm. He decided to attempt to ride it out, lest he lose time and cargo fees. The ship was already being tossed fiercely in the storm, and lightning was crashing all around, when the captain ordered the main sail brought down. Not one man stepped forward to climb up the mast, which was swaying violently in the wind. The captain shouted for Nils. Nils looked to his right and to his left and each of his fellow sailors looked down. As he approached, the captain held out a rope tied with knots at the end. "You'll climb up the mast and take the sails down or taste this," he said. Nils was deathly afraid of the storm, but even more scared of a whipping, so he did as he was ordered. He ascended the rope ladder to the very top of the mainmast as the wind howled and tried to tear him loose, praying every minute that he not be flung into the sea. He was able to lower the sail, but only at great peril to his life. When they eventually reached port, Nils left the life of a sailor, never to return. He found temporary work in a livery stable and married a pretty neighbor girl, Anna, and children quickly followed. The work paid little though, and his family was often hungry, which put Nils in a desperate state.

At that time, an immigration fever hit Norway. There was free land in the United States for those with the courage to emigrate. Nils felt the fever and thought he could better provide for his family in America, so Nils and Anna gathered up their courage and a few belongings and left Norway in 1881, accompanied by their three children. They crossed the North Sea to Hull in England, took the rail to Liverpool, and then a White Star Line Steamer, *The Majestic,* for the fourteen-day voyage. The weather was cold and the steerage quarters cramped and damp. Their youngest child was just two months old, and the voyage was too much for him; he died mid trip. They said a prayer for him, and he was lowered into the sea as Anna wept. "The Lord hath given; and the Lord hath taken. The Lord's name be praised."

Nils and Anna landed in New York City. They did not speak a word of English, but they received directions from some Norwegians who'd come earlier. From New York they took the train through Chicago to Wisconsin, where Nils went to work with his uncle on a farm near the town of Tomah. The land there was rocky and hilly, the best bottom land taken by earlier settlers. Eight more children were born to Nils and Anna, seven of them boys, and it was tough to raise enough food for the family. Nils thought there might be better opportunities yet in North Dakota, where it was said that there were still miles of rich, level land that could be homesteaded for only a small filing fee. In 1892, they packed up and moved in two wagons drawn by oxen, bringing with them four cows, three hogs, and chickens. They staked their claim on the empty prairie near Munich, North Dakota.

Many Norwegian, Swedish, and German immigrants were arriving in North Dakota at the same time. They came to a world that was unlike anything they'd seen before. No mountains, no trees, only miles of waving grass as far as the eye could see. They were far from cities and only close to the stars, the sky, and the wind.

With the help of a few neighbors, Nils and Anna built a sixteen-by-twenty-four-foot sod house. The land near Munich was flat, not table-top flat, but the few low-lying hills were just ripples on the horizon. There was nothing to stop the wind coming down from Canada, so they cut the sod for the house three feet thick. Anna clay-plastered and white-washed the sod walls to make it more cheerful. Nils built a wooden table and benches, and they bought a small stove, which they heated with brush, cow chips, and twisted hay. The first crop in 1893 was a total loss from drought, frost, and gophers. They had dry conditions for a number of years, but they stuck it out. They milked a cow. They tended a garden. They killed a hog every fall. Nils and the boys shot game—deer and jackrabbits—to supplement their larder in the winter. They were resilient, and through hard work they survived until better years came. In 1905 they had their first good crop and they rejoiced and gave thanks to God.

Towns sprung up on what were once the vast empty plains of the Dakotas. Churches were built, and then more churches, as settlers kept coming. Schools were needed, and little white schoolhouses appeared in every township. Children popped out of their mothers nearly every year and the tough ones survived, replacing the homesteaders who moved on, broken by the winters and droughts. The Larsons were among the strong or stubborn ones who stuck it out and made the community. As others moved on, Nils bought more land for his boys; by 1910 they owned eight hundred acres of land. That was a very large farm in those days, but with seven strapping boys they could handle it.

When World War I came, the Larson boys were all caught up in the war fever. Six of the seven enlisted in the army. Two died in the trenches in France. All of the boys who survived went on to farm. Nils could proudly walk out onto his porch on a clear morning and see five of his son's houses.

Edna's father, Johan, was oldest of the seven boys and the only son who didn't serve in the war. He had married a Norwegian neighbor girl in 1905, and Edna was their first child, born in 1906. Five more children followed in the next seven years. Edna remembered her childhood years as idyllic. With so many children so near in age, they made up their own close-knit group of friends. There were always things to do (after their chores)—swimming in the stone water tank, climbing the ropes in the barn, building play forts in the hay, sailing homemade boats in the water-filled ditches, sledding and ice skating in the winter, and endless games. Fox and geese, blind man's bluff, crack-the-whip, drop the handkerchief, shadow tag, hide and seek, jump rope, marbles, jacks.

They were a poor family but ate heartily. The farm provided an endless variety of food—beef, pork, mutton, chicken, ducks, and geese. Produce from the garden was canned or put in the cellar. Wheat from the farm was hauled to the mill and ground for flour. Edna's mother cooked all the Norwegian dishes at home, and the children grew up learning to love lutefisk, lefse, rommegrot, fattigman, cherost, and flatbread. "Store boughten" food was a rare thing. The children would be thrilled to get a small sack of hard candy and an orange in their stocking at Christmas. Edna would never forget eating her first orange and peeling it and the juice running down her chin and its fruity sweetness.

Edna's mind drifted and she remembered another time when she couldn't get up. Torger stood over her. It was best to lie still.

Edna was introduced to Torger Moen by Helen. Helen was Torger's sister and a cousin of Edna's neighbor. That is how the connection was made. Otherwise, they would have likely never met. Torger was a farmer who lived about sixty miles away, near the town of Rolette. His first wife had passed away during the flu epidemic in 1918, and he'd been batching it on his farm since then. He wanted to marry again. It was too hard for one man on a farm to do everything. He needed someone to do the cooking and cleaning, help with the chores, and bear him children.

Edna was twenty-two years old at the time, an age when most women in the community were married, or engaged, or at least with a steady. Women were considered odd if they weren't. It signified that you had too many unattractive features. From a physical standpoint, Edna was not unattractive. She was pretty enough with blond hair, prone to fly about if she didn't braid it, a bright Norwegian complexion, and soft curves. Many men had tried to court her since Martin's death, but she'd put them off in her grief. Now the callers were diminishing, and she was getting pressure from her friends and sisters. "Don't be so fussy," they said.

She was introduced to Torger at Helen's home. They sat at Helen's table and drank coffee and ate spice cake. Edna nervously stole glances at Torger. She noticed he had blotchy skin from the sun and a red nose, although he was not altogether bad looking. He had washed up and worn a suit. He was a big man with a thick torso and thighs like tree trunks. Looked strong as a bull. The suit was too small for him and she thought the buttons at his belly would pop. She noticed his hands, which were big-boned, knotty, and scarred with calluses, burns, and blisters. They were not the kind of hands she preferred on a man.

They talked about the weather, the crops, the neighbors. Edna complimented Helen on the cake. Helen was a ponderous woman with flesh swinging like bread dough under her arms. She evidently liked to eat as well as cook. It was a pleasant enough time until Helen's children playing outside became quite loud. They were yelling as children do when they lose themselves in some game. Helen appeared irritated and she excused herself and went outside. Edna heard a smack and the squall of a child. Helen came back in. "I'm sorry about the noise. Children should be seen and not heard," she said.

"A little noise doesn't bother me," Edna said.

"I told them to be quiet earlier," Helen said. "Those children will have a visit to the woodshed later. The Good Book says that if you spare the rod, you spoil the child. I don't believe in sparing the rod." She took a sip of coffee. "Our parents raised us the same way. We got whumped good if we didn't behave. Torger can testify to that." She chuckled.

Torger nodded his head.

Helen continued, "Why, I wouldn't think twice about giving a good spanking to a month-old baby if it wasn't behaving. All my children are taught that I mean business."

Edna could not imagine spanking a month-old baby. She looked at Torger, studying his face. She couldn't tell whether he agreed or not.

Torger took Edna to the Chautauqua the following week. The Chautauqua was held at Lakewood Park on the shores of Devils Lake and was well known throughout the Dakotas. It featured programs that included religion, education, culture, recreation, and entertainment for the whole family. Over the years its attractions included William Jennings Bryan, Carry Nation, Billy Sunday, and Theodore Roosevelt. *Something Good is Coming to You!* was the slogan of the Chautauqua. When Torger took Edna in 1928, however, its popularity had declined, and its attractions diminished. The Great Depression, which started after the stock market crashed the following year, would spell its doom and that would be the last Chautauqua held in North Dakota.

Even though the show was not as big as it was in the past, Edna enjoyed a speaker who talked about the mechanization of farming to come, a fiddler, and the Fort Totten Indian School Band, which presented lively musical entertainment.

Fort Totten Indian School Band. Photo courtesy of
State Historical Society of North Dakota, Collection 982, Folder 0, Item 1.

"Do you want an ice cream cone?" Torger asked her after they
heard the band.

"All right."

Torger bought her a strawberry ice cream cone and a bottle of
cream soda to boot.

They sat on the grass under a tree, and Edna licked her cone
and thought how nice it was to have a suitor who bought her a
strawberry ice cream cone.

On the following Sunday, Torger took her on a picnic. They
parked his Dodge automobile in a grove of trees and laid out a blanket over the grass. She made fried chicken for him with potato salad,
pickles, hard boiled eggs, and bread. She noticed that he ate his food
quickly and chewed with his mouth open. She didn't know what to
think about him. He wasn't much of a talker, although he tried his
best to carry on a conversation, mostly about farming. He liked to
brag about his farm, describing it like a paradise on earth. He had

just bought a new binder, the newest model. His sleek Dodge automobile was new, too, and made him look well-to-do.

Edna introduced Torger to her parents. Edna and her mother
served egg coffee and almond cookies, while Torger and Edna's
father had a talk about the crops and weather. The next week Torger
took Edna to a tent revival. Torger told her that the preacher was
well known throughout the country for the miracles he'd performed
and the number of souls he'd saved. By the time they arrived, the
tent was already packed with hundreds of people sitting in the
wooden chairs set up in rows on the grass under the canvas. A large
banner at the entrance of the big tent proclaimed, THERE IS NO
HOPE BUT JESUS. Torger found them a seat in the back. It was
hot and people mopped their brows with handkerchiefs in the air-
less confines. Edna was perspiring and worried that the sweat from
her arm pits would soak through and stain her white dress.

A young girl in a starched pink dress slipped onto the piano
bench and began to play as the crowd rose to their feet and sang.

> Shall we gather at the river,
> Where bright angel feet have trod;
> With its crystal tide forever,
> Flowing by the throne of God?

Edna had never heard such loud fervent voices at a church service. When the song was finished, the preacher strode to the wood-
en pulpit. He smoothed back a sandy cowlick and smiled at the
crowd. He shouted, "PRAISE THE LORD!" The faces in the crowd
lit up as in rapture. The preacher started preaching soft and low, and
Edna could barely hear, but soon he was working the crowd, stomping back and forth on the stage, shouting and gesticulating with his
hands in the air. "There are sinners here tonight who are destined for
the flames of hell. Oh, Lord, wake them up. Let them see the peril
before it's too late."

"Amens" and "Hallelujahs" echoed from the crowd. One woman at the front began twitching, jerking, and babbling in tongues, which worked up the crowd into a frenzy. The preacher shouted, "Do you feel the spirit descending?"

Toward the end, the preacher gave an appeal to come forward to the altar rail and repent and be reborn. "Brothers and sisters, have you accepted Christ? Now is the time." He looked to the very back of the tent and it seemed like he was speaking directly to Torger and Edna. "Do you feel it?" he yelled. "I know you do. I know you do." Many rushed forward to be blessed. Edna did not feel the call. She had been raised in the Lutheran Church and was used to a more sedate religion. But Torger's face lit up, and he pushed her forward. The preacher blessed everyone as they approached him in a line. She would always remember how hard he gripped her forehead with his long bony fingers. "Do you accept the Lord Jesus Christ as your savior?" he asked.

Edna hesitated. She didn't like to feel pressured, but she said yes, just to escape his grasp. He pushed her backward with a sharp snap and she almost lost her balance. "Praise the Lord! Another sister saved."

Ushers came down the aisles, row to row, passing collection plates, and coins clinked in. Torger placed a whole dollar bill in the plate when it passed. After the collection, the girl with the pink dress came out to the piano again and they all sang:

> Mine eyes have seen the glory of the coming of the Lord;
> He is trampling out the vintage where the grapes of wrath are stored;
> He hath loosed the fateful lightning of His terrible swift sword;
> His truth is marching on.
> Glory! Glory! Hallelujah! Glory! Glory! Hallelujah!
> Glory! Glory! Hallelujah! His truth is marching on.

After the song, the people filed out into the deep night, roused and refreshed with the spirit. Torger was excited and talkative as he drove her home. God had brought them together he said. He stopped the car before he got to the driveway and asked, "Would you care to be my wife, Edna? You're a God-fearing woman. Decent. Upright. I can see that. I expect you know your duties as a woman. You're the kind of wife I need."

She answered, "It seems so sudden. I don't want to say no. I can see you're sincere, but I don't want to say yes either. We haven't known each other long."

"What's right is right. It doesn't take long to see that."

Edna didn't feel right about it. Not yet. "That may be . . . for you," she said, "but I need a little more time to determine if it's right for me."

"Yah, take some time if you must."

She talked to her parents about his marriage proposal. They were not enamored with Torger. He was considerably older than Edna, almost forty, and they could see she had doubts. But they also knew that sometimes love comes after marriage. He did have a house and the new automobile. That was something. He must be a hard worker. He came from a solid Norwegian family by all accounts. Maybe she shouldn't be so picky. It was her decision.

The following week he came to her house again to see her. He brought her a box of chocolates. That touched her because no one had ever given her a box of chocolates before. He asked her to take a walk with him. He asked her again to marry him. He told her he would buy her anything she needed for the house: a new ice box, a new wringer washer, a new sewing machine. Edna thought about her sisters who were now all grown and married with children. She also thought about the children she wanted to have. She longed for a home of her own. She badly wanted a sewing machine. She thought about all those things. But, the uppermost thing in her mind was that she thought she could escape the grief that held her in its grips for the past six years since Martin's death. She said yes.

The wedding was held in September, 1928, at the Lutheran Church in Munich. Edna wore a wedding dress of white voile, with a high neck, and trimmed with lace. Her blond Norse hair was fixed in a tight coil on the top of her head. As she walked up the aisle she saw Torger standing at the front of the church near the pulpit. She suddenly felt nervous. He looked like a stranger. *What am I doing? Is this what I want?* She had a sudden desire to flee. The wedding ceremony seemed to happen so fast as she remembered it later. The reverend said the accustomed words, they exchanged vows, and he turned and addressed the guests, "Those whom God has joined together, let no man put asunder . . ." They walked down the aisle, man and wife.

After the ceremony, they had a small reception in the church basement. They served scalloped potatoes, ham, baked beans, and sandwiches, along with coffee and cake. There was no dance following the wedding. Torger didn't want to have a dance, saying that he wasn't much of a dancer and it was a waste of money to pay a fiddler anyhow. After the reception, people filtered away to go home and milk their cows.

They didn't go on a honeymoon, and this was a disappointment to Edna. She'd badly wanted to stay at the hotel in Devils Lake. Edna had never stayed at a hotel in her life, but her sister had stayed there after her wedding and said it was grand. Torger said it was a lot of money to spend just to sleep someplace. He had a bed at home. They could spend the money on other things. He asked her if it mattered to her and she said no, which wasn't true.

They drove home in his Dodge. She was worried because Torger seemed a little drunk. She'd seen him go off with two other men behind the church during the reception, and when he came back she could smell alcohol on his breath. *Men will be men*, she thought.

Edna hadn't seen Torger's farm before the wedding. It was some distance away and on a muddy county road that was not always passable, and Torger had always put it off. Now as they approached the farm her heart sank. Even from a distance she could see that the house was small, and the peeling white paint gave it a gray look. Besides the house, there was a barn, a windmill, a stock pen, a pump house, and a chicken coop. She noticed that the outhouse was a long way from the house. It would be a cold run in the winter.

As they drove closer, she tried to imagine living there. The place looked austere. There were few trees around the buildings to stop the wind, just three spindly ash trees on the north side. Was that why it seemed lonesome? She looked at the surrounding countryside. No, she thought, the lack of trees wasn't the problem. She didn't mind the lack of trees so much. All her life, Edna didn't like to feel hemmed in. It was something else. Then she realized it was the lack of neighboring farms within view. In those days, one could usually look out from almost any farmhouse and see another farmhouse only a few fields away. This farm was set so that a few low-lying hills blocked out any view of the neighboring farmhouses. She hoped there were some neighbor families not far over the hills who she could visit from time to time.

Once inside the entryway of the house, her heart turned to ice at what greeted her eyes. The house had a lean-to kitchen, sitting room, and two bedrooms, one up and one down. She could see immediately that the interior of the house needed painting and new wallpaper. The floor was wooden and the planks warped unevenly. She walked into the kitchen and saw that it was sparsely furnished with only a cook-stove, small table covered by an oilcloth, cupboard, cream separator, and a few wooden chairs. Cream cans in the corner took up additional space. The odor of an unwashed fry pan thick with rancid lard came up to meet her nose. Unwashed cups and plates were scattered upon the table. It was the smell of an old bachelor farmer kitchen. He could have cleaned up better she thought. Still, Edna was at the age when young people have unlimited hope and energy, and she thought that with a few days of cleaning and scrubbing with lye soap she could get it clean. Then she could do some painting and put up new floral wallpaper and sew some curtains. It wouldn't look so bad. It would be her own kitchen.

She had one valise and her hope chest when she got married. The hope chest was filled with table and dish cloths, four china cups, towels, sheets, pillowcases, a blanket, handkerchiefs, underwear, and a nightgown. Torger helped her bring it in the house and into the small downstairs bedroom. She pushed down on the bed with her hands to test it. The springs made a rusty, squeaky sound, and she was dismayed to find that the mattress was filled with straw ticking. As she began to unpack, Torger pulled out a bottle of whiskey and took a lengthy swig. "Celebrating my new bride," he said. He tried to pull her onto the bed.

"You just wait," she said. "I need to get ready." She pushed him out the door. Edna was fearful about what was expected of her on her wedding night, even though her sister Katherine had told her not to worry about it. Katherine had been married three years and already had two children with another on the way. "It all comes natural," she said. "The first time hurts a little, but you get to like it. Why, now we can hardly wait 'til the children fall asleep."

Edna took her nightgown out of her hope chest. She'd sewn it herself and she thought it was beautiful with lace and crocheted rings. She put it on and sat on the bed. She noticed that the covering quilt and pillowcases looked dirty. She got up and put on her new sheets, pillowcases, and blanket. She sat down again. Now she noticed cobwebs on the ceiling and dead flies on the sills of the small window, which was covered by a gunny sack curtain. Huge brown water stains seeped down the walls like giant salt-stained tears. A calendar advertising a stomach tonic was the only decoration on the wall, six years out of date. Her eyes welled with moisture. This was not at all how she had imagined her life on her wedding night.

Torger knocked on the door impatiently. "You ready yet?"

"Just a minute," she said. She took a handkerchief and wiped her eyes. A few minutes later he knocked again. She took a deep breath and let him in.

He came in with his red union suit on and his penis poking out like a tent pole. He smiled a dumb grin. She could smell the alcohol on him from six feet away. He kissed her and she didn't like the foul smell. He lifted up her gown and she helped him pull her underwear off. He pressed her legs apart, fumbled, and entered her with a grunt. It hurt terribly and she bit her lower lip to keep from crying out. A minute later he gave a shudder and rolled off and fell asleep. In the morning she would clean the sheets of blood and semen.

After that, for the first year at least, it seemed that he constantly wanted her in that way. He took his pleasure two or three times a day—in the afternoon after lunch, at night, and often in the barn in the morning. He would see her gathering eggs or tending the horses and the breathless look would come over him, and he would push her down onto the hay. He would hitch up her cotton dress, peel down her underwear, and copulate from behind, his dirty fingernails digging into her rump. Afterwards, she would lie there; spitting straw out of her mouth and listening to him fasten the metal clips of his overall suspenders into the buttons.

Keeping up with the household chores seemed endless. Edna established a routine. Cleaning the house top to bottom on Mondays and Fridays. Sewing and mending on Tuesdays. Baking bread on Wednesdays and Saturdays. Churning butter on Thursdays. Washing clothes on Saturdays. She hated Saturday wash day the most. Torger worked outside all day, and his overalls, shirts, and jackets would be filthy and ripe with the smell of manure. It was an all-day job to get them clean. She would bring in the large oblong washboiler and set it on the stove and fill it with buckets of water. She added soap and brought the water to a boil, threw in an armful of clothes, and stirred it with a long stick. Then she would have to transfer the clothes to a washtub and scrub them vigorously on the scrub board. They would be dried on the line outside in the summer and on wires strung in the sitting room in the winter. All the clothes were later ironed with a flatiron heated on the stove. They never did get ahead enough for Torger to buy her the new washer. Nor the new ice box. Nor the new sewing machine.

She cooked three large meals every day. This was especially hard in the summer. She had to build a fire in the coal stove to heat the water, as well as do the cooking and baking, and when it was hot outside, it was doubly hot inside. The sweat would start the minute the fire was lit and would stream down her body and she felt like she could hardly breathe.

Torger seemed to eat endlessly, gulping down whatever she put before him in huge forkfuls. At every meal she served him first. It was the Norwegian custom at the time and signified that he was the head of the house. He was often finished with his dinner and out the door before she'd eaten more than a couple of bites. Then after eating, she would have to clean up, hauling the dishwater from the pump house by the stock tank.

Edna planted a huge garden that first year, and even though it was dry she hauled buckets of water to keep the plants alive. She canned twenty-five quarts of tomatoes, twenty quarts of beans, forty quarts of sweet corn, twenty quarts of sauerkraut, and thirty quarts of pickles. She lined up the jars on the shelves in the cellar, marveling at the sheer quantity.

Every morning and every evening the cows bawled to be milked. Milking was considered women's work on Norwegian farms, and Edna had milked cows as a child. Secretly, she didn't mind it so much. Milking time was the quieter part of her day. The cows were content then, munching their feed in the stalls, and there was something comforting about sitting on the one-legged stool and leaning into the soft, warm belly of the cow. The stillness would be broken by the first jet of milk shooting out of the teat and hitting the sides of the tin pail, making a sharp metallic sound. Then, the spit-spat, spit-spat, spit-spat as a rhythm was established. The two thin lines of milk would slowly begin to fill the pail with the white froth, creating a sense of accomplishment.

She would take the milk into the house and use their Delaval cream separator to collect the cream. The skim milk was fed to the hogs. She and Torger took the cream to town on Tuesday or Wednesday and then again on Saturday to sell. The cream check was hers to buy groceries and the things she needed for the house — sugar, salt, flour, coffee, baking powder, dried beans, prunes, matches, and material for her sewing projects.

She also took care of the chickens. They ran free in the summer, picking at the manure and searching for insects in the garden, but they had to be fed grain in the winter and watered year round. She gathered the eggs every day, selling the extra eggs in town for twelve cents a dozen, although the price would drop to six cents later as the Depression took hold.

Torger made it clear from the start that he expected Edna to help with the farm work, as well as maintain the house. She had infinite energy, and she accepted this without question. It was the way of life on a farm, and her mother and grandmother had done the same. So, in addition to the cooking, baking, cleaning, sewing, mending, gardening, milking, and caring for chickens, Edna pitched hay to the cows, slopped the hogs, hauled manure, groomed the horses, cut and shelled corn, raked and hauled hay to the hay mow, and did the hundred other things that needed to be done on a farm.

In the midst of the work, there was little time for play, but that didn't mean life was totally void of all pleasure. There were some good days, especially that first year—watching the twin calves that were born in the spring frolicking in the pasture, early morning sunrises casting jets of light on the emerald green fields of wheat, and the time she gathered a jar of crickets from the field and threw them to the honking geese. Even Torger chuckled at their antics as they chased after them.

Then, in the late summer, the threshing crew came for a few weeks. Even though it meant more work, she looked forward to this time because the neighborhood women would work together to feed the threshing crew, preparing three main meals and two lunches for the crew every day. She enjoyed having someone to talk to and the companionship of other women to share the work. They would start at four o'clock in the morning in order to have breakfast ready by five-thirty—pancakes, thick slices of home-baked bread, oatmeal, eggs, bacon, and baked beans. At noon they would make fried chicken, mountains of mashed potatoes, gravy, corn or peas, stewed prunes and apples, coleslaw, and more baked beans. In the evening, it would be pork chops or fried beefsteak, more potatoes, bread, dill pickles, three or four kinds of vegetables, and pies. The men worked hard and ate accordingly. During the day between the three main meals, huge cans of coffee, beef sandwiches, potatoes, bread, cookies and cakes were also sent out to the fields by buggy. Edna enjoyed this time too—watching the steam thresher as it roared away, the men rhythmically pitching the bundles into it, and the huge cone-shaped stack rising higher and higher as the straw was blown out the back. She liked joshing with the threshers as they scarfed down their coffee and food. There were all types and all nationalities—small wiry Italians and Greeks, big Danes and Swedes, quiet Norwegians and Germans, and smiling Irish and Scots who were quick to fist fight.

She had a little excitement one day in late September when she drove the buggy out to the field with the lunch. She got to joking with the men about who was the strongest. A big Swede by the name of Ivar bet the men that he could lift "the little lady" over his head while she stood on his hands. The men thought that was perhaps possible—if he used a wagon or stack of straw to assist her in getting up. So, conditions were added to the bet. He could not use any supports. He had to start from a prone position. Ivar smiled and took the bet and lay down, stretched his hands out above his head, and told Edna to stand on them. She was afraid she would crush his hands, but after much cajoling by the men, she complied with his request. Ivar gripped her feet tightly in his mammoth hands and slowly raised her above his head. Other men gathered around to catch her lest she fall. Then Ivar sat up, still shakily balancing her above his head, and moved slowly to his feet, and stood up straight, and raised her into the air, his arms now stiffly extended, and Edna standing on his hands, high above the men's heads.

Edna laughed with delight and shouted, "Look at me. I'm on top of the world." The men all cheered. The wind thrashed her skirt and she knew the men could see her ankles and then some, but she was having too much fun to be overly concerned about that. After Ivar lowered her to the ground, he collected his winnings and gave her half. It was a bit of fun she would always remember.

After the first year of marriage Edna had settled into her new life. Even if she didn't feel a strong attraction towards Torger, they had worked out a rough partnership. She believed that through hard work and determination she could help him build up a farm they could be proud of. And with Torger as randy as a billy goat, children would surely soon follow. When they were grown a little, they could help with the chores. There was hope.

Then, in October 1929, the stock market crashed, and the nation slid into the Great Depression. Things were bad all over, but no place was worse than the Great Plains. It seemed as if the wrath of God came down with full force upon them. Rain ceased to fall. Clouds of grasshoppers darkened the sky and fell to earth, eating the crops and leaving nothing in their wake but a barren landscape, brown and withered like the face of a dying old man. The sky was never blue. The wind blew and blew, drying out the topsoil, and immense dust storms filled the air. The dust rippled through the windowsills, through the cracked walls, and under the doors. It clung to the walls and curtains of Edna's small house. It covered the table, the dishes, and the furniture. Edna tied a wet rag around her face and mouth to keep from choking on the dust and cleaned and stuffed rags into the cracks in the walls, but it seemed futile. The dust always found some way to seep in again.

Even though Edna hauled buckets of water from the well to her garden every day, it was hard to keep up, and the plants withered in the blistering heat. In the end she was only able to keep a few of the potato plants alive. They seemed to thrive in the dry soil, and she covered them with pails when the grasshoppers came.

With the heat and dust, the summers seemed unbearable. The sun bore down in a cloudless sky, making outside work miserable. It was sweltering hot in their house, too, and the heat blistered the paint and wallpaper. In the evening, they sat exhausted and wordless on their steps and watched the horizon for any signs of clouds that might bring rain.

Winters brought snow, sleet, and intense cold. Torger and Enda huddled around their stove as the bitter wind whistled through the cracks of the house. Torger sat sullen and hunched at the kitchen table, holding his coffee cup. Edna sat with a coat on in the house, her hands growing cold and stiff as she tried to mend or sew. They had little money for coal and sometimes resorted to heating the house by burning cow chips and corn cobs. They piled up manure from the barn around the foundation of the house, three feet high and two feet thick, to help keep the house warm.

On top of the poor crops, prices fell. Torger came home from the local elevator one day swearing up a storm. The elevator would only give him forty-two cents for a bushel of wheat! This was far below his cost of production. What were they to do? Torger borrowed money from the bank in 1930 and 1931 to keep them going, but he couldn't pay it back. The bank repossessed Torger's beloved Dodge, and he scrambled to replace it with a used and dented Model A. The bank threatened to foreclose on the land, too, if payments were not forthcoming, and they were delinquent in paying their property taxes. They toiled and scrimped and made do.

Despite their troubles, Edna kept hoping to get pregnant. Torger wanted boys to help him with the work on the farm, and she hoped that having a child might brighten up his mood. But every month would bring disappointment when her bloody flow came.

Edna didn't say anything, but she suspected it might be Torger. She knew that he'd been kicked in the groin by a horse as a child. She had some knowledge of anatomy from watching the bulls and boars on the farm and she suspected that could be the problem. Maybe his seed was bad.

Chapter 9

M a r t i n

There were many of them and there may have been a string of
insanity in the blood, but at any rate their methods of life were
those of the beasts of the field, and they peopled the wilderness
where they lived with idiots and hideous monstrosities. The
tales told of them do not bear repeating. In time they were
systematically hunted out, like wild animals, and fled to the south,
where they disappeared in the trackless regions of tropical Florida.
Some of them stopped over night, during this migration, in a shed
near where I lived. There were two horrible hags in the party,
that ran on the ground on all fours and had faces like things seen
in a nightmare.

> — J.C. Powell, *The American Siberia; Or, Fourteen*
> *Years' Experience in a Southern Convict Camp,*
> (Homewood Publishing Company, Copyright
> 1891, 1893)

Early the next morning, after the trial before Judge Willis, the eight
men who'd been unable to pay their fines were picked up by a driver working for Putnam Lumber Company. The men were to be sent
to a work camp near the town of Clara in Dixie County, nearly
ninety miles away, a two-day ride. The driver was a tall, skinny,
raw-boned man, bald on top and a ragged beard below, wearing

tattered overalls, and his name was Floyd. He drove up to the jail in a four-wheeled wagon drawn by two mismatched mules—one big and a dark brown, the other small and red, with an oozing scar on its flank covered with flies.

"I got orders to pick up some convicts," he said to Sheriff Jones.

The sheriff replied, "Got a wagonload today and more of 'em coming next week. This country seems to be chocked full of lazy, shiftless no-goods."

The men were shackled by ankle chains to an iron bar that ran the length of the wagon, six white men on the right and the two colored men on the left. Martin knew the white men from the jail cell. They were all young, between nineteen and thirty-five years of age, and ordinary fellows, like Martin, men down on their luck and hoping for something better. But they were in a dire spot now, anxious, and facing something unknown and fearful. The two colored men were discouraged looking souls, one tall and angular, the other small and with hardly any teeth. Both were dressed in ragged shirts, trousers, and a pair of brogans without socks. They undoubtedly had a better idea of what they faced, perhaps not the particulars, but they knew it would be a god-awful ninety days.

Once they got started, Martin could see that it was going to be a rough ride. They sat on the bare wooden floor, and the road was in a rutted condition. Floyd whipped the mules to keep them at a steady lope. The men were bouncing about like Spanish jumping beans, shifting from cheek to cheek as their butts became sore in one spot and then another.

Floyd kept up a steady jabber the entire time. He had been working convict camps for twenty-five-odd years, first as a guard, then as handyman and driver as he became older, and the stories he told of the camps put a fright into the men. He confessed about the punishments he'd seen or participated in over the years. He told of convicts being strung up by their thumbs. Men who had been in camps for years with hands like the paws of apes, thumbs as long as their index fingers, deformed from the stringing up. He told of "watering," a terrifying punishment, which was akin to slowly drowning a man and sounded like something out of the Spanish Inquisition. He talked about sweat boxes that were not much bigger than a coffin and where men were forced to stand in the hot Florida summer sun like living mummies. He said that the camps rarely used sweat boxes anymore, however. The guards thought there was no fun in watching that. Nowadays, most of the camps used the strap for punishment. The guards got a big kick out of seeing the stuffing whaled out of a convict. He said that Putnam Lumber had fired the whipping boss of the camp they were going to, J.B. Burch of Perry, Florida, because he didn't whip hard enough. "The new whipping boss, you'll call him Captain Higginbotham, is determined not to make the same mistake."

"Why do they call him Captain?" Nathan asked. "Is he a military officer?"

"Shit no. You're one dumb bunny. Captain is a term of respect for someone whose duties include bossing the niggers in camp. You'll all best obey his every word or suffer the consequences."

"Don't the law mean anything down here?"

"The whipping boss *is* the law down here."

Floyd kept on jabbering. He said that as hard as the convict camps were, they were no worse than rotting in jail someplace. He described a jail in Madison County that was built out of enormous cypress logs. It was two stories high, and the upper story was used as a living quarters by the jailor. The only entrance to the bottom floor, which held the prisoners, was a trap door from the top and when it was shut the cell was completely black. No light or sound could penetrate the walls; it was impossible to tell if it was day or night, and a man could shriek and howl until he was hoarse and no one would hear him. Food was lowered down in a bucket once a day and the men slept on the dirt floor. There was no ventilation and no place to relieve themselves other than a corner ditch. When men came crawling out of the trap door having served their sentence, they stumbled and squinted like moles against the bright light, and it took weeks for them to recover. He talked too about the turpentine camps up near the Florida-Georgia line that men never left alive, living in make-shift shacks and owing their souls to the company commissary. He called the worst of them, owned by Florida State Senator T.J. Knabb, "human slaughterhouses." He did not elaborate further. He sang an old turpentine worker song as he drove along.

> Teppentime nigger got a coal-black woman,
> Brownskin gal, away she run;
> Coal-black woman she shake like jelly,
> Wash her feets in teppentime gum.

> Teppentime man got a lonesome dollar,
> Grits is cold and the snaps is dry,
> Freeze in winter an' sweat in summer,
> Burn in the teppentime hell when he die.[1]

That night, Floyd fed them hard biscuits and cold beans. He let them get out of the wagon one at a time to relieve themselves while he watched over them with a shotgun. Then they had to settle in the wagon to sleep, the men all crowded together, nearly on top of each other, as they tried to stretch out.

The next day, Floyd was gripped by the thirst and he stopped at a log home near the road and bought himself a jug of whiskey. He took an occasional pull as he drove. The reins soon dangled listlessly in his hands and the mules slowed their pace. He became reflective and told the men he was fifty-six years old, although he looked a lot older. He said he had constant bowel problems and couldn't keep anything in. "Life has shit on me. I'm guess I'm giving back what I got," he said. As a younger man, he'd been a sharecropper in Alabama. "Couldn't make a go of it." He said he went into debt to buy a pair of mules and they both died within a few years. Half his hogs ran off and disappeared in a bad storm. His wife got pellagra. Three of his eight children died of the diarrhea within a year of birth. "You ain't never seen trouble 'til your woman loses a young'un," he said. He nearly died himself of congestive chills after being caught out in the rain. He started drinking more heavily and his wife moved back in with her folks. He found himself at thirty years of age heavily in debt to the landlord, and still falling. He heard there was work in the lumber camps in Florida. There was little to be earned pay-wise, but he figured it beat sweating in the fields or breathing dust in a cotton gin. He up and quit in the middle of the night and moved. Been there ever since.

Floyd said he'd been sick often of late, and his liver was bad too, and he was starting to think about the other side. "Some says that when y'die, if you're a sinner, you'll go t'hell and burn forever. I reckon God don't rest with the whuppin' and beatin' I done'. I expect the fire is already kindled for me."

A melancholy mood fell over the men hearing this, and Nathan began to talk to liven things up some, or maybe it was just a ruse to befriend the man and get a drink of whiskey himself. Nathan told Bible stories from the Old Testament. He talked of Job, and the stories he told made the men feel like maybe they didn't have it so bad. Then he got to talking about all the salacious parts of the Bible. When he strung them together, he made it sound like the chosen people did nothing but fornicate and covet after those they weren't already fornicating with. Talk turned to women as it often does among men thrown together, and Nathan asked Floyd if there were women at the camp.

"Not where you're going, but there are women convicts in other camps," Floyd said. "Mostly negresses and they do provide some entertainment." He told of a woman who'd been convicted of killing her husband with a stick'a'stove-wood upside the head and spent some thirty years in a variety of convict camps on the Gulf Coast. She was well known for being able to wander into the woods anywhere and gather greens—nettles, poke, wild mustard leaves, dandelion, swamp cabbage—and cook them up with fatback or hog maws and, "they were mighty good eatin'." She was also known for her fecundity. "Bore more than a dozen little pickaninnies while in the camps, all different shades of darkie from coalblack to brown-sugar to dusky-white."

"Any white women?" Nathan asked.

"We've had a few. Sorry to see them myself sometimes. Thrown together with lonely, desperate men. Ain't no place for a white woman, decent or not." Then Floyd proceeded to tell the story of one innocent woman in a camp to the south. It seems that this woman was well reared and well educated, not a woman of vice, and got caught up in some trouble down at Key West. He said her name was Virginia Simms, and her father was a well-known businessman in New York City. Virginia was apparently a rebellious young woman with romantic notions, and she and a girlfriend caught a boat from New York to Havana in the hopes of meeting a Spanish Don or other gallant Hidalgo. They somehow ended up in Key West after a few weeks in Havana, and Miss Simms had a brooch stolen. There was apparently a case of mistaken identity involved because the man she accused of the theft had an air-tight alibi. He was incensed at having been blamed, and being well connected in those parts, he managed to have Miss Simms arrested for perjury. She was convicted by a local jury and given a one-year sentence. She was too shamed to communicate with her parents and not fully understanding what lay before her. Floyd first saw her when she arrived at the camp where he was employed as a guard. She was forced to disrobe from her fancy clothes and don stripes, and she cried in a paroxysm of wild grief.

Once imprisoned, Miss Simms abandoned herself to the degradation. According to Floyd, she gave herself freely to many men in the camp. "She was like ol' Eve eating that fruit." It stirred up the camp something fierce. One man who took up with her was knifed by another jealous lover in a spit of rage. Eventually, the Captain of the camp had to house her with him to keep her safe. After her year was up, she put her fancy clothes back on, smiled, and waved to the men in camp as she mounted a buggy. All the men cheered. She eventually made her way back to New York City and resumed "the life of a highfalutin' woman." Floyd told this story with a straight face, and swore it was true, although it seemed curious to Martin, and he wondered whether the telling was colored by Floyd's position.

In the early afternoon they entered a desolate looking area. Palmetto trees grew on little hummocks rising above the stagnant brown water, the huge palmetto leaves interlacing overhead, darkening the scene, and endless water weeds tangling in confusion in the gloomy swamps. "The camp is just up the road a few miles," Floyd said. Martin saw his first alligator as they rounded a bend, and it slid into the algae-thickened water from the edge of the road where it had been basking in the sun.

"Look! An alligator!" Martin shouted in his temporary enthusiasm.

"Ain't you ever seen a 'gator before?" Floyd asked.

"Only in picture books."

"Where you hail from anyhow?"

"North Dakota."

"Ha ha ha!" he laughed. "Well, you shore landed in hell, son."

As they rounded the last bend, Martin could see the convict camp ahead. It was set on a broad sand elevation, no walls, but surrounded by a dark jungle of cabbage palms and boggy pine woods. Two long bunkhouses stood on each side of a yard—one for the colored men and one for the whites. The bunkhouses were not old, but already you could see that weather had aged the white-washed pine boards covering the sides. The boards had been put up green and shrunk, and there were cracks big enough to see through and let the cold night air in. On the far side stood the whipping boss's house. Three bloodhounds lounged in the shade of the porch. An outhouse was erected in the back. Another one-story shack to the near side was the kitchen. A series of small ram-shackled huts for the guards lay on the far side. Farther back yet stood a corral for the mules, a harness house, and two pig pens. The yard was beaten down from the footsteps of the men come and gone, hardly a blade of grass to be seen, dusty, with no trees and no shade. Swarms of flies buzzed about piles of mule dung dotting the yard.

It was about mid-afternoon and the convicts wouldn't be back from the forests until dark. Floyd ordered the men out. "You is supposed to line up here and wait 'til the whippin' boss talks to you," he said. "If you know what's good for you, don't move an inch. He might be nappin' or he might be watchin' through the window. Can never tell. But he don't like it none if you move 'til he talks to you."

"Like hell," one of the men muttered softly.

Floyd turned to see who'd said it. "Mind what I sayin'," he said. "I seen men whipped near to death the first day."

Martin stood rock still like a soldier at attention. He would show them right from the start that he wasn't a troublemaker. He expected that his brother would wire the money and he would be free soon. *Either later that day or first thing tomorrow,* he thought.

Still, the way the driver talked about all the whipping had him worried. His father wouldn't hesitate to give him a few swats with a belt, if he misbehaved, or he'd thought he had. It was the common method of raising children everywhere. But there was a fear even in the driver's voice when he warned them about remaining still. *How hard does the whipping boss whip? How many licks? Do you have to drop your trousers?* Martin wasn't sure, but he knew he didn't want to find out.

They all stood there, tense and rigid, their eyes casting about. They waited and waited, looking toward the whipping boss's house. Once, Martin thought he saw someone looking out the window for a second. He couldn't be sure. It wasn't a hot day, but still they got uncomfortable standing there in the sun.

Martin heard the tall colored man whisper to the smaller. "I is almighty skeery of that thar whip he done talk 'bout."

The smaller said, "Just mind yo' own business, humble down and play shut-mouthed, and you might not git whipped."

"I'm thinkin' on runnin'."

"Dam yo' dumb coon ass. Yo won't get a mile. Yo goona git the livin' mule shit knocked out'n you, you do that." Saliva spit out between his few remaining teeth as he talked.

The taller one kept looking towards the woods desperately, but he stayed in his place.

After an hour, Martin heard a door open, and Higginbotham stepped out. He was an ugly oaf with a ruddy face, bushy eyebrows, a patriarchal beard, and cold gray eyes. He scratched himself and stared at the men. He was not as big as Martin had thought he might be, of middling height, five feet and seven or eight inches. But even from a distance, you could see that he was built stocky, bow-legged, with heavy thighs and gristly forearms.

Higginbotham stood there, watching the men, and they felt uneasy in the silence. He scratched himself again and went around the house to the outhouse. The men waited again for what seemed like the longest time before he emerged. Now he walked towards them and stopped ten feet away.

"Name's T. W. Higginbotham," he said. "I'm the whipping boss of this here camp. I'll say this short and straight. You work hard—and I mean blister-raising hard—and you won't get to know me too personal. You shirk and we get more acquainted. No back talk either. I don't take impudence from any 'em."

He paused and looked the men over. "Anything you don't understand about that?"

"There been a mistake in my case," a fellow named Del said. "I . . ."

A mean-eyed glare from Higginbotham seemed to suck the remaining words right out of his mouth. "Let's get one thing straight," Higginbotham said. "Y'all been convicted in a court of law. Square and legal like. Complainin' 'bout that is the same as shirkin' far as I'm concerned."

Del looked down at the ground.

Higginbotham directed his attention to the two Negroes. "Name?"

The taller one replied "Elihu Swift, suh." Martin noticed that he said "suh" loudly with the most deferential tone of voice he'd ever heard. Higginbotham nodded and looked at the other shorter Negro.

"Andy Johnson, suh . . . marster suh," he said, shuffling and scraping.

Higginbotham nodded again as if he liked what he'd heard. "You men will do some hard time here," he said. "I reckon you know your place." He nodded once more as if to confirm his own words. Then his expression changed and he snarled, "But you's still niggers. I ain't seen a nigger yet that don't benefit from a good whippin'." He glared at the two of them watching their reaction. "Shiftless, lazy," he said. "Born that way. The mark of Cain is upon your race, I expect."

Both men hung their heads.

"I'll teach you some," he said. "There's a lot of things I don't know anything 'bout, but there is one thing I do know, that's how to make mules and niggers work."

"Yas, suh," the two Negroes said in unison, but more softly. Martin noticed that there was a quiet tone of resignation in their voices now.

"One more thing. We got us a whore come Saturday nights to take care of the guards. She's ugly as a dead possum, but she's got a big, wide bottom. Smooth as a sow's ass. You so much as look at her, and I'll have you castrated right then and there. If there is one thing I won't tolerate, it's you tailless monkeys gawkin' at white women."

"Yas, suh."

Higginbotham turned to the six white men. "Name?"

"Fred Werlitzer."

"Delbert Smith."

"Nathan McLaren."

"John Gardner."

"Jeb Neuhaus."

"Martin Tabert."

Higginbotham took a quick step towards Martin, looking him hard in the face. "Sounds like we got us a Yankee here," he said.

Martin wasn't sure how to respond and said nothing, which was a mistake.

"You a Yankee, boy?" he yelled.

"Yes . . . I guess."

"You guess! You guess! Where you from boy?"

"North Dakota."

"North Dakota. That's 'bout as far north as you can git, ain't it?" Higginbotham spit a chunk of dark tobacco chew at Martin's feet. "You best mind yourself. I'd just as soon kill a man from the North as a nigger."

All the new arrivals were given stripes and a pair of heavy shoes or boots, pulled out of a gunny sack by Higginbotham. He would size each man up with a quick glance at his feet and throw him a pair. Most of the men's boots were too large, but they could later stuff them with cypress moss to take up the slack. Martin's boots were snug the first time he put them on. He could see that. But he didn't dare say anything and he figured they might stretch some with time.

The new arrivals were put to work that afternoon splitting firewood for the kitchen. It was dark by the time the rest of the convicts came back from the forest. The arrivals looked up when they heard the shuffling sound of their footsteps. The convicts walked at a fast pace and in a line, guards riding mules in the front and back. Martin thought he never saw a sorrier lot of men. They were haggard, gaunt, and clad in filthy clothes, some in tatters, with dark perspiration stains spread under their arms and on their chests and wet to their waists from working in swamp water. Many were infected by skin maladies, and open pus-filled lesions could be seen on them. They all collapsed around the yard. No one said a word to the new arrivals, wouldn't even look them in the eye.

That evening they all lined up for their supper: black-eyed peas, cornbread, and a little salt pork. Martin would find out that sometimes the meals were worse. If the guards had spent the grub money on whiskey, they might be fed only a sorghum dish that tasted like crude oil and a sort of mushy bread for three or four days in a row. Other days they would be served turnips riddled with green-gutted worms.

The evening meal was eaten out of a bowl as the men squatted on the ground about the yard. While eating, the men were constantly swarmed by flies from the nearby soil pits and middens. Each man used a single spoon. Knives and forks were not used, as it was thought they might be used as weapons for a fight or escape attempt. The noon meal would be the same, except brought out in a wagon to the forest where the men were working. Breakfast was molasses and cornbread and coffee, without sugar, and scarfed down in a hurry while it was still dark in the morning.

Every evening a bonfire was lit in the middle of the yard for the guards and Higginbotham to sit around. Martin noticed that they didn't share the same food but had hunks of boiled pork with beans, or a meat and rice dish they called "perleu," and they ate with plates, spoons, and knives. On Sundays, the guards ate fried chicken and sweet potato pie. They washed it down with water, to which was added some type of liquor out of big brown jugs. After supper the convicts were ordered to the bunkhouse. No one was whipped that first night, but Martin would find out that this was a rare occurrence.

The new arrivals were told the rules by the guards. There was no getting up from the sleeping platforms once they went to the bunkhouse unless they raised their hand and yelled "sir," and were acknowledged by the night watch guard who slept at the far end of the bunkhouse in his own roped off area. Loud talking, gambling, fighting, and any insolence or other conduct drawing attention of the guard would be punished by a whipping. They would be counted every hour and the night watch guard was required to ring a gong on the hour to indicate that he'd done so.

Martin was assigned a bunk by the guard. These were platforms with a space for each man, two feet wide and not more than six inches apart, all in a row down each side of the bunkhouse. A thin, sour-smelling corn-husk mattress was laid on each one, and when Martin lay down he could see the vermin scatter. The walls around the bunkhouse were stained a dusky red, about as far up as a man could reach while lying down, from the vermin the men picked off them in the night and crushed against the boards. A single greasy lamp hanging from a beam glowed all night, flickering and sputtering in the wind that came through the bunkhouse cracks.

The man on Martin's right only gave him a scowl, but the man on the left whispered, "Name's Glen Johnson. Just do what you're told and work hard as you can whenever they is watchin'. You'll get whipped. No avoiding it. The whipping boss likes to test the mettle of the new men. Don't cry out, it only makes him mad. I've seen men whooped 'til they had to be toted to the bunkhouse."

Martin felt a sickening chill listening to that talk, and Glen saw the fear in his eyes. "Hey kid. You can make it. You look strong enough. What's your name?" he asked.

"Martin Tabert."

"What you here for?"

"Vagrancy. Jumping the train, I guess."

"Most of the men are here for the same thing. It's a scam they got going. Cheap labor for the Putnam Lumber Company, and they is all in on it."

Johnson lay down and Martin did the same. His mind was whirling, and he couldn't sleep. After a few minutes he stirred, and Johnson whispered again, "Try to get some sleep; we work from can see to can't see—five o-clock in the morning to eight o'clock at night—and we work as hard and fast as we can. The guards are there to see you do it."

"I sent a telegraph. My brother will be sending money for my fine. I should get out of here tomorrow," Martin said.

"I heard that before," Johnson replied. "Don't be countin' on it. Putnam already paid for your labor. I doubt they will be letting you go before your time is up."

"They can't do that. Why, it would be like slavery."

"It's slavery by another name, but it's legal in Florida. And Georgia, and Mississippi, and Alabama, and Arkansas, and Tennessee, and the Carolinas. They gots to have cheap labor and no one would work here if they didn't have to. Only difference with slavery is that they have whites working too. Wait until tomorrow. You'll see. Colored and whites together in the swamps. Color don't boot with the big white cats; they only care about the money. The white convict and the black convict is sittin' in the same saddle here. The control of the power, the control of the man is all the rich cares about."

Martin sighed. It was too much for him to comprehend. Too much beyond the small world he'd known in North Dakota.

"One more thing," Glen said.

"What?"

"Check the water for the wigglies. You'll be sorry if you don't. If you do get sick, keep up the best you can. Don't let them see you shirkin'."

The next day Martin was assigned to a squad shoveling mud to make a grade to lay the tracks for a rail line that would carry the logs to the mill. It rained every day, and the men worked in water up to their knees. If they needed to change positions or pick up another tool, they were required to call out and get permission from the guard first. It was back-breaking, exhausting work with no rest periods. Even stopping to scratch your louse-eaten flesh could bring a rebuke from the guards and a possible whipping depending upon their whims.

Water breaks were few and when they did come the men had to line up quickly and take turns using a common dipper, gulping the water down and handing it to the next fellow. One guard also did double duty as the water carrier, driving two gray mules infested with horrible looking harness sores. As bad as Martin felt, he felt even worse for the mules. He'd worked around horses on the farm in North Dakota all his life and he could tell when they were thirsty.

Mules hauling logs using high-wheelers from logging site in Dixie County, Florida. Photo courtesy of State Archives of Florida.

Even after a few hours on the first day in the ditch, he could see that these mules needed some fresh water. They were glistening with sweat and he could see the beginning of muscle tremors. At one point, the smaller mule balked and tried to stop and take a drink of swamp water. The driver jerked back viciously on the reigns. The mule turned his head toward the driver and brayed, "Hauggggg-ggggghhhhhhhhhhhhhhhhhh." The driver swore something fierce, locked the brakes, stepped off the wagon with some sort of club, and beat the mule over the head and nostrils until it was bleeding at the mouth.

As Martin took in his surroundings the first few days, he realized he was in a different world. It was nothing like the prairie of North Dakota, which now seemed to him like a pristine paradise in comparison. Tall cypress trees towered up from the swamp blocking out the sun. Below, thick undergrowth and vines climbed skyward trying to catch a ray. Rotting tree trunks were everywhere, often hiding fat, bloated water-moccasins. Big spotted red-and-black spiders ran across the rotted logs in the water. Occasionally in the distance he could see the snout of an alligator rise out of the ooze. An awful stench permeated the stagnant air, and poisonous winged insects clouded around any living thing. Martin was constantly swatting and scratching, and the bites were far worse than the prairie mosquitoes he was used to.

The men would occasionally raise a song as they worked to ease their worries. The guards didn't seem to mind, bored as they were with their monotonous duties.

> Cap'n got a mule, mule on the mount called Jerry;
> Cap'n got a mule, mule on the mount called Jerry;
> He won't come down, Lord: Lord he won't come down.

> I don't want no cold corn bread and molasses;
> I don't want no cold corn bread and molasses;
> Gimme beans, Lord; Lord, gimme beans . . .
>
> If I can just make January, February, March,
> If I can just make January, February, March,
> I'm going home Lord; Lord, I'm going home.[2]

Martin was determined to keep up with the work, but after the first day his feet swelled up from standing in the water and began to develop sores and blisters from his boots. This made it hard to walk and each step was agony. His trousers were soon torn and frayed from contact with the sharp palmetto leaves. He lay in his bunk at night hoping his brother would wire the money for the fine, but as the days wore on it was hard to hold on to that hope. He felt homesick and terrifyingly alone.

On the third day a convict by the name of Max Grimm was in a section gang hauling heavy logs through the swamp. Max was a Brooklyn fireman who'd been arrested near Greenville, Madison County, for stealing a ride on a train bound for Jacksonville. He was clearing the way through the swamp, as he was told, when his grubbing hoe handle broke. Martin saw Captain Higginbotham come riding up a half hour later, get off his horse, and call him out of the ditch. He called Max a bastard son-of-a-bitch for breaking his hoe handle and told him to lie down. He gave him twenty-five licks right there. After his beating Higginbotham told him to get up and get back to work. As it was the custom to run back to work always, Max got up running, but crazy with pain, he ran the wrong way. Higginbotham ran after him and gave him another dozen lashes on his back, neck, and head.

There were twelve guards for the eighty-five prisoners. The guards were all profane, coarse, and brutal; Martin could see that from the beginning. During the day they walked or rode mules, watching the men. They carried shotguns or rifles lying across the horn of their saddles and they weren't afraid to use them. At night the guards gathered in a shiftless mob in the camp yard—sweat-stained straw hats and dirty, cheap overalls—biting off chews of tobacco, spitting, and snorting the rotgut whiskey. Their talk was of nothing but the food they ate, the liquor they drank, or the whores they'd had. Putnam Lumber didn't want to pay the guards much, so the job attracted some of the rudest, foulest dredges of society. Men that no one else would hire. Men with no choice. Men who'd abandoned their consciences.

The isolation of the camp encouraged wanton, sordid behavior. The guards looked forward all week to the local whore who came every Saturday night. She went by the name of Buttercake and she arrived in a fine surrey pulled by two matched percherons and driven by her pimp and husband, a scrawny, swarthy man, possibly of Spanish or Italian blood. You could hear them coming a quarter mile away as the husband announced their arrival by shouting: *Jelly-Roll! Jelly-Roll! Jelly-Roll! Jelly-Roll!*

Once inside the camp, Buttercake stepped off the surrey, painted up and showing her fleshy leg, and that further got the guards' attention. She was dressed in a red cotton shift and she had an old rag, likely a baby's diaper, tied around her head. Buttercake was ugly, that was true, as Captain Higginbotham had said, with a big broad nose, a swelling on her right cheek, and a nearly toothless mouth. But she had watermelon breasts, thick thighs, and wide, deep hips built to take a pounding. The guards lined up and took turns with her in a shack, and she was done with all twelve of them in less than an hour. She handed her roll of money to her husband who pocketed it and they drove off.

Martin had been at the convict camp only four days before he received his first whipping. He'd stopped for just a moment to pull his right boot off. He wanted to spit on the spot where it was chafing the worse and a bloody sore could be seen. He thought the saliva might bring some relief. He had only just pulled his boot off when the guard rode up fast on his mule. "Get that damn boot on. You shirkin' boy. I'm reporting you to the whipping boss. You won't be stopping tomorrow to take a rest."

"I'm not resting, my feet hurt something fierce. These boots are too tight," Martin said.

The guard rode away without responding.

That evening at supper Martin could barely eat, despite his hunger. He'd seen the whippings the previous nights. One night three men had been called out of line. The next night it was seven, including both the Negroes who'd come the same day as Martin.

All the men had been whipped unmercifully. In turn, they were ordered to drop their trousers and pull up their shirts and lie down on the ground. The whipping boss would take his time, forcing them to lie there until the strap from Black Aunty came cracking down. The strap was three or four inches wide, three-ply at the handle and two-ply halfway down. The whipping boss would clench his teeth and rise up on his tiptoes as he wound up in order to deliver the hardest blow possible. When the strap hit, every man in line winced with the sound. The men were struck so hard that the force of the blow drove the man being whipped into the ground.

Most of the men put a piece of wood between their teeth to bite on and keep from screaming out in pain. They would get ten to twenty strokes for most offenses, but Martin heard that men could receive fifty or more if Higginbotham was really mad or liquored-up. Their backs would turn black and be riddled in bloody red welts when he was finished.

Convicts leased to harvest timber.
Photo courtesy of State Archives of Florida.

The hardest whipping was delivered to the Negro Andy Johnson. A guard, by the name of Henry Stevens, had claimed he was shirking. Henry was a loutish, chuckle-headed fellow, who was as likely to lie as tell the truth, just for the fun of it.

"You been shirkin' boy?" Higginbotham asked Johnson with a glare of malevolence.

"No, sir," he said quietly. Johnson had a resigned look of desperation on his face and his arms dropped to his sides in a helpless gesture. He should have known better, but he spoke again, almost under his breath, "He jus' sayin' that cuz I'm a nigger."

"You callin' Henry a liar?" Higginbotham yelled. "Henry, was he shirkin' or not?"

"Yes, sir. Sneaky like, but I saw him." Henry smiled.

"A sneakin', shirkin' nigger," Higginbotham said, his jaw now trembling. "I'll teach you." Then to the guards he said, "You watch the other niggers in line. Any one of them looks away, they get the same. You will see some hard work out of these niggers tomorrow. No shirkin' tomorrow. No-siree."

He had his fetching Negro, Jessup, apply syrup, and Higginbotham ran the sticky strap through the sand to increase the sting. One of the guards snickered, "Whooey. You gonna whoopem good with that there one boss."

"When I do things, I do things right," he responded.

All the guards hee-hawed.

"I bet I can bust this peckerhead open in three licks," Higginbotham said, looking around for any takers.

Not one of the guards took the bet. They'd seen how he would turn the strap in the air so that it came down on its edge and aim for the same spot on a man's buttocks. In a few strokes the skin would be cut open and you could see the dark red blood oozing out, even in the fading bonfire light.

Johnson was ordered to spit out the piece of wood someone had handed him and told to count the strokes out loud. This was part of a game the guards liked to play. They would yell out the counting with the man and then purposely mix him up. "Ten, eleven, twelve, thirteen, ten." This was quite the night's merriment for the guards.

Good to Higginbotham's word, Johnson was cut open on the third stroke, and after twenty licks he was a bloody mess from his thighs to his upper back. Pieces of skin were completely flayed off and his rump looked like jellied beef. The strap became wet with blood, which also flowed down Johnson's side and splattered the ground. Johnson was howling, begging him to stop. When he cried out for mercy, he was given ten more licks. Higginbotham was red with fury, with beads of sweat popping out of his face and running down in rivulets. He gave an audible snort with each lash.

Having seen that, Martin knew what he was in for, and he'd had all afternoon and most of the evening to think about it. As the bonfire was stoked he tried to control his trembling. His name was the first to be called out.

"I knew from the moment I heard you speak, you was goin' to be trouble," Higginbotham said. "You Yankee boys don't know the meaning of work. Come down here in the War and stole the food of the good Southern folk. Come through my pappy's farm and stole his hogs when he was jus' a young'un. I heard him tell 'bout it, many a time."

"I can work," Martin said. "I grew up on a farm. I was shocking wheat when I was ten years old. I got a problem with my boots is all. They're too tight. My feet are blistered something fierce."

"You talkin' back boy?" Higginbotham shouted. "Quit complainin'. Those are fine boots. I can see that from here. You gettin' ten extra licks for complainin'." He stared hard at Martin.

"Let that be a lesson for all of you," he yelled out to the men in line. "I won't have any complainin' in this camp. Specially not from no damn Yankee from *North* Dakota."

Martin received twenty-five strokes that night. When the first stroke hit, it hurt worse than anything he'd ever experienced before. He bit down on his piece of wood as hard as he could and it was still all he could do to keep from screaming. Tears came to his eyes and there were twenty-four to come, delivered just slowly enough that a man had time to contemplate each one. He could hear Higginbotham grunt as he winded up and the strap whistling though the air, so he knew it was coming. He cried to himself, "Oh, God. Why are you allowing this to happen? Please don't forsake me."

Martin was determined never to get whipped again. The men walked seven to ten miles a day to the work site, then worked shoveling dirt for road embankments, hauling railroad ties, cutting down trees or building roads, often wading in water and with the rain pouring down. By quitting time every limb of the body would ache, and they would trudge back to the camp to try to dry out their clothes by fire, eat, and wait for the whipping boss to whip someone or not. Usually he would. One night he whipped an entire squad of twenty men for not getting enough work done. It seemed like once he got started he couldn't hardly quit; he would be panting like a heated dog from the sheer effort.

At night Martin would sit with the other men. They would have thirty minutes to an hour before the lights were put out. The men who'd been whipped would lie down in the bunkhouse and the other men would gather in small groups on the far side of the yard and talk quietly. Often the talk turned to food. Food that they would eat once they got out. The conversation always started with the ordinary and grew to the extraordinary as the conversation flowed from one man to another.

"I'm dreamin' of hog-chitlins and hot cracklin' bread."

"Gravy and biscuits."

"Eggs swimmin' in fatback grease."

"Chicken and dumplings."

"Scalloped potatoes and ham."

"Steak and thick slices of homemade bread with butter."

"Duck in orange sauce with fresh vegetables."

"Waldorf salad and all the oysters I can eat," Martin said.

The men laughed. "You dreamin' big," Nathan said. "I like that."

The men talked too of women they'd known or wanted to know. Wives, girlfriends, acquaintances, strangers. Farm girls lifting up their skirts in the hayloft, fancy-dressed women they'd seen walking down the street, whores and dance hall girls. Tall women, short women, skinny women, and fat women who kept them warm at night. Women with breasts pointing up, sticking straight out, or swinging down like clock pendulums. Asses that were small, soft and smooth, and asses that were stout and wide. Anything with skirts on. Breed didn't matter. White, brown, black, yellow. They were all desired.

Martin kept his mouth shut. He thought about Edna, but she was sacred in his mind. He was not about to besmirch her name by sharing stories with these coarse men.

As they got to know each other better, talk turned to escape. They talked in low voices speculating about the possibilities. The men who'd been there the longest always discouraged it. Maybe it was because they thought they could make it to the end of their sentences. Maybe it was because they'd seen men brought back after being run down by the dogs. Maybe it was because they'd seen men shot. "If you make a move that looks suspicious they don't hesitate to pull the trigger cause that's the orders an' the chance is that you'll be buried in the swamp that night."

Nathan was one who was always talking-up escaping. He said that he wasn't going to stay in camp and be whipped. "No one has whipped me since my mammy and no man ever will." He thought that a man could escape if he got a good enough jump on the dogs. "You would need to keep moving in a straight line northeast across the swamp," he said. "Set your direction by the sun or stars. Eventually you'll reach the Florida Central Rail line. Then follow the track north to Georgia."

Glen was one of the men who discouraged it. He'd spent some time as a linesman for the telegraph company before he was laid off. He knew the country all the way across Florida from the Atlantic to the Gulf. He laughed when he heard Nathan talking. "*Now* you're dreamin' big, but you're deceiving yourself," he said. "It's a jungle out there, infested by wild beasts, alligators, and horrible reptile life. Quicksand too, and muck pools, and mile after mile of toothed sawgrass taller than a man's head. Make no bones about it. No one can get through those swamps. You can wander for days and never make any headway."

Glen told stories of the people who populated the swamp country. They were outlaws he said. People who'd fled to this remote area because they were wanted men or could not abide others. "The outlaw population live in the rudest possible manner. Their usual habitation is a rough log hut with a dirt floor and a skin bed in the corner. Everything they live on is obtained from the wildness. They eat gar, frog legs, tortoises, gator, possum, coons, turkey buzzards, ducks, cranes. Anything that crawls on the ground or flies in the air. Occasionally they go into a settlement to trade for gun powder, shot, and salt. They have no morals, and they will turn you in for a half-dollar or a mess of corn pone. Lynchings and burnings are a regular form of recreation for them. Moonshiners and gator-poachers hide too in secret spots all through the swamp and forest and will not hesitate to shoot anyone they see with their long-barreled rifles."

"Furthermore," Glen said, "the country is full of degenerates of the worse sort who breed with each other without regard to familial relationship. Some of their offspring are monstrosities and are thrown into the swamp to die when they're born. Others grows up with hideous deformities and run around on all fours. You would have nightmares forever if you ever met up with 'em."

Nathan listened, but Martin could see by the look in his eyes that the warnings were not settling in his mind. What was settling in his mind was the thought of the food they'd talked about, a taste of whiskey, and libidinous women with soft bottoms.

The day after Martin's first whipping, Nathan attempted his escape. He and Martin were working on the same crew, digging with shovels at the roadbed. Martin was hurting something fierce after his whipping and trying to keep up, shoveling hard, and not saying much. There was a sticky, persistent drizzle of rain all day, dampening the men's spirits further. He could see that Nathan had the itch to flee and he was looking about and working at a slow pace.

They were watched by a guard named Gabe that day. He was a heavy man with a big neck and a fleshy face and he took guff from no one. "You there, why you tarrying?" Gabe asked Nathan.

"I ain't tarrying," Nathan responded. "This here mud is thick with vines and roots. You get off your mule and see if you can do better if you think it's so easy."

"Shet your mouth, don't you be back-talkin' me."

Martin heard Nathan say quietly, "Hell to him." It wasn't loud enough for the guard to hear, but he knew Nathan had said something.

"Are you vexing me, you bastard? I'm reportin' you to the whippin' boss. He's gonna beat the cow-walkin' hell out of you."

After that Martin knew that Nathan would run for sure. He could see that the dread of a whipping was preying greatly on his mind. "You heard what the men said about trying to escape. You can't get far," Martin whispered to him.

"I seen what happened to you and the others. No man will whip me like that. I'd sooner die. I'm bootin' it when I get the chance."

"There are alligators out there bigger than you are."

"I'll be runnin' too fast for them to bite me."

Martin noticed the guard watching them and he shut up and shoveled as fast as he could until he had a sudden ambush of diarrhea. He raised his hand and the guard nodded his head indicating that he could step out of line. He squatted behind a low brush and his bowels rumbled and let loose. At that moment, he decided that if Nathan made it, he would try to run too.

As he walked back, Martin could see Nathan studying the guard. The guard was sitting on his mule whittling on a piece of wood with his pocketknife. Martin saw Nathan look to the thick woods, which were within hollerin' distance. He was likely thinking that if he could make it that far he might have a chance. The guard sheaved his knife and took out his flask of water and took a swig. Nathan saw his chance, threw his shovel down, and ran. He was surprisingly fleet-footed and was about halfway to the woods before the guard saw him. He raised his rifle. When the shot rang out, every man's heart jumped, but he failed to bring him down. Perhaps his line of shot was obscured by a palmetto tree. At any rate, he put his rifle back in his scabbard, took out a dirty handkerchief and wiped his brow. "God dermit," he said. He didn't ride after him, just turned his mule around and rode back to camp.

An hour later the whipping boss came riding up on his big bay horse, slobber foaming at its mouth, followed by the three bloodhounds. He talked to the guard and surveyed the situation and turned the dogs loose. In no time, the dogs struck the trail and were off barking.

Higginbotham galloped after them on his horse. For over two hours the men listened as they worked. The barking of the dogs grew fainter and fainter and the longer it went on, the more the men thought that Nathan might just make his escape. Some of them were smiling now, thinking about Nathan—running free.

After a time, they could hear the dogs in the far distance letting up a raucous baying. The men knew by the sound that they must have cornered their game. There was no wishing that fact away. The baying went on for some time and then there was silence. The men strained to hear anything, but there wasn't a sound. Even the dust-stained trees in the distant woods seemed to hang still and lifeless.

Higginbotham came back a half-hour later with the hound dogs panting and trailing behind him. He rode right past the convicts working in the ditches and didn't look at them or say a word. They saw a pair of muddy boots, speckled with blood, strung up from his saddle horn. Later, high in the pale gray sky, the men could see buzzards swooping and tilting and wheeling over the spot where he'd come from.

That night the men speculated on what happened to Nathan. They didn't know how he'd died, but they all knew that the whipping boss had "kilt him." They could imagine a hundred ugly ways it could have happened. Fear of the unknown is worse than fear of the known. For days the men all withdrew into themselves and their own thoughts. And, for the first time, Martin sensed the beginning of his own death.

At 6:00 a.m. Nicole walked outside and to the lobby. No one was at the desk, but the coffeepot was on and half-full. Whether it was fresh that morning or from yesterday, it was impossible to tell. She poured herself some coffee, added the sugar and powdered cream, and returned to her room. After she drank it, she fell asleep. She woke up at noon. A large fly was buzzing overhead. She lay in bed,

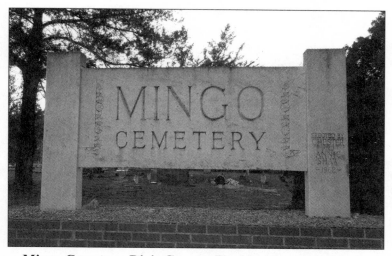

Mingo Cemetery, Dixie County, Florida. Photo by Paul Legler.

watching it. It alighted on the ceiling in one spot and then another. It seemed like her mind had slowed down to a more normal pace and she felt calmer. A plan seemed clear. She would spend a few days more looking for Martin's grave, then she would tell Edna she hadn't found anything, fly back to Washington D.C., go back to work, and find a way to slip the Abbu Al-Nasser photos back into the file. She called her grandmother again. This time Edna answered, "Hello."

"Is that you, Grandma?"

"Yes, dear. How are you Nicole?"

"Okay. I've been trying to reach you for a while. I was worried about you."

"I'm sorry. It's these tubes they have sticking in me. I can't always reach the phone when it rings."

"What tubes?"

"Well, I don't know exactly. Tubes. Just a minute."

Nicole heard her talking to someone in the background. "Nicole wants to know what these tubes are for."

She didn't hear the answer, but then Edna was back on. "They're to make sure I have enough oxygen."

"Okay. Who is there with you?"

"Cathy. The nurse. Checking on me. She's just leaving now."

"How are you feeling?"

"I'm fine, dear."

"It sounds like you were sick for a while."

"Yes, but I guess the good Lord isn't ready for me yet. Not sure why. Goodness knows. I've done my share of dancing here on earth."

"Are you eating okay?"

"Yes, I'm eating . . . some . . . you don't eat so much when you're older."

"Are you getting up and moving around with your walker?"

"Oh, quit worrying about me. How are you?"

Nicole hesitated. She wanted to say, *I'm depressed and I hate my work and I feel like I'm losing it.* But she couldn't do that when her grandmother was so ill. She would worry too much. "I'm doing well, Grandma. I'm in Florida."

"Oh, are you looking for Martin's grave? Humph . . . I probably should never have asked you to do that. It may not be safe down there in Florida for a woman by herself. Maybe you should go back home. I'll send you some money to pay for your expenses."

"Don't worry about that, Grandma. I just got here two days ago. I haven't done much actual looking yet. I'm just getting my bearings so far."

"Oh. What's it like there?"

"It's hot, Grandma. Swampy."

"I've heard that. I still get sick thinking about my poor Martin working in those swamps. And you know, that whipping boss Higginbotham didn't even go to jail. Some jury down there let him off scot-free. That's the worst of it. I expect Higginbotham was sorry when he met his maker and he had some explaining to do. We wish for justice on earth, but it doesn't always happen. Sometimes the worst evil goes unpunished. People have to be willing to step forward and say, 'This is wrong.' That doesn't always happen."

"No, it doesn't, Grandma." She thought about her work. "Sometimes things are complicated at the time though . . . it seems like it anyhow. They taught us in law school to always be able to argue both sides of a case."

"Phew. Don't believe that. Don't let anyone tell you not to make your own judgments about right and wrong. Listen to your head and your heart. They'll tell you what to do."

Nicole didn't immediately respond.

"Are you still there, dear?"

"Yes, Grandma. Just thinking . . . I'll let you know what I find out about Martin's grave."

"Okay, but take care of yourself. Always be mindful of your surroundings."

"I will, Grandma. Bye. I love you."

Nicole jumped out of bed with a sudden burst of energy. She reviewed her notes about the Martin case. Three cemeteries had been mentioned in the historical accounts as the possible burial sites of Martin—at Perry, Clara, and Mingo. Clara and Mingo were not on her highway map, so she decided to start with the cemetery in Perry. Perry was forty-five miles away, up Highway 19. The drive took her through the heart of Dixie County—nothing but mile after mile of swamps and second-growth pines. She passed a small lumber mill with piles of wood chips, sawdust, and shavings scattered in a muddy yard. Trucks towering with spindly logs passed her at high speeds, heading to the mills. Occasional breaks in the forest revealed the smoldering fires of tree skeletons and blackened stumps bulldozed into piles. This was obviously still an area dependent on lumbering, although now in a post-digestive stage.

Perry was a small town, and once she drove past the half-empty strip malls on the outskirts and reached the older, mostly closed buildings in the town center, she quickly found the cemetery, two blocks off Main Street. She parked her car and walked out. The cemetery was the size of a square city block, but she thought she could easily check all the gravestones in an hour or two. She started on the west side walking up and down the rows of gravestones, peering at the names and dates of death. Nicole had only been to a few funerals in her life and never spent any real amount of time in cemeteries, and she found the experience oddly disturbing. The dates of birth, dates of death, and occasional short epitaph on the gravestones telling such a brief story. Husbands, wives, and children come and gone. One person lived seventy-eight years. The next sixty-three. Another forty. One gravestone was for a woman who died at the age of twenty-three. Next to it was a pair of silver high heels — faded, weather-warped, and rat-chewed. Then there were the gravestones with no name, simply "Infant." Another gravesite interned a mother and infant with the same date of death. The infant's gravestone had Jesus's little lamb carved on top, splattered with white bird-droppings.

Nicole quickly passed the gravestones that looked newer and concentrated on the older, smaller gravestones in the northeast part of the cemetery. There were a few with the date of death of 1922, but none with the name Martin Tabert. Some gravestones had names and dates too faded to read; years of erosion, moss, and algae having taken their toll. *Could one of these be Martin's grave?* She found a concrete bench and sat for a long time. She thought about how quickly our names fade and we're forgotten. *After I die, who will care? Will anyone come to visit my grave?*

On her way back from Perry, she noticed a highway sign for the Forest Capital Museum State Park, home of the Cracker Homestead. The museum was near the highway. She pulled in and paid the two-dollar entrance fee. A brochure explained that early settlers were called "Crackers" because they used whips that made a cracking sound to herd cattle. The museum was small, and even though she took her time, she was through it in thirty minutes. The exhibits were brief and mostly talked about all the products that came from lumber and the importance of forestry to the area. No mention was made of the convict labor of the early days. She asked the woman at the desk if they had any information about the lumbering camps of the 1920s. "No, just what's in the exhibits," she said.

"Any information about the convict labor?"

"What convict labor?" she asked.

That evening she drove to the Dairy Queen to eat. She hadn't eaten at a DQ since she was a teenager, but she wanted some comfort food and there weren't a lot of choices in Cross City. She ordered a chicken strip basket and a large chocolate-dipped cone. After she ate the chicken strips and fries, she wasn't so hungry, and the ice cream was dripping down the cone making it a sticky mess. She ate a few bites of the chocolate and threw the rest out. She drove back to the motel. She turned on the television and flipped through the channels aimlessly, unable to find anything she wanted to watch. She started feeling anxious again. She concentrated on taking deep breaths. *Why am I such a wreck? What am I doing with my life? Why am I here?*

The next morning Nicole forced herself out of bed and decided to go for a run to clear her mind. She hadn't brought running clothes, but she could wear her shorts and t-shirt and wash them in the sink later. Nicole wasn't sure where to run. She hadn't seen a running path, and she didn't feel safe running down the roads outside of town where she would quickly be surrounded by woods. She stayed on the major streets in the town, doing loops around a six- or seven-block area—past the electric cooperative, consignment and gift shop, beauty salon, barber shop, fire department, city hall, farm supply, laundromat, bank, discount furniture shop, service station— then back around again. It was sunny and the black asphalt was already giving off blasts of heat. On her third loop, a man came out of the laundromat, walked out on the sidewalk, and looked her over as she passed. It made her uncomfortable, just like it did when she was at the gym and she saw some man paying more attention to her workout that his own. The man wore a big dumb grin, a battered baseball cap over long stringy hair, and a goatee like Uncle Sam's.

The goatee look got her thinking about her Constitutional law professor at Yale Law School, who was also the faculty advisor to the *Yale Law Journal*. He was in his forties, recently divorced, and trying to look younger than he really was. He was always hitting on her. He was careful not do anything that would be evidence of sexual harassment, but he was constantly asking to meet with her late in the evening and go out for a beer to talk about this or that law review article. Brushing up against her accidentally or staring at her breasts. When she made it clear she wasn't interested, he started being hypercritical of her work. It still pissed her off and it ruined her run thinking about it.

Nicole showered and walked over to the Taste of Dixie Diner for breakfast. She had worked up an appetite. The waitress asked, "Do you want the breakfast buffet or order from the menu, hon?"

"Let me look at the buffet."

Nicole walked up and down the steam table line, perusing the calorie-rich display — scrambled eggs, ham, sausage links, piles of fatty bacon, biscuits and gravy, grits, fried okra, chicken-fried steak, pancakes. It was so overwhelming she couldn't deal with the choices. She sat down in the back and ordered coffee and orange juice. She watched as the locals began to gather, sitting at a large table near the buffet line. They were mostly men, all exceedingly large in girth, and loading up plates with enormous mounds of food from the buffet. There were bottles of hot sauce on every table and the men doused their food with it. They all seemed to know each other, and they dressed the same—faded blue jeans or overalls, t-shirts, and camouflage baseball hats with the brims bent in a semi-circle. Their faces had a rounded, jowly look, as if they came from the same genetic pool. Nicole didn't like to think of herself as the kind of person who would stereotype people, but she thought that they looked like the type who could be descendants of mean guards at a convict camp.

Nicole thought about her next steps. The previous day she'd seen a Florida Forest Service administrative building along the highway, and she thought that perhaps someone there would know the location of other cemeteries in the county. She was at the administrative building when it opened at 9:00 a.m. The man at the desk said they didn't have a cemetery map, but he could direct her to where a few cemeteries were located. The Mingo and Clara cemeteries were not far, but located on dirt roads off the main highway.

"Are you driving alone?" the man asked.

"Yes."

He peered out the window. "Is that your car?"

"Yes. It's a rental."

"Well, hopefully it's in good mechanical shape."

"It should be."

"Do you know how to change a tire if you have to?"

"Yes." Nicole remembered how her father had spent an afternoon teaching her how when she first got her driver's license. *I hope I can remember.*

"I'm not trying to scare you," he said, "but some of these back roads are pretty isolated. Let's say you had car trouble. You wouldn't want to walk up to an unknown place. Some of the houses stuck back in the woods have meth labs or marijuana patches. People might poke a barrel through their screen door and shoot at anyone who comes close. Might be over your head, might not. If you stayed with your car, someone might not come along for some time. And, if someone did, you can't always be sure of the people who might stop. There are some nice folks that live in this county, but there are others you can't trust, if you know what I mean. I know I wouldn't want my daughter to meet up with them on some back road someplace. Some of those men act like buck deer in rut."

"I have my cell phone."

"Don't count on that. The reception can be spotty."

Nicole put on a brave face. "I'll be careful. Thanks for the warning though."

Nicole found the roads leading to the Clara and Mingo cemeteries matched the description given to her. Small, red-dirt roads weaving through swamps and forests, the trees close to the road and rising up to block the sunlight. A light rain had started too, and she wished she had four-wheel drive on the slick surface. She checked the Clara Cemetery first. The mill town of Clara had been near there once, but it was long gone, the people relocated and the scrub brush and pine forest reclaiming the land. The cemetery was small. She walked between the rows of cracked gravestones now turned a grimy gray. She noticed a dry snakeskin near one. It was large and transparent. The snake must have rubbed himself against the gravestone in order to free itself of its old skin and slither away. She was studying the gravestones in the far end of the cemetery when a pickup truck drove past, a man at the wheel, slowing down and looking at her. A few minutes later he drove by again the other way, even slower. She looked around and saw a thick branch fallen from a tree. *If he comes in here, I'll pick up that branch and smash him in the head.* She was determined to check the remaining gravestones and threaded her way between the rows of graves, glancing up frequently toward the road.

She drove to the Mingo Cemetery next. It was along another narrow dirt road with an occasional trailer house stuck back in the woods surrounded by junked cars, bald tires, and rusted bedsprings. One home had a hand-painted sign out front, CHOW WOLF MIX 4 SALE. The homes looked lonely and forsaken or totally abandoned. It was sometimes hard to tell. She parked next to the Mingo Cemetery sign, stepped out of her car, and walked into the cemetery. She spent some time there, wandering in the twilight as the trees began to cast thin shadows across the scattered gravestones. It was quiet and still, and she was struck by a profound sense of loss, although she didn't know what the loss was for.

She walked back to her car, wondering what to do next. There were areas in the Mingo Cemetery where simple stone markers showed the location of graves, but they were lacking gravestones, and Nicole realized that if Martin was buried here, it could likely be in an unmarked grave. *Could there still be cemetery records somewhere?*

That evening, she drove to a roadside restaurant, the Cypress Inn. She needed a drink terribly and was surprised when she went inside to find that the restaurant didn't serve alcohol, not even beer

Grave at Mingo Cemetery, Dixie County, Florida.
Photo by Paul Legler.

or wine. She excused herself and drove to the package store a few blocks away and bought three miniature bottles of vodka and guzzled them in the parking lot while sitting in her car. She reentered the restaurant, feeling slightly buzzed, and ordered the barbeque chicken special for seven dollars. The three sides included stewed tomatoes, macaroni and cheese, and coleslaw, and it was accompanied by a gigantic sweet tea. She sat there feeling depressed. She looked about. Fox News was playing on the only television in the place. Deer-head mounts decorated the walls, but the deer are small in Florida and not much to look at. There were only two elderly white couples and one family of four in the restaurant. A few Black people wandered in from time to time to pick up take-out from a side room. She picked at her food until she felt the need to leave.

After that, it was another long, lonely night. Nicole felt like her hearing was heightened and she noticed every door slam and every dog bark outside her motel room. Her mind raced as if fueled by an accelerator stuck to the floor. She must have looked at the clock a hundred times. She didn't like the smell of her pillow, but she couldn't sleep without it either. Somehow around 5:00 a.m. she drifted off.

When she awoke it was late in the morning and the day was already sweltering hot. She walked to the motel lobby and rang the bell on the desk. A woman came out of the back office. Nicole said, "I'm sorry to bother you, but I'm looking for a gravesite of someone who was buried in Dixie County many years ago. Do you happen to know if there is anyplace, like a county office or church that would have cemetery records of people buried back in the 1920s?"

"I get my husband."

A man came out in a few minutes. Nicole explained again what she was looking for.

"We are new here," he said. He had the same accent. "I will call for you." She heard him talking to someone on the phone in a foreign language, and when he got off, he said, "There is a history center in Old Town." Nicole hadn't thought about the possibility that there might be a local history center. He pulled out a local map and showed her the spot. "Take County Road 51, ten miles south."

Fifteen minutes later, Nicole pulled up to the Dixie County Historical Society. It was located in a yellow and white brick building that had once been a school. The place was empty except for a woman at a desk in the rear. She was a tall, elderly woman with white hair and wearing a red embroidered sweater, blue slacks, and white tennis shoes. She greeted Nicole, "Good morning. How can I help y'all today?" Nicole thought her pleasant voice had the sound of the South in every syllable. She said her name was Doris, and she showed Nicole around the building, which housed a small historical exhibit in the lower level and a genealogy resource center on the second floor. Hallway walls featured old daguerreotypes of original county residents, all wearing grim faces. Nicole and Doris spoke at length. She'd never heard of Martin Tabert, but she was familiar with the Putnam Lumber Company. She said that it was well known in north Florida. The company headquarters were now in Jacksonville, and they still had an active operation in the county.

Nicole was excited when she found out that they had all the cemetery records going back some hundred years. They sat at a table and Doris searched through each of the cemetery records with Nicole looking over her shoulder. There were nearly thirty cemeteries in the county, although many were small and now abandoned. Doris asked, "Do you want me to check the old Negro . . . excuse me . . . African American cemeteries too?"

"I think we should, just in case. If it's not too much trouble."

"No, no trouble at all. It was a different time back then, and the races were generally separated, but not entirely."

After they searched the last one, Doris said, "I'm sorry there is nothing in any of the records about a Martin Tabert."

"So, it's no use then. If he wasn't buried in a cemetery he was buried in a field or swamp someplace. Who knows where that would be?"

"I wouldn't necessarily jump to that conclusion. Folks sometimes didn't have the money to pay for a cemetery plot. So, there were lots of unofficial cemeteries. Usually they were clustered in small groups in forest clearings. Most don't have gravestones. They used wooden crosses and those would all be rotted now. However, you can sometimes see where the graves were because the ground settled, and when it rains the water gathers, and you see these six-foot long depressions. The old folks sometimes know who was buried in those graves, and some of them might have hand-written records too. You might want to check with some of the old folks in the county. See if anyone knows anything."

"How would I do that?"

"You would just have to start asking. I can give you some names to get you started."

Doris compiled a list of elderly people in the county who might know something. There were only fourteen names on the list. "People generally don't live that long here," she said.

The mission seemed somewhat overwhelming to Nicole. She wasn't entirely comfortable knocking on doors of people she didn't know. And she knew that in this rural area people might not be all that friendly to strangers. It was the kind of place where everyone had a guard dog and they weren't chained. Still, she felt she had to make an effort, and once she made a list, she didn't stop until it was all crossed off.

Nicole visited three homes that afternoon. She had to travel a long distance to some of them over long baked-dirt roads, which gave her an uneasy feeling. She realized that she'd seen too many movies where people get lost on some back road and end up being carved up with a chainsaw or something. The stops she made were fruitless. One of the three people was too sick to have visitors. The other two knew nothing.

That evening Nicole drove to a roadside bar and grill for something to eat. She ordered a cheeseburger with "freedom fries," along with a side salad and several cans of Busch Light. She had another restless night and spent the next day searching again, concentrating on the people who lived in or near Cross City. Every house she went to seemed to be the same. Mailboxes without a name. Trees casting a shadow over the house set back from the road. Spanish moss hanging from the trees like spider webs. Potted gravel or dirt driveways. Carcasses of rusted cars and washing machines and refrigerators out back. Homemade no trespassing signs nailed to posts.

Every time she got out of her air-conditioned car, the heat hit her like a furnace blast. She threw a piece of cookie to the dog to make friends. She walked up to the house. Then, the long wait for someone to come to the door. The shuffling as someone rose from their La-Z-Boy and peered out. The bewildered look and suspicion on their face as she explained what she was looking for. The sound of the screen door shutting behind her. No one knew anything.

While she was driving back to Cross City, she noticed a sheriff's car following her. *What's that about?* She felt like she was in every movie about a redneck Southern sheriff she'd ever seen. He followed her for several miles before he turned his lights on. She pulled over. She waited. She thought that was the thing to do, even though it made her uncomfortable, and she wanted to ask him what he wanted. She could see him in the rearview mirror as he got out of his car, hitched up his belt, and walked up to her car. His face was hidden in the shadow of his Stetson hat. He said, "Good afternoon, Miss Nicole." Nicole wondered how he knew her name. He probably got it from calling in the license plate number to the rental car company, but it was still unnerving. He asked to see her license. She gave it to him along with her DOJ identification. He studied them for a minute and handed them back to her. He stood there looking her over, his feet planted far apart, and one hand resting on a wooden baton hanging from his belt.

"Have I done anything wrong, officer?" she asked.

"No, I just wanted to make sure you were the person I was told to look out for."

"Who told you to look out for me?"

He didn't answer. He took out a handkerchief and wiped his brow. "Nothing for you to worry about. Have you found the grave you're looking for?"

"How do you know about that?"

"I talk to folks. I know you've been going about the county asking about some fellow who was buried eighty years ago."

She didn't know how to respond.

"That's a long time ago," he said.

"Yes, I know it is."

"Well, good luck with that."

He started back to his car. About halfway he turned around and strolled back. "Forgot my manners. I didn't introduce myself. I'm Sheriff Speckhauser." He handed her a business card. "If you need anything don't hesitate to call me. And I'll keep my ears open too. If I learn anything I'll be in touch."

He started back to his car once again. Nicole stuck her head out the window and called out after him. "Who told you to look out for me?"

If he heard, he didn't respond or even look back.

That evening she went back to the Cypress Inn. She ordered a grilled Shrimp Po' Boy with a side salad. When the food came, the smell of the fried shrimp was nauseating. She took a bite of the salad. She saw the fork rise to her mouth and she felt the sensation of the greens entering it and the cold metallic feel of the fork as it came cleanly out from her lips. She couldn't swallow and discreetly spit the salad into her napkin. *God, please make this feeling go away.* Her hands were shaking again and she hid them under the table so that no one could see.

She stood up and walked to the restroom. She leaned over the toilet and gagged. There was an empty feeling in her throat and nothing came up. She sat on the toilet. The waitress came in sometime later. "Are you okay in there, honey?"

"I'll be fine. A touch of the flu, maybe. It's not the food. The food is good."

"If you need anything, just let me know."

"I will. I'll just stay here a minute." She held her head in her hands and closed her eyes.

Was it the next day? Or sometime later? She was confused. Where was she? The sheriff's car was following her again. He turned his flashing lights on, and she pulled over. He walked up to her car and she rolled down the window. He looked like a different officer than the one who had stopped her before, heavier. Or was he the same one?

"Lordy, lordy, it's a hot one ain't it," he said.

"Yes, sir. Did I do something wrong?"

"You tell me that."

She was hit by a feeling she had but couldn't remember what.

"It's too hot out here to sit and jaw. You follow me to the office, and we'll talk there."

What's this all about?

He turned his lights off, and she followed him.

He parked outside the sheriff's office and held the door open for her and ushered her into his office. He said to another officer at the desk, "You better come in. Me and Miss Nicole is going to have a chat, and it would be good to have you as a witness. We don't want no misunderstandin' about what's said."

He sat down in a large swivel chair behind the desk and she noticed the brass name plate, SHERIFF SPECKHAUSER. He motioned for her to sit down. "I expect you know my name. I been the sheriff in this county nigh on twenty years. This is Deputy Clayton," he said. The deputy looked like an actor she'd seen in a movie once, but she couldn't place him.

The sheriff reached into a small fridge next to his desk. "You like a cola or a Dr. Pepper, ma'am?"

"I'll have a diet coke. Thank you."

"I don't think I have anything diet in here. How 'bout a 7-Up?"

"Sure. That'll be fine. What do you want to talk to me about, Sheriff?"

"Well you goin' door-to-door and people call me. They expect I know something, which I usually do."

She cracked her can of 7-Up open. *Where is this headed?*

"I understand you're looking for a grave of one Martin Tabert. Supposed to have died eighty years ago. That's a long time ago. Now don't it seem far-fetched to you that you could find someone who died and was buried that long ago?"

"I understand that. I know it's a real long shot." She told him about the request from her grandmother and what she'd done so far in her search.

He sat there and nodded his head while she talked. When she finished he said. "Now that's a touching story. Let me save you some trouble and you can go on your merry way. I don't expect anyone knows anything, so you can go back and tell your grandma that you looked like a good girl and you didn't find anything."

"I have a few more names to follow up on."

"Where do you think that will get you?"

"Maybe someone knows something."

"No one knows anything. I can tell you that right now. Sometimes it's best to let things lie and not stir up ol' mud. People forget eventually. That's the way it should be."

"I expect you're right," she said. *Why am I talking with a Southern accent?* "Still, I'd like to tell her that I did everything I could. My grandma Edna's not well. She might not live much longer."

"You did plenty already. You can be proud of that. Mighty proud. Pat yourself on the back."

He looked her over, his eyes resting on her crossed legs for some time. She wondered if her skirt was too short. He looked back up and said, "The other thing is that I've been told to keep tabs on you."

"Who asked you to keep tabs on me?"

"Don't worry your pretty little head. Anyhow, I said my piece. I expect you'll be leaving the county now."

"I'm not clear about what you're saying."

"I expect you do. My piece generally carries a little weight in this county seein' how I been sheriff for so long."

"I respect that."

"I bet you do."

"Like I said, I just have a few more leads to follow up on and I'll be leavin' in a few days."

He looked red and flustered. "Are we not communicatin'? I suggested you leave now!" He glared at her.

She gripped the side arms of her chair. She took a deep breath. *One. Two. Three.* "There is something called freedom of speech and association. Even in Dixie County," she said. "I believe I have the legal right to talk to people."

"Yep, and if you go around talkin' to people dressed like a slut, you're liable to get raped or somethin' worse."

"Don't talk to me like that."

"I'll talk to you any way I want. Maybe that's the real reason you came down here from your Sodom and Gomorrah up north. You're cruising around lookin' for a big black buck to take on."

"You bastard." She reached into her purse and pulled out her Department of Justice I.D. "I'm with the U.S. Justice Department."

He sat back in his chair and rocked slowly. "You don't think I already know that. That don't hold shit down here. God damn feds." He turned to Deputy Clayton. "We don't like feds down here, do we? Specially not some damn Yankee fed." He turned back to her and shook his head. "Don't flash that goddamn ID at me. It won't mean diddlysquat if I take a notion to shove this here baton up your lily-white ass." He took his wooden baton out of his belt and thumped it against his other hand.

Deputy Clayton chimed in. "Let me at her with the baton, Sheriff."

"We'll all get our turn."

They grabbed her. Nicole screamed.

She heard a knock on the stall door. *Did I pass out?* The knock came again. "Are you sure you're okay in there? I thought I heard someone scream."

"I'm fine."

"You've been in there a long time, honey. Your food is cold, and we need to clear the table."

"You can clear the table. I'm not hungry now."

It was another God-awful night at the motel, and when she woke up in the morning a little light in the back of Nicole's head told her that maybe she needed some professional psychiatric help. A hazy image of a peaceful-looking sanitarium with nurses dressed in starched white uniforms and lounge chairs neatly arranged outside in the garden rose up in her mind. She took some deep breaths. She decided to take a long, hot shower. Maybe that would help. She closed her eyes in the shower and turned the knob until it was almost scalding. The steam rose and she felt she was in a dream. She stood there for a long time until she heard her cell phone ringing. She stepped out, threw a towel around her and sprinted for her phone. It was Doris from the Dixie County Historical Center.

"Are you still looking for that Martin Tabert grave, hon?"

"Yes, I am."

"Well, I might have a lead for you. I know a teacher in town, Elsa Shaw. She's at the elementary school. My son was in her class many years ago. She's a good teacher. She has an elderly uncle. He's very old and he knows just about everything there is to know about Dixie County. Would you like me to make an introduction?"

Nicole arranged to meet Elsa on Main Street in Old Town. Elsa was a short, matronly-looking Black woman with high hair and tortoise-shell glasses. They chatted for a few minutes about her work and family while standing on the sidewalk. She had three boys and three girls, all in the local schools. She was obviously very proud of them, and she proceeded to tell about each one and their school activities — drum line, softball, volleyball, Beta Club, choir, track. Her two oldest boys were on the Dixie County High School football team. "Fall football season is the only time the community comes together," she explained. "We only have one high school in the county and everyone comes to the games. Everything else closes down, even the gas stations." Nicole offered to drive her to her uncle's house, but she said, "I best drive myself, ma'am."

Nicole followed her on State Highway 349 for twenty miles and turned onto a dirt road for ten more miles. There was nothing but trees and scrub brush. They veered onto a rutted track and drove up to a yellowing house with a rust-streaked tin roof, sitting on cement blocks at the edge of the pinewoods. The yard was brown and beaten down, and a few chickens wallowed and fluffed in depressions in the dirt. A scruffy mutt of a dog barked to announce their presence. A man came to the screen door. He looked the right age to Nicole, patchy white hair, wrinkles and a stoop. He had to be at least ninety. He led them into the house to a table in the kitchen.

Elsa introduced Nicole. "Uncle John, this is the lady I told you about. She's doing some historical research. She's interested in some things that happened back in the 1920s. I thought you might be able to help her."

"I'll do what I can. I still remember those days." He shook his head as if he was already traveling back in time. "Hard times, hard times. Then the thirties came along and they was even harder."

"Did you live in Dixie County in 1922?" Nicole asked.

"Yes, ma'am. I lived here all my life."

"Can I ask, how old were you in 1922?"

"I was born in 1908, so I would have been . . . fourteen years old." She could see he was still sharp enough.

"I'm looking for the grave of a man named Martin Tabert who was buried somewhere in Dixie County in 1922. Does that name ring a bell?"

"You got to give me a moment to recollect myself." He was silent for a moment and then shook his head. "No, no, I can't say I remember anyone by that name." He coughed a raspy cough and picked up a pack of Pall Malls, packed it down, took one out, and lit it. "The cemetery records might have something," he suggested.

"I checked those and I didn't find anything."

"Some of the poor folk used to bury people in a grove of trees down by the Suwannee River. It wasn't an official cemetery."

"Would someone have a record of who was buried there?"

He looked at her questionably and raised his voice. "Why you tryin' to find him? Is he a relative of yours? We don't need no one snoopin' around and disturbin' our dead folk."

"I'm tryin' to find him for my grandmother. She is ninety-eight and lives in North Dakota. Martin was her beau back in the day."

"As I said, I don't remember the name, and I knew everyone in the county. How did he die?"

"He was at a convict camp. He was whipped to death."

He looked at Elsa and then back at Nicole, fear now in his eyes.

"By who?"

"A whipping boss of the Putnam Lumber Company."

His head shook rapidly. "Putnam Lumber . . . I don't know nothin'. Nothin'."

Elsa spoke. "Uncle John, you don't have to be scared of Putnam Lumber anymore."

"No, no, I won't have anything to do with it."

"Uncle John, please."

"No, you best be goin'."

"You don't have to be scared anymore."

"No. No. Go now. I need my nap."

Outside, Elsa walked with Nicole to her car.

"I'm sorry he wouldn't tell you anything. Even if he knew, which I doubt. The old folks are still scared of Putnam Lumber. They controlled the whole county at the time. Still own a good chunk of the land. Black people learned to keep their mouths shut and not talk about company affairs."

"Surely it's safe to talk about the company now."

"Probably, but who knows? The South hasn't changed as much as folks think. It could slide back to its old ways. Some folks think it's already slidin'."

Later that day Nicole went to visit the Putnam Lodge, a hotel and restaurant that had been erected in the 1920s for use of Putnam

The dining room in the Putnam Lodge, Shamrock, Florida.
Photo courtesy of State Archives of Florida.

Lumber Company visiting executives in the city of Shamrock, a company town founded by Putnam. Workers were busy restoring it, but she was allowed to enter and look around. It was a huge building, beautifully refurbished inside with the original unpainted cypress paneling. She stood and read the posted historical information: "The reconditioned pecky cypress paneling of the lobby and dining room along with the elegant furnishings evoke the genteel charm of an earlier era. The Putnam Lodge is now considered a centerpiece in the county's promotion of nature and heritage tourism."

She looked at the photo and thought about Putnam company executives eating there with their white tablecloths and napkins and shiny silverware while innocent men were being brutally flogged in a company camp not far away. Nicole drove back to her motel, stopping at the package store on the way for more vodka and ice. She bought a quart bottle and several miniatures in case she needed them later. Once in her room, she quickly tore the thin paper from the plastic cup next to the sink. She filled it with ice and cracked the quart bottle open.

That night she woke with a roaring sound at the back of her head. The clock read 4:30. She got up and poured herself a cup of water and drank it in great swallows. Then another. She lay back in bed, not able to sleep. She knew she was getting nowhere and she was on the brink. She decided to drive to a beach the next day. It was supposed to be a sunny day and perhaps she could relax and regain her equilibrium for a final push of her search.

When she awoke again at 10:00, she stepped into the shower to shave her legs. Her hand was unsteady, and she nicked herself badly. She stopped the bleeding with multiple swaps of Kleenex and put on her smelly shorts and t-shirt and studied herself in the mirror. She always had one of two thoughts when she looked at herself in the mirror—I look terrific or I look terrible. Nothing in between. Today she thought she looked terrible. Her face appeared tired. The dark shadows under her eyes were disconcerting. There appeared to be small lines at the corners of her lips. The blond streaks in her shoulder-length brown hair were almost totally faded.

Nicole knew she didn't want to go back to Horseshoe Beach, so she looked on the map and found Keaton Beach in Taylor County, just north and west about an hour away. The drive took her through more thick pinewoods, and they were starting to give her a claustrophobic feeling, like being wedged into a tight coffin. There wasn't much to see anywhere, only scattered dwellings stuck back in the woods. She wondered where these people worked. There didn't seem to be any businesses and no farms. She passed a ten-foot sign in someone's yard, BEWARE THE FLESH, and a short distance later, THE END IS NEAR. She drove on faster. *Is there such a thing as a Judgment Day?* she wondered.

Nicole arrived at the beach at noon. She sat in her car in the parking lot for some time before stepping out of the car and taking her beach bag out of the trunk. This beach looked only marginally better than Horseshoe Beach, with lots of seaweed washed up on the sand. She started walking along the water's edge. She saw a dark-skinned boy with a group of other young people throwing a Frisbee around. The image of Abbu Al-Nasser rose in her mind. She tried to force it out by counting seagulls. She walked faster. She started thinking about her arms and hands. Was this the way she usually swung them when she walked? She didn't know what to do with them. She walked south along the beach for a long distance, swerving between the sunbathers and loud children with sand buckets. She wanted to get away from the tourists.

Nicole eventually reached an area where there were few people. She couldn't walk anymore. She could hear the beachgoers farther up the beach, but just barely. A few gulls cawed; otherwise the only sound was the waves rhythmically lapping against the shore.

It was warm and the air felt as liquid as the ocean. She lay down on her towel, closed her eyes, and fell asleep.

When she woke it was nearly 2:00 p.m. She took out her paperback to read. She couldn't concentrate, the words fluttered past like specks of dust floating in light without a pattern. She turned a few pages and threw it back down. *What's the point?* She sat up and looked out to the ocean, squinting her eyes at the shimmering heat waves on the horizon. The sun was bright, a harsh light that seemed to emanate from her skull. She fumbled in her beach bag for her sunglasses. She couldn't find them and thought she must have lost them. Her fingers touch something else, something glass. A miniature bottle of vodka. She hesitated, screwed off the lid, and gulped it down. She searched her bag again frantically and found another bottle and drank that too. She lay back down and closed her eyes. She was possibly sleeping, or near sleep, when images began floating across her eyelids—Martin Tabert on the ground being whipped unmercifully; Abbu Al-Nasser hung upside down, electrodes being attached to his testicles. Then, the piercing sound of his screams in her head. She sat up abruptly. For the first time, she realized that she would never be able to shut out those painful scenes in her mind. She gasped and bolted up and dashed into the ocean.

The water felt warm. She stood there for a moment, waist deep, and she saw herself splash water on her shoulders and torso. She started walking out farther and saw the water rise above her waist and her body swimming towards the horizon. She swam until her legs and arms became very tired. She didn't know how long or how far she swam, but when she looked back the people on the beach looked like tiny specks. She floated on her back, bobbing with the waves, and treading just enough to keep her face above the water. She listened to the somatic sound echoing in her ears. *My heart?* She felt the depths pulling at her. She quit treading. The water pressed her eardrums. She saw herself sinking.

And the sun became black as a sackcloth of hair.
    —Revelation 6:12

As the Great Depression continued and their lives spiraled downward, Torger took out his despair on Edna. The first time came
when they'd been married less than two years. He'd been in town
and he came home late in the evening stinking of liquor. Prohibition
was still in effect, but it was easy to find a bootlegger to sell you
a bottle brought down from Canada. He had muddy boots and he
stomped around the kitchen angry because she didn't have a plate of
food ready for him. She was warming his pork chops in the fry pan
when he said, "These floors are dirty. What do you do around here
all day? Can't you keep the house clean?"

    "Listen mister," she said. "Don't come in here late all liquored
up and talk to me like that. You tracked the dirt in yourself. Just look
at your boots."

    "Don't sass me."

    "You won't even look at your boots because you know
I'm right."

    "It ain't my boots. The floor was dirty when I came in."

    "No, it wasn't."

    She could see his face turning flush with red. He yelled now.
"No woman of mine is going to sass me."

"Call it sass if you want to, but I'll say what I want."

He pointed a fat finger at her. "I'm the man of the house and you'll mind your back talk or else."

"You're drunk. You can fix your own pork chops."

"I'm not drunk."

"Then you're just stupid."

"Why, you bitch. I'll fix you." He started unbuckling his belt and then stopped. "Bring me the razor strop," he said.

"The what?"

"You heard me."

"Don't you dare touch me!"

He strode into the bedroom and came back carrying his razor strop. He slapped it hard against his hand. "I'll learn you not to talk back," he said. "Bend over and take your rightful punishment."

She stomped her foot. "I shall do no such thing, you brute."

He grabbed her and threw her to the ground. The first swing hit her back and side. She cried out and curled up in a ball. She turned her head and looked at him, "Don't! Stop!" He came down with the strop again. She screamed. He struck her several more times, the strop cutting the air and coming down with a loud swoosh.

When he was done, he silently took the fry pan and sat down at the table to eat. She could hear him chewing his food. She lay there for a minute weeping and then pushed herself up off the floor and ran outside to escape the house. She kept running, far out into the pasture, stumbling in the moonlight, until she was too winded to go on. She stood there and looked at the sky and screamed and beat her fists against the wind.

Torger was apologetic for a time, but as the Depression wore on, his drinking only got worse. He began to travel to town alone to sell the cream, refusing to take her. Then he would take the cream check, cash it, and buy a jar. Several ne'er-do-wells in the county had set up stills to brew moonshine. It was cheaper than the rum the bootleggers ran down from Canada, and Torger now bought his whiskey from them. This made Edna furious. *I will not milk those cows and haul those heavy cream cans around for some damn moonshiner,* she thought. *I will pour the cream into the ground before I do that.* She was too fearful of Torger to carry out her thoughts, however.

When Torger was drinking he had a deep slow-seeping rage inside him that she could feel across the room. He swore about the weather, he swore about the banks, he swore about the grain companies, he swore about the "gover'mint." Then he would find fault with her housekeeping or her cooking—it was overcooked or it was undercooked—and he would push her into an argument, which always ended badly for her. He took to hanging the razor strop on a hook next to the front door so she would have to see it every time she went in or out. When he was angry he would order her to bring it to him. To her that was worse than the beating itself.

They rarely talked anymore. Sitting quietly without a word at the dinner table. He would be eating and farting as if she wasn't there. She would ask him if he wanted this or that food and he would grunt or simply reach for it. He would often leave in the evening, disappearing to drink and falling asleep at a moonshiner's house or in their hayloft. On the long winter nights when he didn't come home, she sat in the house alone. It would be nothing but darkness all around and the wind howling. The house lit by the single kerosene lantern. She would fret about her fate, lonely and scared. When he did come home, it was no better, because he would stink of alcohol and want to take her. He said it was his right and she let him, but it was a mean, furious rutting, as if he could somehow get rid of his anger if he just planted his seed deep enough. *Am I only an animal for his animal pleasure?* she thought.

Once Torger started cashing the cream checks, Edna no longer had money to buy the things she needed for the household. She had to beg him for any small amount. She hated that. It was humiliating to her. Edna was a capable seamstress and she could even sew herself a fashionable dress, but her dresses gradually became tattered and holey past the point of mending. She thought about a time when she wouldn't have been caught dead in them. All her life she'd liked to dress in style. Now, she didn't have any money to buy buttons, let alone material. Holes wore through the soles of her shoes, and she had to cut the cardboard back off a writing tablet to put inside. Her underwear wore out, and she was forced to make herself new underwear by tearing up and re-sewing Pillsbury Best flour sacks. Every time she wore them she could feel the rough cloth against her skin and her resentment grew.

Edna seldom went to town anymore. She often had bruises and she didn't want people to see her. She received letters from her sisters and mother inviting her to visit, but she was too ashamed to see them in her condition. She didn't have any neighbor ladies nearby who were friends or confidants. The closest neighbor was an elderly German woman who didn't speak English, and the next closest farm was owned by two unmarried Norwegian brothers. The only time she got off the farm was when she went to church. No matter how drunk Torger got on Saturday night, he would rise on Sunday morning and drink a pot of coffee, and they would go to church together. It was as if in his mind the act of going to church would wipe away the drunkenness and beatings for the week. They sat in the hard, wooden pew and listened to Reverend Thomas give his sermon, and Torger would nod his head like a pious man.

Edna found her only refuge in writing. She began to keep a journal that she would write in whenever Torger was gone. It was like having someone to talk to. At first, she would write down her daily activities—the chicks or piglets that were born, the weather, what she cooked, when the plants in the garden emerged. She soon found that she had little to write about that didn't seem dull. So she started writing about her previous life before she was married and especially about Martin. She could still remember everything they'd done together like it was yesterday, every voice and gesture, and she spent weeks recording what she could recall.

She wrote about her first kiss. It came on May Day. May Day was the one day of the year when the girls could formally flirt. Edna had made a May Day basket out of pieces of colored paper woven together and with a paper handle fastened to the basket with glue. She filled it with homemade treats of candy and cookies. The tradition was that the girls would knock on the door of the boy they liked early in the morning and set the basket down on the steps. Then they would run, but not too fast. The boys would run after the girls and grab them and try to give them a kiss.

When Edna set her basket on Martin's step she knocked and ran very slowly, occasionally looking over her shoulder. She didn't see anyone. After she ran a hundred yards, she thought that maybe she had not knocked loud enough, and she crept back to the house. The basket was still on the steps. This time she knocked louder and again she ran. She was just past the barn when Martin came out, saw her, and ran after her. Edna was a fast runner, but she made sure that she ran slow enough for Martin to catch her. When he finally grabbed her, he hesitated in his shyness, so she moved in close and puckered her lips. He got the idea and planted a quick kiss on her lips. Then she noticed that Martin only had one shoe on. He explained that was the reason he didn't come after her when she first knocked. He couldn't find his other shoe. After that, she would always tease him when they saw each other by looking down at his feet and saying, "It's good to see that you found both your shoes today."

When Edna couldn't remember anything more to write, she began making things up. Naughty things that would make herself blush. Things she wished she'd done with Martin. Stories of passion, soft caresses, and lovemaking. She could lose herself for hours in this fantasy life, the words flowing across the page as fast as she could write. She hid the journal under her underwear at the bottom of her chest.

One day she was in the barn tending a heifer and its calf that had just been born. The calf needed clean straw in the pen and the mother needed hay and water. Torger was cleaning the horse stalls. She lost herself in the animals' care and didn't notice he left. When she was done tending the mother and calf she looked for Torger. She couldn't find him in the barn or farmyard. *He must be in the house.* That was unusual for him during the daytime. A nervous feeling came over her. *Maybe he is just going over his farm account ledger,* she thought. She would have to be careful because when he was working on his bookkeeping it always put him in a bad mood.

She fed the chickens and then the hogs, now peering out the big barn doors every few minutes towards the house. *He has been in the house a long time.* Her uneasiness grew. She walked to the house, and as she entered she saw him sitting at the kitchen table with his back to the door. She saw her journal on the table. By his silence she knew that he'd been reading it. Her heart began to beat wildly in her chest.

"Why do you have my journal? That is private," she said.

He turned around, his eyes glaring at her. His face was red, blood veins pulsing on his forehead.

"It's not true. None of it is true. I just make things up," she said quietly.

"Who is Martin?" he demanded loudly.

"No one."

"I will not ask you again. Who is Martin?"

"Martin Tabert. He is someone I knew years ago. Before I met you."

He jumped up. His chair slammed to the floor. The first blow from his fist hit her on the side of her head. She went down. He grabbed the razor strop next to the door.

She begged. "No, Torger. Please don't. None of it is true."

He raised the strop and she turned and faced the floor. The first blow hit her backside. She curled up in a ball covering her face. He grabbed her dress and tore it down exposing her bare back. The blows came like never before, driven with a crazed fury. Swishing, flaming, cutting. She struggled, jerking and twisting, but couldn't escape the blows. He hit her again and again, burning the bare skin of her back and thighs. She screamed in agony. She could hear him grunting and breathing heavily. He stopped. His whipping arm was sore and he rubbed it. "Stay there, don't move an inch," he said. He went out to the barn to get his jar. He came back in and stood over her. He took a swig. Then another, and another.

"Please stop," she wept. "I won't write again. Ever. Please."

"You whore. You dirty filthy whore. That is why you cannot bear me children. You have whored too much with this Martin." The strap rose again and again until he was too tired to raise his hand.

When she regained consciousness sometime later, she could feel her lip cut and bleeding. She had a terrible pain under her left eye. Her back and buttocks and thighs were burning in pain. She lay on the floor, not daring to move. When he went outside to the barn she would try to get up. She heard the chair squeak. She knew he was sitting at the table watching her. She heard him take another snort of whiskey. She waited. The floor felt cold.

"Get up you damn hussie," he said. "You ain't hurt that bad. Get to work. You got what you deserved. Whore thoughts. Shame on you."

She could hear him get up out of his chair. He picked up the journal. "I'm going to burn this trash," he said. The screen door slammed behind him as he went outdoors. She knew he would be gone for a while. She picked herself up from the floor. She felt dizzy and stood still, feet anchored apart, until the spinning stopped. She went to the icebox and took out a piece of cold meat and held it to her eye. She calculated in her head. Four more days until Sunday. Most of the swelling should go down by then. Then she thought, *Why do I worry if everyone at church knows.* Surely many of the ladies had seen her bruises before. They would turn their heads and pretend not to notice.

The Sunday after Torger found her journal, they did attend church as usual. Edna could not rest against the pew back without searing pain. She still had a purple-yellow bruise on her face, too. She tried to hide it by bringing her hand up to cover it if someone looked in her direction. After church, as the women gathered outside to gossip, she stood far to the side, her bruise facing away from them. Mrs. Kowalski saw her and waved and began to walk over to say hello. Mrs. Kowalski was one of the few women in the church who took the time to regularly speak to her. Edna's sister-in-law, Helen, saw that and made a beeline to get there at the same time. Edna knew that Helen knew. Mrs. Kowalski made a comment about the weather and then looked at her face inquisitively.

"What happened to your face?" she asked.

Helen butted in and answered quickly. "The wind blew the door into her face. Torger told me about it. You need to be more

careful," she said to Edna. Edna gave her a cold look. Helen took
Mrs. Kowalski by the arm and led her away. She could hear her
asking about her flower garden.

Edna went and sat in their car, waiting for Torger. Helen came
over to her and motioned for her to roll down the window. When
she did so, Helen said, "You should be ashamed of yourself. Torger
told me about your journal. Here he is already worried sick about
losing the farm and now he has to find out about your impurity. It's
more than any man can bear."

"I was not impure."

"Don't lie. It was right there in your journal. He told me all
about it. 'Dreaming of his soft caresses on my breasts.' A proper
woman does not write such things."

"It wasn't real. It was just writing."

"Who writes things that aren't real? What foolishness. Anyhow, even if it wasn't real, you had thoughts. It says right in the
book of Matthew that having lustful thoughts is the same as com-
mitting adultery in your heart."

Edna was silenced. She hated it when people threw Bible passages at her. How could you answer them unless you knew another
one to counter it, and she could never remember them when she
needed to. "Torger had no right to tell you what I wrote in my journal," she said.

"A man has every right when he's married. Remember that.
And let me give you some advice. Forget about that old beau of
yours. He's been gone for a long time. I found out all about him.
Probably got what he deserved anyhow. Gallivanting about the
country. All the way down to Florida. He should have stayed in
North Dakota."

After that day, Edna decided she would ask the preacher, Reverend Thomas, what she should do. The reverend was a solemn,

self-righteous man, and she did not think highly of him. Nevertheless, he was a man of God, and Edna thought that he would surely not approve of a man beating his wife. She needed to find a time to talk with him alone. Wife beating was hardly the kind of thing she could mention to him in the narthex as he greeted the parishioners leaving the church.

A few weeks later, in the spring of 1934, she found her chance. The Ladies Aid Club was organizing a church luncheon to celebrate the children who had completed their confirmation classes. The women of the church were asked to arrive early to set up the tables and make preparations. They were serving the community favorites — lutefisk, meatballs, and lefse — and the whole congregation would be there. Edna told Torger that she needed to go prior to the church service. He never let her drive the car by herself, but she arranged for a neighbor lady to pick her up on the way to church. When she arrived, Edna helped the ladies for a short time, putting tablecloths on the long tables set in the yard on the side of the church. When she had a chance and no one was looking, she drifted away and into the back of the church and knocked on the door of Reverend Thomas's study.

"Come in."

Edna entered and shut the door behind her. Her nervousness and apprehension increased when she saw him because he looked irritated at the interruption.

"I'm working on my sermon. What is it that you want Mrs. Moen?" he asked.

She gathered herself. "I need to ask your advice on a personal matter."

He frowned. "Yes, what is it?"

"Please don't tell Torger that I came to see you."

"I cannot make such a promise until I know what it is you want."

She answered in a quiet voice, tinted with a sigh of anguish. "Torger and I are having some troubles and I thought perhaps you could help me."

"Speak up. You need to talk louder."

"I said that my husband and I are having some troubles."

"Of what type?"

"He gets angry. The drought. The Depression. The bankers. That's not all . . . he thinks I did something . . . which I did not." She stammered now, "I don't know how to say this . . . he-he beats me . . . with a razor strop." She was unable to control her voice, which turned to a sob. "I can't take it anymore."

"Now, now. Don't cry. I don't need to see that. Pull yourself together."

"I'm sorry."

He handed her a clean handkerchief from his desk drawer. "Take this."

She wiped the tears from her face.

"Your husband is a drinker, Mrs. Moen. I know that. I hear everything that goes on in this community. You have my sympathy. Liquor is the devil's elixir. Always has been, always will be. Many men are seduced by it. I have preached against it many times. Were you in church last winter? Second Sunday in January, I believe."

"Yes, I was there. Torger sat right beside me. It was a good sermon. Torger was sober for six days after that."

"Good, good."

"The following Saturday he bought a jar of moonshine and came home drunk again."

"That's regrettable. I see that I will have to give my temperance sermon again next January and pray that God does not let him forget it so quickly."

"But January is a long way off. What am I to do now?"

"I cannot interfere with what happens between a man and his wife."

"So I am to be beaten whenever he gets drunk?"

"No, that's not what I'm suggesting." He sat silently for a moment, as if thinking carefully, and then inquired, "Perhaps you are doing something that agitates him."

"No, I'm not. Why would you ask that?"

"Often times I see that the men who are drinkers have wives who agitate them."

"I don't try to agitate him. Of course, times are hard. Sometimes I do, I suppose."

"A wife can always do more to please her husband. Cook him good meals, keep the house clean. That is the role that God has made for women."

Edna was miffed. She did not feel that he had a right to criticize her homemaking. "I do all those things and he still beats me," she said.

"I don't mean to pry, but I must ask. Are you submitting to him? The Bible says that a wife must submit to her husband. Perhaps he is angry because you have not borne him any children."

Edna answered sharply, "I am submitting to him. Whenever he wants. It's not my fault that we don't have children."

"Perhaps so, but perhaps it is and you don't know it. You must have a calm disposition to bear children. You don't seem to have a calm disposition."

Edna didn't know how to respond. She bit her lip and looked out the window.

"I cannot interfere with what happens between a man and his wife," he repeated. "Practice humility and maintain a calm disposition. That is my advice. I'm sure it will all get better in time. Remember, it is always darkest before the dawn."

He got up and began to show her toward the door. "I'll pray for you," he said.

"Don't bother," she said quietly.

"What! I have never heard such impertinence."

Edna summoned up all of her courage and looked him in the eye and said, "You're the one who is impertinent. I shall not be treated like an ox. I do not believe that is what God intended for women. I know the difference between right and wrong, even if you do not!"

She slammed the door in his face.

As the beatings continued, Edna began to think about a divorce. Divorces were rare, considered a sin, and a deathly stigma for a woman. A divorcee could be expected to be looked down upon in the community for the rest of her life. Still, Edna was at a loss of what else to do, so she decided to see a lawyer to ask about it.

She told Torger she needed to go to town and buy baking powder and sugar and other things, and she would bake him some biscuits and pies. He agreed to take her and she shopped at the grocery while he went to the hardware store. After her shopping, she gave him a few nickels that she'd saved hidden in a crock in the house. She told him that he'd been working so hard, he deserved to have a drink. She would walk up the street and have a soda. He looked at her suspiciously, but she knew that once she suggested he have a drink, it would play on his mind, and he wouldn't be able to resist. "I'll just have one and then we'll go home," he said. He headed off to a residence where a moonshiner sold jars of whisky out of his garage. She knew he would be gone for some time.

She waited a few minutes and then walked up the street. She bent down and pretended to fix her shoe, furtively looking up and down the street until she could see that no one was looking, and she dashed into the lawyer's office. The lawyer, Fred Williamson, was in his forties. He was known as a drinker around town, so Edna wondered if he would be sympathetic to her, but she had little choice. There were only two lawyers in town and the other one was a drinker too. He greeted her warmly, perhaps thinking that there would be the possibility of receiving a fee that day. However, when she explained her situation and asked about a divorce, he was not encouraging.

"You need to have legal grounds to seek a divorce. It is true that habitual drunkenness is grounds that the law recognizes. But it is often hard to prove if he denies it, which I expect he would. Buying an occasional jar of whisky is not enough. Why, if that were the case, every woman in the county would have grounds for divorce. I take an occasional nip myself for medicinal purposes." He chuckled but grew quiet when he saw that she didn't smile.

"Well, I can see that your mind is made up," he said. "If you are determined to file for divorce and you will pay me fifty dollars I will represent you."

"Fifty dollars! Fifty dollars! I don't have that kind of money."

He looked at her up and down and thought for a moment.

"Perhaps we can make other arrangements."

"What would those be?"

"I could use someone to clean my office every week or so."

"I can do that."

"Are you fit?"

"Fit as a fiddle."

"Stand up. Walk across the room."

She did so. "As you can see, I am perfectly fit, although I don't know what walking across the room proves. Anyone can do that."

He arched an eyebrow at her. "Let me see you bend over."

Edna bent over.

"Now turn around slowly," he said.

Edna became flushed. *So that is what he wants.*

Edna rose up and left, slamming the door behind her. She took a few steps down the sidewalk before turning around and yelling, "You can go to hell." She saw him look out the window and scowl at her. A couple walking across the street craned their necks to see what was going on. "You too," she yelled at them. It felt good.

Edna decided to return to her parents' home, divorced or not. The problem was that they only had the one car, and Torger wouldn't let her drive it. She didn't even know how to drive. Shifting gears with the clutch looked difficult. She sat at night staring at the red-hot glow of the stove and thinking what to do.

On Saturday night Torger went to town as usual. She went out to the car on a pretense as he was about to leave and watched him carefully as he started the car and drove away. He came in late in the evening drunk as Edna knew he would. He sat down on his chair at the table. "Woman, get me my food," he barked.

"Get it yourself."

His face grew red. "You worthless whore," he shouted. "Get me the strop! I'll learn you once and for all."

Edna walked to the entryway where the strop hung near the door. He was facing away from her, and she picked up the iron skillet that she'd hidden under a coat earlier in the evening. With one sudden movement she pulled it back and swung, using her forehand with all her might, and striking him alongside the head. Torger went down, falling to the floor. He lay still. She checked to make sure he was still breathing. He would have an egg on his head, but he would live. She quickly gathered up a bundle of her best things and went out to the Model A. She started it just as she'd seen him do. She didn't want to risk using the clutch more than she had to and perhaps stalling the car, so she left it in first gear, driving not much more than ten miles per hour.

When Edna started out that early November night, the sky was clear, but it soon grew cloudy and then the snow started. At first it was only a few flakes dancing into the headlights, but soon the ground was covered in white. The wind came up and the snow began to drift. It seemed terribly dark, and it was hard to see where the road ended and the ditch began. She had to keep rolling down the window and craning her head out to see the side of the road. *Perhaps I should turn back.*

She thought she heard a noise outside, a whooping sound. She stuck her head farther out the window. She listened. There it was again! It sounded like cranes high in the sky heading south. Perhaps it was just the wind coupled with her imagination, but it reminded her of Martin and it gave her a renewed sense of determination.

She arrived exhausted at her parents' house six hours later. It was still dark but the sound of the door slamming woke them, and her father peered out the window and saw her walk up to the house red-eyed and pale. "Edna!"

Chapter 12

M A R T I N

Just prior to the time of [his] death the same kind of boils as were on the legs of said Martin Tabert, broke out on his face, around the mouth, nose and eyes.

> Affidavit of John Marino, May 8, 1923, Gudmunder Grimson Papers, records of the State Historical Society of North Dakota, Collection Number: 10120.

The Captain was under the influence of liquor at the time he whipped the said Martin Tabert for I could smell it . . .

> Affidavit of Tom Wiggins, February 3, 1923, Gudmunder Grimson Papers, records of the State Historical Society of North Dakota, Collection Number: 10120.

. . . no State is more humane to their prisoners than Florida.

> Governor Cary A. Hardee, letter to Gudmunder Grimson, Gudmunder Grimson Papers, records of the State Historical Society of North Dakota, Collection Number: 10120.

Day by day, Martin struggled to do his work. He shoveled in a ditch, standing in water to his thighs. He was sweating in streams, and his wet shirt clung to his back. In the late evening it would get cold, and he couldn't get warm. Biting mosquitoes woke him at night. He had continuing stomach problems, too, because of the water parasites, and constant diarrhea caused him to lose weight. He had to tie his pants up with a rope.

Martin's feet got worse day by day. They were swollen grotesquely now, and boils began to appear on his feet and legs. Raw festering wounds discharged blood and pus. When he took his boots off at night it was all he could do to keep from screaming, the blood and pus having crusted and stuck to the leather, and pieces of bloody flesh tore off. One day he begged a guard to be allowed to take his boots off from time to time in the swamp to get some relief.

"Those boots are jus' fine," he said. "Quit your complainin'. I never heard a boy complain so much in my life. Why, most men be grateful for a pair of boots. They got big ol' cottonmouths out there in the swamp."

Martin had seen the cottonmouths that the men had pointed out, thick around as your arm, so he knew there were snakes, but he didn't see how boots would protect him anyhow, since he was often in water above his boots.

"Shit . . . I'm taking them off. I'll take my chances with the snakes," he said.

The guard jumped off his mule and hit Martin upside his head with his rifle butt. As Martin struggled to get up, the guard shouted, "White boy, you ain't so white now. Shet your mouth hole and keep a goin'."

Martin began to develop a boil on his groin now, too. If he stood with his feet apart it was bearable, but whenever he walked it made him wince. Within two days it had grown to the size of a walnut. The guard Gabe noticed him wince one day and asked him, "Shit, now what's your problem?"

"I got a boil here." Martin pointed. "A big one."

"Pull down your pants, let me see."

Martin did as he was told and Gabe let out a whistle.

"Doc Jones will be here tomorrow. I'll ask if he kin look at it."

This was the first that Martin had heard about a doctor, and it gave him some hope. He asked Glen about it that evening. Glen laughed, "I wouldn't call him a doctor. Maybe he uses that title, but he don't deserve to." Glen told him what he knew. "Doc" T. Capers Jones had been hired by Putnam Lumber to care for convicts in several of the north county camps. Too many convicts were dying in the swamps and camps, and the company lost money on them, so they were looking for someone to keep the convicts alive until their time was up. Judge Willis had persuaded Putnam Lumber to hire Doc Jones, a distant cousin. That was a dirty bit of nepotism, because Doc Jones was a drunk and medicinal abuser, and it was well known that he'd received less than a year of medical training at the Atlanta Medical College when he was drummed out for being too intimate with a cadaver. He'd drifted back to Florida and set up a small practice in southern Leon County, where he treated patients with various medicines, usually including alcohol as a major ingredient. Other than the most desperate or ignorant, he had few patients. Knowing women avoided him entirely once word got out that he routinely conducted rough pelvic examinations. Doc Jones was supposed to visit the Putnam Lumber convict camp once a month or more often if someone couldn't go to work in the morning. He often failed to show up as scheduled or showed up smelling of liquor.

That evening Gabe asked Captain Higginbotham if the Doc could see Martin for the boil on his groin.

"That damn Yankee's a no-good son-of-a-bitch, always complainin' of something. To hell with'em," Higginbotham said.

"Yes, sir. He's a complainer. But I seen it. It's one dang big boil."

Higginbotham shook his head. "By his pecker, you say. Most likely he got the syphilis. We don't waste the Doc's time on that. Hell, all these vagrans got it."

"Don't look like syphilis 'xactly."

"I 'spect you'd know about that."

Gabe was silent.

"Hell, he can see the Doc, but he don't take no time off. I won't have that damn Yankee layin' in bed. I don't like 'em. Ain't our kind. Lazy bastard, too. I'll own his hide before his ninety days is up."

"Yes, sir."

"And one more thing. The Doc don't treat his back for the whippin's. I ain't whippin' men so they can loaf around with salve on their backsides. When I whip 'em I want 'em to remember it. You got that?"

"Yes, sir, Captain."

The next day Martin was seen by the Doc, and his boil was lanced. The entire process lasted two minutes. The Doc told him to drop his pants and made a quick cut with a scalpel. Martin clenched his teeth to keep from screaming out as a stream of yellowish pus, tinged with red blood, flowed down his leg. Brown disinfectant was splashed on the boil and the sting hurt as much as the cut.

Martin asked the Doc if he could look at his feet too. Doc Jones said, "I don't do feet. Why, I'd be here all day if I had to treat every damn foot sore. They'll heal up by themselves anyhow. Stuff some moss in your boots."

"I can't. They're too tight."

"That ain't my doin'."

Martin was back to work the next day and he felt somewhat better having the boil lanced, but his feet only festered worse. Then, after he'd been in camp for a month, the malaria hit him. The first cycle knocked him hard at night in the bunk—fever, chills, head-aches, fatigue, sweats. He felt he was drowning in whirlpools of vertigo. He told Glen Johnson that he was sick that morning. "What should I do?"

"Shit, nothing you can do. The whipping boss drives everyone hard and it don't make no difference if a man gets sick or not. You get worked the same."

Martin dragged himself up and to his work with the other men. He was dizzy, trying to keep up with the shoveling and moving mud. The guard rode up to him on his mule, "You slowin' up boy. Pick up the pace."

"I'm not feeling so well. I can't stop sweating. I think I'm sick."

"Hell, the sweat will cool you off boy. Yo' ain't sick boy; just a shirkin'. What yo' good for? Gimme a strong black nigger instead of a white Yankee like you. There's no lammin' out at this camp. You work or you die. Sweat boy, before I report you to the boss."

That night Martin was called out of line and received twenty licks. They were delivered without mercy and with the strap cov-ered with syrup-stuck sand. He lay on his stomach on his bunk af-terwards. Turning his head to the side, he strained to draw in the putrid air of the bunk house. He felt nauseated from the malaria and thought he would retch. Glen Thompson came in and sat beside him. "I asked about the Doc," he said, "but I was told he ain't comin' back for a time." He lifted up Martin's shirt to look at the bloody cuts from the whippings and Martin clenched his teeth. "We ought to get something on that," he said. "Alligator grease will heal that up in no time. Maybe one of the men can catch a small one, and we can squeeze the grease out of him. And one of the colored men knows how to make a poultice out of swampwillow bark if'n he can find some. That'll take care of the chills some."

Martin retched and a brownish-green bile came up. Glen wiped it up with a rag. He watched Martin. Martin's teeth were chattering and he was silent, waiting for the attack of shakes to abate so he could speak. *Maybe it's already too late*, Glen thought. Glen cocooned him in a blanket, lying down beside him, holding him tight, trying to stop the shakes. Later, Martin looked up with half-opened eyes and said to Glen, "I-I-I never knew men could be so evil. Evil as devils. Why-why is that?"

"I don't know Martin. I thought on it many time myself since I've been here. I reckon we all have a little of the devil inside, but it's a small piece of us, and it keeps tamped down. Out here in the swamps there is nothing to keep it tamped down. Then you have the bigwigs of the Putnam Lumber Company. Don't think they don't know what happens out here. They do. But they are too blinded by greed to do anything about it. They could tamp down the evil, but they look the other way to the almighty dollar."

Martin was quiet for a minute thinking on that. "I'm not sure I can make it, Glen. If I don't, tell folks what happened here. They oughtn't to get away with it."

"I will, Martin. I promise."

"I'm never going to be able to see the whooping cranes."

"What?"

"Whooping cranes."

"Hush. You're delirious."

The malaria abated slightly for a day and then hit hard with a vengeance. Two days later Martin received twenty-five licks and then almost every evening the same. The pain was worse every time, the whipping opening up skin that never had a chance to heal. Often his shirt and pants would stick to the bloody ooze on his backside. Both legs were covered with risings and boils, running and festering, and he couldn't get around as he was having difficulty even walking. He was constantly muttering for water. Later, convict Max Grimm would tell how Tabert worked in a ditch next to him and they stood in water to their thighs: "He was weak and trembling so he could hardly lift his shovel. His eyes glittered like those of a half crazy man and he could hardly speak."[3]

Prisoner Gardner later reported: "One day Martin was working beside me we was in water above our hips shoveling sand to make a grade to lay the track on. Martin would get dizzy and fall down and could not work very much and Cap. Higginbotham wipped him two times that day and almost every night when he came in from work he would get wipped."[4]

A few of the men tried to give him help for a time, covering him with their own thin blankets at night to stop the shaking chills or giving him extra coffee, but there was nothing to clean his festering wounds. They were not allowed to procure any alligator grease, and the wounds began to emit a rank, cheesy odor. Flies buzzed around Martin's eyes and the raw wounds constantly. His limbs took on a corpse-color. The men began to stay clear from him, knowing he was a goner.

At night, after his whipping, Martin would lie in the bunk-house trying to sleep. His body was burning, then cold penetrated his bones and he would have the shakes, then his body was burning again. He slipped in and out of dreams. He dreamt of soda fountains and burying his hot face in an iced soda drink. He dreamt of a long white train taking him home. He dreamt of Edna.

Martin had been in the Florida convict camp for less than two months when he was whipped to his death. Sometime later, a former convict guard by the name of A.B. Shivers testified about Tabert being called out of line for the last time:

> Tabert looked at [Higginbotham] in complete despair and lay down on the ground at his feet. The whipping boss swung that "Black Aunty," a whip 5 ½ ft long . . . 3 ply leather . . . and brought it across the raw flesh. Tabert screamed for mercy. Thirty times the whip curled. Tabert was twitching. Walter Higginbotham put a foot on his neck and held him quiet, then added forty lashes. In the weird, unholy light of the campfire eighty-five prisoners stood in line until it was over. This was on Friday. Saturday he couldn't rise and was flogged in his bunk. On Sunday he couldn't swallow water. Scalding hot coffee was tried, and it seemed cold to him. He couldn't be washed on his bruised and sliced and inflamed body. On Wednesday, the first day of February, he drifted into a stupor and died that night.[5]

"Is That All There Is?"
— Peggy Lee

She heard a voice coming from above. "Hey, are you okay?" The water had spat her out and she realized there was a boat nearby. "Need some help?" She located the sound of the voice. A man was yelling from a long, flashy, Donzi speedboat.

She coughed and tried to restart her mind. "Yes . . . I mean no. I guess I swam out farther than I meant to." She looked to shore. "I think I can swim back."

"Are you sure? You could get hit by a boat out here. I almost didn't see you."

"I'm sorry about that. I'll swim back now."

"I'll stay here for a while, just to make sure. If you need any help, just raise your hand and I'll come and pick you up."

"Thank you."

She began swimming. Her arms and legs felt dead. Twice she felt like signaling to him. She kept swimming, slowly and steadily, switching to a side stroke when she tired. When her feet touched the bottom she stood up, turned, and waved to let him know she was okay. She lay down on her towel. She was exhausted and no longer felt she was floating above herself, and she fell asleep again for some time.

She was awakened by a cell phone ringing. It took her a second to realize that it was hers. She found it in the bottom of her beach bag. It was Paige. She answered, "Hi Paige."

"Hey, Nicole. I've been worried about you. I tried calling you earlier, but there was no answer."

"Sorry. I didn't have my phone with me."

"How's it going?"

"So, so. I haven't found out anything for my grandma."

"That's not surprising."

"I guess not."

"You should come back. Catch the next flight. There's a little shin-dig on Saturday at Sonoma's. A campaign fundraiser, of course, but no pressure. I need someone to go with. It should be fun. They always have the best food. Great wine. Not the cheap stuff. It'll be loaded with eligibles. Who knows? Maybe you'll meet another congressman."

"I didn't like that last one I met."

"Congressman Buckner?"

"Yeah. He was a jerk."

"Don't be so fussy. He was handsome as hell."

"He was married."

"They all are. Think of them as broken-in. Mature. Rich." She laughed, but Nicole knew she was being only half-facetious.

Paige continued talking about some new guy she'd met earlier in the week at the gym, and how buff he was, and what a cute smile he had, and how he was ex-military and had an important position in a defense contracting firm. Nicole's mind wandered. She remembered the political function where she'd met Congressman Buckner. It was at a reception room in the House Rayburn Building. Paige had dragged her there as usual. Paige loved these types of events. She was drawn to men with power and they were often drawn to her.

She could talk expertly about anything—the Washington Redskins, politics, or arcane details of congressional legislation. Nicole was not in the same league as Paige when it came to conversation, but she had her own assets, and it was not uncommon for men to look her way. At the reception she was wearing her sophisticated little black dress—an Armani sheath—zipped up in the back and tight at the waist and hips. She could hardly breathe for the Spanx she was wearing. Paige was dressed almost identically, although she never had to wear Spanx.

Paige had deserted her to talk to some people she knew, and Nicole was standing awkwardly alone. She noticed Congressman Buckner across the room. He seemed young, with boyish good looks, and she didn't know he was a congressman then. She thought he could be a staffer until she noticed his suit. It was a Brooks Brothers, not a suit a staffer would wear. She guessed he was a high-paid lobbyist. He looked her way and started to move in her direction when he was interrupted by a small group of men. She could see him laugh loudly at something they said. She walked over to the buffet line. She took a small plate and a few veggies. Then a chicken wing. Then another, and a spoonful of blue cheese dressing. She moved to the side of the room. She had a glass of wine in one hand and the small plate in the other. She looked for a place to set down her wine. She placed it on the edge of a windowsill. She tore the meat off a chicken wing and chewed it. She turned around and he was in front of her.

"Hi. I'm Congressman Buckner," he said. Nicole swallowed, slow to respond, and somewhat dumbfounded that he was a congressman.

"And you are?" he asked.

"Nicole Knutson. It's nice to meet you." She wondered if she had blue cheese and wing sauce on her lips.

"The pleasure's all mine. I'm glad you could come. Who are you with?"

"No one. Well . . . I mean . . . I came with my friend Paige."

"No, I mean who do you work with?"

"I'm in the Justice Department."

"Staff or attorney?"

"Attorney."

"What branch?"

"OLC."

"Really!"

She could tell he was impressed, and she liked that. They talked for a few minutes. He offered her a napkin, and she wiped her lips. There was a tell-tale bit of sauce on the napkin. He smiled at her. Before he excused himself, he asked for her phone number. She wrote her private cell phone number on the back of a card and handed it to him.

Paige came over. She was busy working on a plate of hors d'oeuvres with plastic picks sticking out. "Who's that?" she asked.

"Congressman Buckner."

"Ooh la la, girl. Nice catch. He's a real panty-melter."

"You think so?"

"Yes. Totally. I'd do him."

When she got home, Nicole googled him. She found out he came from a wealthy beer brewing family in Wisconsin. He served on the Armed Services Committee and was known as a bit of a hawk. He ran on a "family values" campaign. The Madison liberals hated him. She possibly could have overlooked some of that, but then she found a recent photo of him with his wife and three children. They were all smiling with perfectly coifed hair and straight white teeth, like the All-American family. When he called the next day and asked to get together, she said she was too busy and quickly hung up.

Paige interrupted her thoughts, "Are you still there, Nicole?"

"Ah, yeah. What were you saying?"

"I said I want to go to the gym again to see if I can run into him. You said you wanted to work out more this year. Come with me."

"Maybe."

"When will you be back?"

"I'm not sure . . . maybe I won't even come back."

"What are you talking about?"

"Nothing. Just babbling. But I need to tell you about something else. Something serious."

There was a slight pause before Paige said, "Sure, go ahead."

She confessed, "To be honest, I didn't come down to Florida just to help my grandmother. I was trying to escape work too."

"What?"

"You need to promise this doesn't get out if I tell you."

Silence.

"Are you there?"

Damn it! Her phone reception had dropped. Now she felt a desperate need to talk to her. She ran up the beach back to her car and drove to an open area where the reception was better. She called Paige and swore her to secrecy, then she told her about the Al-Nasser case and the photos, her voice rising and falling with her emotions as she poured it out.

"My God," Paige said. "That's nuts. Why would someone take photos of something like that? They must have been awful."

"Worse than that."

"I bet. Just come home. I'll have the pinot chilled. We'll go to a spa and get a massage or something."

"I don't want a massage. I'm past that. I can't get the photos out of my mind. Shouldn't something like that be investigated?"

"I suppose, but lots of things should. You can't take on everything, Nicole. It'll drive you nuts if you start worrying about everything wrong in the world. Book a flight home tomorrow. We'll go to the party."

"I told Lee that I needed a few more days. I have to finish looking for the grave for my grandmother. I just won't feel right about it if I don't."

"How did he take that?"

"Not well. I think he wants me there to keep an eye on me."

"Why?"

"I guess he thinks I could go to the press with what I know."

"But you wouldn't do that. Your career would be toast."

"No, I don't think I could. I've worked so hard to get where I'm at in OLC. But someone has to do something. We're torturing people. I can't get that out of my head. Doesn't that bother you?"

"Torture is a loaded term. No one is using that word. Not even the *Times*."

"Maybe they should."

Paige spoke up more loudly. "Nicole, I'm telling you for your own good, you can't take that on. That's for the White House. I'm sure they're just doing what's necessary under the circumstances. They don't want another attack on their watch."

"But they want OLC to endorse their dirty work. Lee is licking their boots. I'm caught up in this and I don't want to be. I feel responsible."

"Why would you be responsible? You were just doing your job."

"Paige, I'm the one who signed the opinion allowing Al-Nasser to be deported to Syria. Cheney wanted a quick sign-off. Lee was out of the office, giving a talk at some law school. I was back-up. Lee told me to give the White House whatever they wanted. So, I signed it. Me. Nicole Knutson. He's dead because of something I did."

"You're making too much of it. If you wouldn't have signed it, someone else would have. No one dares buck Cheney. Everyone knows that. When he wants something, he gets it."

"That doesn't change the fact that I signed it." Nicole was close to bursting into tears and she mumbled, "I think we're losing reception again. I have to go. Bye."

Nicole drove back down to Dixie County and the Sun Shade Motel. She showered and noticed that she'd gotten sunburned from falling asleep on the beach. She studied her red neck and thighs in the mirror, pressing down on her flesh to see how bad it was. The pain from the sunburn made the night even more miserable. The next morning she forced herself out of bed at 9:00 a.m., not knowing whether she had actually slept that night or not. Over the bad coffee from the lobby she reviewed her notes and lists of names. She was determined to check the remaining names of elderly folks on her list. Then she would head back to Washington, D.C. Three or four days, at most, she thought. She had two names to check in Steinhatchee, a small fishing town on the Gulf Coast. It was just over the border in Taylor County, but not far from the old towns of Clara and Mingo. It took her most of the day to track down the two residences. One person had recently passed away and the other had Alzheimer's. His caretaker said he couldn't remember the names of his own children. It was discouraging. The leads were getting thin.

Nicole drove back to the motel and walked next door to the diner. She passed by the window as she walked up to the door. *What the fuck?* She instinctively ducked. It was Mr. Lee with two other men sitting at a booth on the far side. She hoped she hadn't been seen. *Shit, shit, shit.* She walked around to the back of the diner, took the manila envelope out of her purse, and stashed it under the metal trash container reeking of grease.

Nicole entered the diner, acting startled to see Lee, and walked over to his booth. "What are you doing here?" she asked, trying her best to speak in a cool, calm way.

"Hello, Nicole." He stood up, smiling, and shook her hand, grasping it for a little too long. "Good to see you. This is Mr. Benson and Mr. Smith." They both wore gray suits and they did not stand but nodded their heads. Mr. Lee motioned for her to sit. "How are you, Nicole?"

"Pretty much the same as when I last talked to you."

"Have you found out anything about that kid's grave for your grandmother?"

"How do you know so much about what I'm doing?"

"Well, it took us some time to figure it out and track you down here to Dixie County. I wish you would have told me about that earlier. It would have explained a few things."

"It's personal. I don't have to explain everything to you."

"Of course not. But you didn't have to lie about your grandmother living in Florida when she lives in North Dakota. It makes me wonder."

"It wasn't a real lie. It was just easier than trying to explain the whole story to you."

"It's always better to tell the truth."

"You still haven't answered my question. Why are you here?"

"I'm flying down to Guantanamo. I thought it would be wise to make a quick stop on the way and tie up some critical loose ends."

"Guantanamo?"

"Just advising."

"What 'critical loose ends' are you tying up here?"

"Listen Nicole, we checked out David's office and apartment. So far he looks clean."

"I could have told you that."

"Well, we still have the problem of the missing photos."

"I told you I don't have them."

"I believe you. But we have to make certain. We need your motel room key, your car keys, and your purse."

"I don't believe this shit."

"Just make this easy, please."

She took out her car and motel keys and threw them on the table. They looked at her purse and she handed it to them. Benson turned it upside down and emptied it on the table. Tums, tampons, lip gloss, birth control pills, two miniature bottles of vodka, piles of used Kleenex, gum wrappers galore. She felt flush with embarrassment. Benson and Smith took her keys and left.

"Where are those two characters from?" she asked as she tossed everything back in her purse.

"The agency. Good men. Professional. Thorough."

"Did you have my townhouse searched too?"

"What do you think?"

"This is ridiculous."

"I'm sorry about this, Nicole. I really am. We just have to make certain. You're a smart woman. You can understand that."

"Don't try to flatter me. This is utterly humiliating."

"Like I said, I'm sorry."

She looked him in the eye, and he looked contrite, and she almost believed him.

"Are you coming back to work soon?" he asked.

"I don't know."

"I'll be forthright with you. I would feel more comfortable if you were back at work and I could see every day that you're still on our team."

"I'm on the team, Lee. That's not the issue. I'm just not sure if the team is doing the right thing sometimes."

"See, that kind of talk concerns me. I have no doubt we're doing the right thing. Everything we've done is legal."

"Right and legal aren't necessarily the same thing."

"They are under these circumstances."

"Bullshit! How do you think history will judge us in fifty years?"

He maintained his calm voice. "I think history will show that we did what we had to do."

"Torture?"

"It's not torture. What we've done is to their minds, not their bodies."

"What about in Syria?"

"We're not doing that. The Syrians are."

"We transport them there."

He scanned her face. "Where is this coming from all of a sudden?"

"I'm just not as certain as you are. About what we're doing. I have some reservations. Anyhow, I need some more time to work on my grandmother's issue. A few more days."

"Fine, I'm going to go out on a limb here. I'll give you a few days, but then you need to get back to the office. You got that?"

"Yes, I got it."

Mr. Lee ordered the grouper. Nicole couldn't eat. They sat and he talked about routine office affairs as if everything was normal. After an hour, Benson and Smith came back in and shook their heads.

"Good. I knew I could trust you," Lee said.

She looked him straight in the eye and pursed her lips.

"Unless you stashed the photos somewhere. Which would be stupid and you're not stupid."

"No, I'm not."

They handed her keys back.

Lee got up. "See you in a few days, then?"

"I expect you will."

He walked out the door. Benson and Smith trailed behind. She looked out the window and watched them drive away.

Nicole ordered a coffee and waited an hour, sitting still, except her legs were jiggling, and she frequently glanced out the window to make sure they were truly gone. Then she rose and walked out and to the back of the diner and retrieved the envelope. She hesitated, pulled the photographs out, and looked at each one for only the second time. She quickly stashed them back into the envelope and her purse. Her breathing was uneven and she had to clench her hands to control the trembling.

Nicole found Jerry's Bar on the highway towards Perry. It was an old wood and tin structure, and a wooden rail extended around the walk in the front. Two dozen pickup trucks were parked outside. She walked in, and the strong odor of cigarette smoke hung in the air. A maze of tables filled the front and there was a long wooden bar and row of barstools along the far wall. On the right was a small stage set up with a drum kit and stacks of speakers and an area for dancing. The floor was sticky and littered with peanut shells, which crunched as she walked. She sat on a barstool, her tan legs crossed in her cream-colored pleated skirt. She knew she looked out of place. Everyone in the bar looked at her. It wasn't the kind of place to order a martini. She ordered a whiskey and coke.

Nicole wished that Paige was there with her. Paige would help her forget. She would joke about the "local yokels" and try to make her laugh. Nicole downed her drink and signaled the bartender for another. A small birdlike woman two stools down moved over to sit next to her. The woman was of an undistinguishable age—between thirty and fifty. She was painfully skinny, heavily rouged, and her hands were fidgeting. She mumbled something.

Nicole said, "Pardon?"

"I lost my purse. Can you buy me a drink?"

"Sorry. I don't normally do that sort of thing."

"Oh, come on. I ain't got no money. My husband's in prison, my boyfriend's in prison, and my new boyfriend just got sent to jail."

"Sorry to hear that. We all have problems."

"What kind of problems does a pretty lady like you have?"

"You'd be surprised."

"One."

"What?"

"One drink. Can't you buy me one drink?"

Nicole didn't respond, but motioned to the bartender to get the woman a drink, and excused herself and walked to the ladies' room. When she returned to her stool, the woman was gone, her glass empty. A minute later, a man took the abandoned stool. He was tall and thin with a scruffy beard. He wore an American flag muscle shirt, with the stars on the left and the bars on the right.

"Can I buy you a drink, angel?"

"No thank you."

"You change your mind, you let me know. I'm feelin' good tonight. Just got off a twenty-three-hour drive and I'm still buzzin'." He was a truck driver, and he launched into a long-winded story about his trip down from Wisconsin. Something about his boss making him cheat on his logbooks, and how he needed money for insurance, and how they had repossessed his car illegally, and how he was behind on his child support payments.

Nicole tuned out and signaled the bartender for another drink. The man tried to pay for it, but she refused. He started talking again, something about his ex not letting him see his kids. Nicole was studying the amber color of her drink and her mind started shuffling rapidly—a cavalcade of memories from her first day on the job when she'd proudly hung her diploma and bar license behind her desk, to the legal opinions she'd written, to her last visit with Mr. Lee. *How can he be so damn sure of himself all the time?* She gulped her drink down.

She heard the man say, "Sorry to talk your ear off."

"No problem."

"You look a little down."

"No, I'm fine."

"You look like you could use some lovin'."

"No, I don't. Really."

"A little sugar in your bowl, if you know what I mean. Ha. Ha."

"I might need a whole lot of sugar in my bowl, but not from you. Sorry."

"You're a stuck-up bitch." He jumped off his stool and walked away.

Nicole's mind started in again about her work. The legal citations she'd researched for Lee. The memos he'd written for the

White House. How Lee had ignored the legal precedents and objections that didn't fit his theories. Then, Abbu Al-Nasser. His duct-taped body. His blackened puffed-up eye. His smashed-in nose. She looked down and realized that she'd twisted the bar napkin into a tight spiral.

Nicole had five or six drinks, she couldn't remember for sure, when the band took the stage and started playing. Southern rock and country and loud. A few people got up to dance. After two songs, a tall man wearing a cowboy hat, jeans, and white t-shirt asked her to dance. He had the good-ole boy, awe-shucks look of a country western star. Nicole said no. He hovered. Her thoughts returned to her work. *I went right along with it. I never questioned myself. I might as well have applied the electrodes myself.* She tossed down another drink. *Deep down, I'm a piece of shit.* She pulled the good-ole boy onto the dance floor. He was a good dancer, and once she started, her thoughts about work slowly began to crumble. The band started playing "La Grange," by ZZ Top. The booze was starting to kick her ass and the music throbbed and made her feel better. She remembered what a good dancer she was. She put everything into it, gyrating her hips, and leering at the man.

He shouted over the music, "I'm Lucious. You're pretty. What's your name?"

"Maribelle," she shouted back.

After the song, they sat at the bar and he asked her what she was drinking and he ordered her a double. She drank it straight down. Then another. She swung her stool around, her leg bumping his leg, then did it again. He smiled and pulled out a pack of Marlboros and offered her one. She let him light it for her, and she blew the smoke in his face as he flashed her a knowing look. A slow song started. "I Cross my Heart," by George Strait. "Let's dance some more," she said. As they danced, he slid his hands down and squeezed her ass cheeks under her skirt and pulled her tight. She felt him hard against her as they swayed across the floor. She could see the two of them from above. The last thing she remembered was Maribelle leaving the bar holding onto the wooden railing with both hands.

Nicole woke up in the morning with the sun filtering through the blinds. She had a dry, stale taste in her mouth, and she lay there for a moment, trying to remember where she was. A musky smell hung in the air, and the sheets felt slick with the night's sweat. Then someone moved next to her. She looked over. He was sleeping. Nicole studied him for a moment. She saw he had grimy nails and a wedding band. The feeling came creeping in. She watched the two of them lying in bed from above, looking very small.

Later, when he stirred awake, she closed her eyes and pretended to sleep. She could hear him get up and put his clothes on. She imagined that he was looking at her and thinking that she looked terrible in the morning. He walked into the bathroom and closed the door. The toilet flushed and he came out and left, closing the outside door softly. She groped for her underwear. *Where are they?* She couldn't find them. She looked about the room and saw them draped from the top of the television like a distress flag. She swung her feet to the floor and balanced dizzily for a moment. When she regained her equilibrium, she slid her underwear on and found her bra on the floor and walked into the bathroom. She had to stop and stare at it a minute in order to comprehend it, but yes, there was a message on the mirror. Luscious had written on it with her red lip gloss, THANKS FOR A GOOD TIME MARIBELLE. His phone number was underneath, then below that, ANYTIME.

She saw her reflection in the mirror, too. She pushed her hair back with her hand. Her face seemed to have the green-gray pallor of a drug addict, the cheeks oddly dark. She hated the face in the reflection. *If I smash the mirror, there will be very sharp shards of glass.* She turned around, looking for something heavy. Blood thumped her temples and a feeling of nausea hit her. She sat down on the toilet and rocked back and forth until she felt the need to turn around and spew the contents of her stomach into it. She stood up and wiped her mouth with the towel. Her mouth had a sour taste and she leaned over the toilet again and spit into it again and again. Her stomach contracted again, violently, but she only had the dry heaves now. She walked back into the bedroom and lay down and cried.

Nicole must have slept several hours when she was awakened by her phone ringing. She found it on the nightstand.

"This is Doctor Brownson in Devils Lake."

"Yes, what is it?"

"They told me that you would like to be updated on your grandmother Edna's status."

"Yes, yes I do."

"I'm afraid she's had another heart attack. We had her transferred to the hospital here. We have her on a heart monitor, but the readings aren't steady."

"Oh my God! I'll be up there as soon as possible."

It was 4:00 p.m. the next day when Nicole peered into Edna's room at the Mercy Hospital in Devils Lake, North Dakota. Edna was asleep. Edna's cardiologist, Dr. Brownson, was watching the readings on a monitor. He introduced himself when he saw her in the doorway. He looked to be in his mid-thirties, good looking, with a friendly disposition. He said, "She's a tough woman, but we're concerned about her heart rate. It's too fast. We're trying some new medications and we'll see how she does on those. The medications can cause drowsiness."

Nicole sat down on a chair at her grandmother's bedside. She studied her face. She looked very pale. A metal stand holding intravenous bags fed the tube sticking into her arm. Another tube supplied oxygen through her nose. It all looked so mechanical and cold. "How are her spirits?" she asked.

"Good. Her mind drifts away now and then. But she comes back. She seemed lucid this morning."

Dr. Brownson took the time to get Nicole a cup of coffee and sat with her and talked for a good twenty minutes. He had a Northeastern accent and Nicole asked where he was from. He said he was originally from Boston and that he'd come to love the prairie country of North Dakota. She was taken aback at that disclosure and surprised he took so much time to talk to her. After he left, Nicole was alone with her grandmother. She may have dozed off herself, she wasn't sure, when an aide arrived with a food cart and woke her grandmother.

Her grandmother looked around confused until her eyes settled on Nicole.

"Nicole. Why are you here?"

"Hi, Grandma." She gave her a hug and kiss. "I came back to see you. I heard you had some medical problems."

"Oh." She had a bewildered look on her face.

"Grandma, do you feel like eating something?"

"I don't know. I'm not too hungry. Maybe a bite or two."

The aide cranked her bed up so she could sit upright, and the tray of food was placed in front of her. Chicken, gravy, mashed potatoes, and peas. A single slice of white bread. Nicole noticed that Edna's hands were trembling, and she had a difficult time getting the fork to her mouth without spilling. "Can I help you with that?" she asked.

"Yes . . . it's pathetic, isn't it? I can hardly feed myself anymore."

"Well, you helped a lot of people in your life, there's no harm in letting someone help you for a change."

Her grandmother ate most of the mashed potatoes but refused even a bite of chicken.

"Are you sure you don't want any chicken, Grandma?"

"No, dear." She leaned towards Nicole and whispered. "The chicken here is terrible."

A short time later Edna said, "When I get back home, I'll butcher a young fryer and cook us up some real country-fried chicken. And real mash potatoes too, not the ones that come out of a box."

"Grandma, you don't have chickens anymore. You had to sell your chickens when you moved to the nursing home, remember?"

"Oh . . . I don't have chickens anymore?"

"No, Grandma."

The nurse came in with a little cup and Edna took her medications. Her eyes closed and she fell back asleep. Nicole closed her eyes too and thought about easier, more innocent times.

Edna had chickens on the farm when Nicole had stayed with her in the summers. Edna was already in her seventies then and living alone. Nicole still held fond memories of those summers. The white farmhouse, the big yard, and the red barn with a hundred places to play. Edna rented the farmland out, but she still kept chickens: Leghorns, Plymouth Rocks, Rhode Island Reds, and small colorful black-and-red Bantams. They ran free in the barnyard. Edna gave Nicole grain or scraps of food to feed them. In June, to mark Nicole's arrival, Edna would purchase a couple dozen baby chicks for her to care for. They were just little yellow fuzzballs when they arrived. Nicole loved the way they bonded to her after only a few days, so desperate for a mother that they came running when she opened the chicken coop door. She loved to watch them pick at their feed and drink water with their tiny beaks, tipping their heads back to let it flow down their throats. By the end of the short summer they had already grown, and they were not so cute, but they still came rushing to her every time she went outside, and they would follow her around the yard.

Nicole's chores those summers included gathering the eggs every day from the barn. The chickens had two long rows of crates filled with straw, and Nicole would look for the eggs there first. But the hens would sometimes lay eggs in other nooks and crannies of the barn, too, so Nicole would have to search high and low for where they might be hidden. Occasionally she would find abandoned eggs that had been undiscovered. She would shake them to feel whether the contents shook. If they did, she knew they were rotten. "Throw out all the rotten eggs," her grandma said, "far from the house." Nicole took them down to the rock pile a quarter of a mile away and tossed them. She loved to throw those rotten eggs against the rocks. They would have turned color by then, blue or green, and she liked the rainbow of colors. She learned to get upwind from them.

The good eggs she would bring up to the kitchen and Grandma Edna would always ooh and ahh at her find, like finding an egg was a great thing that never grew old. She and Nicole would wash them with a wet rag and put them in egg crates. Edna used a lot of the eggs for her baking and often cooked eggs for breakfast. The yolks of those eggs were bright yellow and the eggs tasted nothing like the eggs Nicole now bought in D.C., even the "free range" ones from Fresh Fields Market.

Besides the twenty-five or so chickens that Edna kept, she had anywhere from twelve to twenty cats at any given time. They were not housecats. They lived in the barn, but Edna fed them every day, and between the food she gave them and the mice they caught, they appeared to be a fat and happy lot. Every summer there would be several new litters of kittens. It would be a challenge to find where the mother cats had hidden them. This search was even harder than finding eggs. The kittens would often be under a pile of boards or junk someplace in the barn. Nicole would stealthily follow the mother cats with their teats showing to see where they disappeared. Then she would search until she found the kittens. Often they still had their eyes closed and they would be tiny little fur balls. She would run and get her grandmother, and they would spend hours gently picking them up and petting each one. Edna said you had to give kittens a lot of attention when they were little or they would be wild and never love people. At first, the mother cats would look on warily, but if you were patient they would come around, and you could pet them too until they arched their backs and purred, seemingly proud of their offspring.

Nicole remembered one summer when she discovered a litter of baby kittens that were dead when she checked on them. She ran up to the farmhouse crying. "Grandma, Grandma, the kittens are dead." Edna ran out with her and gently checked each one for a sign of life, but they were limp, their necks broken. Edna explained that a tomcat must have come around from a neighboring farm and killed them. "They do that so the mother cats go back into heat and they can breed them," she explained. Edna told Nicole to watch out for any strange tomcats.

A few days later she saw an unfamiliar big gray tomcat slinking around the barn. She ran to the house and told her grandmother. "I'll deal with him," Edna said. She took some meat out of the fridge along with a sharp kitchen knife and some disinfectant from the closet.

"What are you doing, Grandma?"

"We're going to fix that cat. Cut off his testicles, so he's not so aggressive." She walked out to the barn and befriended the tom cat with the meat until it was purring at her side. Then she picked him up and carried him over to an old stove pipe. She forced him into it so that only his legs were hanging out. She explained that this was so the cat couldn't turn around and scratch them. She had Nicole hold the cat's struggling legs while she made a quick insertion in his nut sack with the knife. The cat howled and shrieked horribly. Her grandma quickly pulled out his testicles and cut the connecting tissue. She splashed on some disinfectant and let the cat loose, and it slinked away. Nicole watched with some satisfaction. She knew that cat wouldn't be bothering any kittens anymore.

In addition to the animals, Nicole would never in her life forget Edna's cooking and baking. If she closed her eyes, she could still see her lifting a tray of fresh-baked cookies out of the oven. Gosh, how she could eat in those days. A dozen was nothing to her, still gooey and soft with melted chocolate chips. Besides chocolate chip cookies, Nicole remembered Edna baking sugar cookies, gingersnaps, oatmeal cookies, thumbprint cookies, peanut butter cookies, monster cookies, date-filled cookies, and lemon coconut dainties. Her grandmother taught her how to make sticky buns, too, and jelly rolls, potato donuts, bars galore, and an endless variety of pies.

Nicole had other warm food memories, too, like her grandmother's huge garden where she would spend afternoons eating fresh peas off the pods and stuffing herself with raspberries. Then on Saturdays, her grandmother would kill a chicken for the Sunday dinner. Edna nabbed a leg with a hooked stick and cradled the chicken in her arm and brought it up to the shed where she had a pan of scalding hot water and a chopping block ready. Their heads would be cut off in one quick strike with the cleaver, and the chicken would tumble across the yard, sometimes trying to run or fly without its head. Nicole thought this was gross at first, but she got used to it. Edna told her they didn't feel a thing without their heads, it was just their nerves reacting. Once the chicken was still, she would dip it in the hot water, and the two of them would pluck it. Edna saved the soft breast feathers for pillow stuffing. On Sundays, after church, Edna would dip the cut up chicken in her special buttermilk batter and fry it in lard. Nicole became a careful eater as she grew older, avoiding fried foods in favor of salads, but she knew that if she could ever get fried chicken that good again, nothing would stop her from eating it and licking the grease off her fingers.

She remembered too her grandmother looking out the kitchen window and scanning the sky.

"What are you looking for, Grandma?"

"I like to look out and see the birds. Sometimes I see geese and cranes flying." She pulled Nicole close into her apron and hugged her.

The memories comforted Nicole. She knew she would always be able to evoke them whenever her mind went to the dark place.

After an hour or so, Edna woke up. She seemed more alert, talking about a television show she'd seen recently and the tennis star, Serena Williams. "Did you see her win at Wimbledon? She has a terrific forehand." Nicole was amazed she knew about such things.

As they were chatting, Nicole noticed a photo by the bed.

"Is that Grandfather Ted?"

"Yes, dear. I always keep his photograph with me. It reminds me of how the Lord blessed me. Blessed me with Ted, and children, and grandchildren."

"I never met him, did I?"

"No, he passed away before you were born."

"How long were you married?"

"Nineteen wonderful years. He was my savior, Ted was. I was having a hard time in life before that. I don't know that I ever told you about that. I don't like to dwell on those things."

"No, you never talked about the hard times, Grandma."

"Well, you heard about the Dirty Thirties I expect. Those times were tough for everyone, especially the farmers. Uff da. And I got divorced and times were tough after that too."

"I didn't know you were married before Grandfather Ted. Dad never said anything about that."

"I think your dad knew, but it wasn't something we ever talked about much at home. My first husband was a real bastard. I don't like to use that word, but he was."

Nicole sat at Edna's bedside for over an hour while Edna told her the story of her first marriage with Torger. She ended by saying, "He hurt me, and hurt can stay in the human heart for a long time—a lifetime really."

"Yes, I think it does, Grandma."

Her grandmother slowly reached out and grasped her hand and held it. "I want you to remember something important though."

"What?"

"Love can overpower hurt. Don't ever forget that"

"I won't, Grandma."

She asked for a sip of water, and Nicole held it up to her with the bent straw. Edna appeared visibly exhausted; Nicole shut off the lights and left for her hotel so her grandmother could get some rest. Later that night, Nicole lay in bed thinking about her grandmother's story. Her feelings were mixed up. Sadness and anger that Torger would treat her grandmother like that. Mad at the world for being such an evil place at times. But she marveled at her grandmother's resilience. As long as she'd known her grandmother, she was always bright and full of life. *How is that possible after what she went through?*

In the morning, Nicole was at the hospital at 8:00 a.m. Dr. Brownson was at Edna's bedside. He'd come in at 5:00 a.m. to check on her. "She had a good night," he said. "I've been monitoring her closely. Her heart rate has finally gotten down close to where it needs to be."

"Thank God. I was concerned yesterday. She told me about some of the hard times she went though in life. I started thinking it might not be good for her heart to relive all that."

"I wouldn't worry about that. It's good for people to tell their stories to others."

"It was tough to hear."

"I'm sure. You learn from listening though."

"Learn what?"

"How to get through your own hard times."

Dr. Brownson left and Nicole sat by her grandmother's side until she woke up. She looked confused, but smiled when she saw Nicole. Nicole brushed her hair. It was soft and white and still with a surprising amount of body for someone her age. Nicole asked, "How did you make it through those hard times you talked about yesterday, Grandma?"

"Didn't have any choice, I guess. Sometimes all you can do is just put one foot in front of the other and try to get through the day. You draw strength from someplace. My parents tried to help me the best they could, too. I could always count on them. And they taught me right from wrong. I had that to fall back on."

"How did you meet Ted then?"

Edna asked for a sip of water and cleared her throat.

Chapter 14

E D N A

Darkness cannot drive out darkness; only light can do that.
    —Martin Luther King

When Edna left her husband Torger in 1934, she moved back in with her parents. Torger tracked her down and drove up with his sister, Helen, a few days later. He knocked on the door early in the morning while Helen sat in the car. Edna went to the door, but kept the screen shut between them. "Edna," he said. "You're still my wife. You need to come back home now."

"I'm not coming home with you," she said. "I told you I would not be treated like an animal and I meant it."

"I'm sorry. I lose my head sometimes. I know that. But you're not blameless either. You brought a lot of it on yourself. The things you wrote in your journal. Harlot words and you know it. No one should write those kinds of things."

"I'll write whatever I damn well please."

"You're a hot-headed woman, cussin' like that."

"Damn right."

He frowned at her but took another tact. "Think about your friends at church. What will they think? And the reverend? Getting a divorce is a sin."

"Well, I guess I'll be going to hell then, because I'm not coming back to you."

"Why, I ought to bust you right now."

"Try it, mister."

He clenched his fists, but she knew that he wouldn't dare come into the house with her father there.

He turned around abruptly and walked away. After a few steps he turned his head and yelled at her. "Don't come a crawlin' and a'whinin' for me to take you back."

She yelled back, "You and your sorry farm and your shack of a house will rot and turn to dust before I ever come back to you, Torger!" She slammed the door shut.

Edna never saw Torger again. Edna's father paid for a lawyer in another town to represent her in her divorce. It was a bitter proceeding, and she didn't receive any property, but she was relieved when the divorce was granted.

Torger was embarrassed and angry that she'd divorced him. He thought it damaged his reputation, whatever it was, and he began to tell lurid lies throughout the countryside that he'd kicked her out when he found out she was cheating on him. He told folks that he caught her in the barn with a big Swede from the threshing crew. Over time the stories grew in that small community, every teller adding a few more details to make it sound more salacious. Within months, Edna was the butt of jokes of all the men in the community. They talked about how she'd taken on the entire threshing crew in the barn, the men waiting in line as she leaned over a barrel with her skirt thrown over her head.

In short order, Edna was shunned by the women in the community too. They called her a bad woman, a floozy. She couldn't even get a job as a domestic because the women didn't trust her in their households. She quit attending the local church because she could no longer abide the way the women looked at her, whispering their gossip as they clustered outside the church after the service. For years afterward, decent men would not talk to her because she was a divorcee. Only the louts and drunkards would try to talk to her when she occasionally went to town, and when she rebuffed them, even they cussed at her.

For a long time, Edna withdrew into herself, seeking solace in the land. She would take long walks on the prairie roads near her parents' farm every day. It was flat, desolate country, and she could walk for miles in any of four directions. At first, the occasional neighbor's automobile or farm truck passing by would stop and ask if she needed a ride. They assumed she needed help—maybe her auto had broken down up the road. It was in the day when walking for exercise was not yet in fashion, and no one walked down the road without a good reason. But soon the neighbors ignored her, and when she saw an automobile she would simply pull up her collar and turn her head the other way as it drove past. She knew that they called her crazy or insane, but she no longer cared.

Most people would not see much on these roads: crops, pasture, stubble, fences. Edna saw more by opening herself to the small wonders. She liked to take notice of just a tiny piece of wonder each day that she could hold in her mind. Wildflowers in the spring and summer—small pink prairie roses, yellow and orange coneflowers, wild sunflowers, delicate prairie smoke flowers, purple thistle, small wild crocus. Sunrises and sunsets—subtly changing from fiery reds and oranges to muted pastels. Sounds of the prairie—the song of the meadowlark, the croaking of frogs, the orchestra of chirping crickets, the lonesome rustling of the dry grass thrashed by the wind. And always, she looked for birds. Killdeer, faking their broken wings. Pintails, teal, and mallards in the ponds. And, of course, the geese and cranes migrating high overhead in great V-shaped formations.

A favorite activity was to walk down to the big slough south of their house in the evening. There was always something to see. Giant purple dragonflies skimming over the water, red-wing blackbirds settling in the rushes, baby ducks and coots scooting to hide behind a clump of reeds. Even in the winter she could find something if she looked carefully enough: burst seed pods, frosted cattails on a slough, milkweeds in seed. She walked in almost all weather, wearing a large men's sheepskin coat in the winter to keep warm.

The first few years she was back home were years of poverty for her family. The Great Depression still raged, and Edna and her parents had little extra money to spend on anything except essentials. She took to sewing all of her own clothes again, taking remnants or cloth she bought on sale and fashioning beautiful dresses for herself. She rarely had anyplace to wear them, but it was part of her fantasy life.

As the years crept by and the Depression abated, she increased the size of the family chicken flock, and with the help of her father, built a larger chicken coop. The egg money was her only source of income. She always gave half of it to her parents to help them with her keep, but as her flock grew, she began to have enough income for a few things, and she bought hats to match the dresses she sewed. She also spent money for magazines and books, something that was also considered odd in the community. Most Norwegian farm homes didn't have much more than the King James Bible and a few animal husbandry books. She bought *Harpers, Life, The New Yorker*, and glossy fashion magazines like *Bazaar* and *Vogue*. She liked poetry as well as fashion, and she would send for books by the poets she read about. She particularly enjoyed the poetry of Marianne

Moore, E.E. Cummings, Hart Crane, William Carlos Williams, and Emily Dickinson. They had just received electricity on the farm and she read late into the night, huddling in a quilt close to the dim bulb.

After a time, Edna tried writing her own poems. The words would careen around in her head as she walked the roads. She wrote them down when she returned to her house, and as she gained more confidence in her writing, she brought a few poems into a local newspaper, the *Rolette Record*. The editor, who was new in town, liked them and published one poem, paying her a dollar. Edna was thrilled. *A published author!* But then some of the women in the community complained. She was a bad example for the young people they said. The editor would not publish any more poems by her.

Edna began to keep a journal again. This was an escape for her and she wrote in it every day. Once it sunk in that she would never again have Torger to pry into her journal, she began once more to record her fantasies. These were more elaborate now. Her heart was still haunted by the memory of Martin, and she would write as if he were still alive and now her wedded husband. If she walked up the road and saw a badger she might go home and write about it, recalling the time they'd seen a badger near the grove of trees where they met so many years ago. Her stories would be embellished with intimate details of the most risqué nature. She talked to herself sometimes, too, carrying on imaginary conversations as she walked the roads.

As these years went by, Edna became resigned to being a spinster, not happy, but she'd grown content with her lot in life. She saw no use for real flesh and blood men. They only caused grief and hardship; she preferred her fantasy life with Martin.

It was unexpected when she met Ted Knutson in 1944. Edna noticed a strange man occasionally driving by as she was taking her walks, and he always tipped his hat. One day he passed her by and then stopped a hundred yards ahead. Edna was wary and she looked up and down the road to see if any others cars were coming. *Why is he stopping?*

She turned around and started back the other way. She heard his steps running up behind her. She turned to face him and was startled to see that he only had one arm, his empty sleeve pinned to his coat.

"I don't mean to scare you," he said.

"Then please leave me alone."

"I'm Ted Knutson. You're Edna, right? My folks mentioned that you were the one who walks the roads."

"Yes, I'm Edna and you best leave me alone or I'll report you to the sheriff."

He laughed. "Gosh, do I look that scary with only one arm?"

"No, I didn't even notice that."

"You're being polite."

He continued to walk beside her. She gave him a look as if to warn him away.

"Gee lady, is it okay if I walk down the road? It's a free country last I heard."

"Suit yourself, but don't you try to 'lady' me."

He smiled then and she noticed that his smile was wide open and sunny, the type that said he was glad to meet you and you would probably be glad to meet him. Having heard his name, she placed him. He was a few years younger than her and had recently returned from the war. She'd read a story in the local newspaper. He'd seen action in the Pacific, was badly wounded at Iwo Jima, and lost his arm. After spending six months in a military hospital, he returned home and they'd had a parade down Munich's Main Street in his honor.

"How far do you walk?" he asked.

She wanted to get rid of him. She did not trust any man. "None of your business," she said.

"Really," he said, "I'm harmless. I'd just like to get to know you better. We're practically neighbors you know. I only live five miles up the road."

"Have you not heard about me?" she said. "I'm a fallen woman they say. I'm crazy."

"You don't seem crazy to me."

"If you knew me better, you'd know. Believe me, I do crazy things."

"Like what?"

"Like walking up and down these roads every day. Like talking to myself sometimes."

"I don't think that's crazy."

He continued to walk with her and moved a little closer.

She moved to the far side of the road. "Maybe you're interested because of what they say about me," she said. "You think I'm good for a roll in the hay. Well, get that out of your mind. I don't like men at all. In fact, I don't like anyone . . . except my parents. I like to be left alone."

"I respect that. I expect you have your reasons. No one can know what another person has gone through. What brings them to a point in life. We're all just like cottonwood seeds blown by the wind, I suppose. Still, maybe I can cheer you up some."

"How would you do that?"

"I could tell you a joke."

"I don't like jokes."

"A story then?"

"I don't like stories either. Just leave me alone."

"Perhaps a poem. *If I can stop one heart from breaking, I shall not live in vain; if I can ease one life the aching, or cool one pain, or help one fainting robin, onto his nest again, I shall not live in vain.*"

"Emily Dickinson!"

"Yes! Do you like poetry?"

"I love poetry."

"Me too!" He was quiet for a second. "Oh, don't tell people about that. They wouldn't understand around here."

"I know. I won't."

Ted was soon walking the roads with her every day. They would walk and talk for hours about everything in the world or nothing at all. Ted liked to joke, and the two of them would often end up bubbling with laughter. One day he asked her, "Do you like to dance?"

"Well, truth be told, I've never danced before."

"Never danced? Why a pretty woman like you was just made to dance. Do you want to try it?"

Edna surprised herself by saying yes. He was soon taking her to neighborhood barn dances where they learned all the square dances. Even with only one arm, Ted could swing her around the floor with authority, and she thought she never had so much fun in her life. Six months after they met, he asked her to marry him. She said yes with delight and he was so excited he danced a jig on the spot and whooped so loud that their neighbors in the farmyard a mile away could hear it.

They were married six months later on June 10, 1945, before the Justice of the Peace in Devils Lake, just the two of them, their parents, and a clerk as a witness. Ted looked handsome in a gray suit and wore a spiffy felt hat. He gave her a gift of a pearl necklace. She wore an ivory chiffon dress with a semi-fitted bodice that flattered her figure. It had a simple neckline — perfect to show off the pearl necklace — and she didn't wear a veil, wearing her blond hair pulled loosely back in waves, with wildflowers interwoven in the strands.

After the wedding night at the hotel in Devils Lake, he took her on a honeymoon to Yellowstone National Park. They were gone a month and every day they camped and every night they made love in his old army tent. He was gentle and slow and for the first time, she luxuriated in the carnal joy that a kind heart and a tender touch could bring from a man.

They settled down on the farm where Ted grew up. His parents retired from farming and moved to town. Ted was a bit of a dreamer, not lazy, but not the best farmer in the area. He didn't have to be. He planted his seed and the rains came and the crops were good. Grain prices were high after World War II, and in a few years they built a big white house with a wrap-around porch. Edna was thirty-six years old when she married Ted. They had two daughters in quick succession and then to their surprise a son, Tim, in 1950 when Edna was forty-four years old. Tim was Nicole's father.

The years skipped by for Edna. She was happy and they were good years, the late 1940s, the 1950s, and early 1960s. Prosperous times for those who worked the land. Edna would look back on those years as the best of her life. Her children grew up happy and healthy, and Edna always saw to it that her daughters dressed beautifully, sewing their dresses herself when they were small, and when they became young women, taking them on a dress shopping spree to Fargo every year. Both daughters went on to college and one eventually became a manager of the Dayton's Department Store in Minneapolis and the other a fashion designer in New York City. Edna and Ted traveled around the world, visiting the capitals of Europe, the pyramids of Egypt, and twice flew all the way to Hawaii.

In 1964, Ted died unexpectedly when he got off his tractor on a hillside to remove a rock and the brake on the tractor slipped and the tractor rolled back over him. Edna grieved Ted's death terribly. For a time, she took to walking the roads alone again, but she had her children now, and they were a supreme source of comfort and support. Over time she realized that God had given her a gift by bringing Ted into her life, and they'd had nearly twenty wonderful years together.

When her son left to attend Carleton College, Edna was once again left alone on the farm. She had her chickens and cats and garden and reading and poetry writing. She started attending church again. She made new friends. Then in 1979 she found out to her delight that her granddaughter Nicole was coming for the summer. Edna cherished those summers with a smart, inquisitive grand-daughter, so full of promise.

The astonishing thing is that some people are good, and many others try to be.
— Katherine Boo

Nicole was still in Devils Lake, North Dakota, when she received a telephone call from her mother. It was late at night and Nicole was in her hotel room, lying on top of her bed, staring at the ceiling and thinking. She hesitated when she saw who was calling, but picked it up and answered.

"How are you dear?"

"I'm fine, Mom. I'm up in North Dakota visiting Grandma Edna." She told her about Edna's condition.

"She's a strong woman. Led an admirable life," her mother said. "I hope she recovers and has a few more good years."

Nicole was taken aback that her mother could be so sympathetic.

"What's up, Mom? Why are you calling?"

"I've been thinking about some things we talked about when you called me last."

"Like what?"

"About me not being there for you when you were younger. I know I wasn't a good mother."

"That's not what I said, Mom."

"You don't have to say it directly. I know it's true. I don't know why I am the way I am. Sometimes I wish I could do it all over again."

"Would you still divorce Dad?" Nicole asked.

"I wish I could say I wouldn't, but I would. Oh, he was a good man. We were just too different. Look at him now, living in Hong Kong and being a successful corporate attorney. Could you see me as the wife of a corporate attorney?"

"Not exactly."

"No, of course not. But after the divorce I should have spent more time with you. It was wrong of me. I was selfish. I know that now."

"Thank you for saying that, but it's a little late for that now, right?"

"Yes, I suppose so. I'm sorry, dear. Sometimes it takes a long time for revelations to break through the surface. Years."

Nicole was silent for a moment trying to comprehend. She couldn't yet. "Anything else, Mom?"

"I just hope that you find someone who can make you happy. I wish I had set different expectations with Devlin from the start. I know I told you I don't mind him running around with those young groupies, but I do. It tears me apart sometimes. I cry when he's gone. I worry that he'll leave me for a younger woman and I'll be all alone."

"What about you and the swami in India?"

"Oh, I just made that up. I want people to think that I am still desirable but I know I'm not."

"Of course you are."

"No, I know I'm not. When you reach my age, men look right through you like a piece of glass. You can't bank on your looks forever. It all goes south."

Nicole wondered if she was warning her.

"I hope things will be better for you," Ginny said. "You're still young enough to make choices."

Nicole woke up later that night again. She couldn't sleep and she put her coat on and walked outside. It was dark, only a few streetlights casting a yellow haze that intensified the lonely stillness. She paced the parking lot and thought about her life ever since she was a child. She thought about her mother. She realized that much of what she had done in her life was out of anger that her mother had left her. She would get back at her by being everything that her mother wasn't. That anger was fading now.

Before she went to sleep, she called her father. She calculated the time zone difference with Hong Kong in her head. It was morning there. He answered on the third ring. He'd been in contact with Dr. Brownson and knew about Edna's medical condition. They talked for a long time and Nicole now told him about Edna and Martin and how she'd been searching for the grave, something he knew nothing about.

"Nicole, I'm so proud of you trying to help your grandmother," he said. "Not many people would go to all that trouble to help their grandmother like that."

"Well, she's special. You were lucky to have a mom like that."

"I know. That's why I sent you up there in the summers to be with her."

"I really wanted to find Martin's grave for her. It would bring her some peace."

"Sweetie, there might not be much you can do. It was a long time ago. Not many people live to be ninety-eight like your grandmother. Any witnesses probably passed away long ago."

"I know that, Dad, but I feel like I need to try my best."

"I understand that. But I know how you are. You never want to give up. You've always been so persistent in everything you do."

"I get that from you."

"I guess so. Remember when you did that Science Fair project in middle school? Something about pollution levels in creeks flowing into the Potomac. You insisted on checking every creek. We must have spent weeks driving around and obtaining water samples."

"I remember."

"You got first place, too."

"That was in the regional competition. I only placed third in state."

"Third is great."

Nicole had never forgotten how disappointed she'd been with the result. "I was mad because I wanted first place so badly."

"You did fine, honey. You don't have to be perfect all the time."

"I'm not, Dad. That's one thing you don't have to worry about."

"You're perfect enough in my eyes, honey. Whatever you do."

"Thanks, Dad."

"One more thing."

"What?"

"It's probably not safe down there in that part of Florida by yourself."

"Don't worry. I'm done with that anyhow. For now, at least."

"Good."

"I should go. It's late here. I love you, Daddy."

Nicole awoke early in the morning. She'd slept better. She took a shower and noticed the skin was peeling where she'd been sunburned. She dried her hair and put on a light touch of makeup. She spent the day in the hospital with her grandmother. Dr. Brownson said her grandmother's condition seemed to be stabilized. Nicole was sitting by Edna's bed when her phone rang. She looked at it and noticed the number had a Florida prefix. *Now what?*

"Hello, this is Sheriff Speckhauser."

Nicole thought she'd misheard.

"Who?"

"Sheriff Speckhauser, from Dixie County, Florida."

"Oh."

"I guess you would be surprised to hear from me. We only had that one short conversation when I pulled you over in your car. Hope I didn't frighten you."

"You didn't frighten me."

"Well, good. I told you I was asked to look out for you. Doris from the Historical Center asked me to. She was worried about you and said you might need some help. She gave me your cell phone number, too. I know a lot of people so I've been asking around some."

Nicole was quiet as she processed this new information.

"I located two elderly people you might want to talk to. One is a man by the name of Edgar Sneldon. He was an employee of Putnam Lumber for most of his life. The other is a woman, Netta Tuck. She's a good lady. I've known the family for years. Anyhow, she knows all the old unofficial graveyards in the county. She might be willing to talk to you if you want to meet her."

"I'm up in North Dakota now."

"Oh, is that where your grandmother lives, the one who asked you to find the grave?"

"Yes."

"How is she?"

Nicole was struck by his tone of concern. "She's in the hospital, but she's stable for now. Thank you for asking."

"Good to hear that. Maybe you don't want to come back down now. It's probably not a good time."

"No . . . I do . . . I don't like to leave things unfinished. I'll fly back tomorrow."

"If you want, I can pick you up at the airport in Tallahassee and drive you back down to Dixie County. I have to go up that way to deliver a prisoner anyhow."

"Oh . . . that would be okay, I guess."

Sheriff Speckhauser picked Nicole up at the airport. He was driving a sheriff's marked car and it seemed strange to Nicole to climb inside with the computer and a short-barrel shotgun between them. He had a suit and tie on, however, not a sheriff's uniform, and he didn't look intimidating. He looked to be forty at best. Dark hair, dark eyes. Handsome actually, Nicole thought. "Call me Jim," he said.

As they drove, he inquired about her grandmother and what it was like in North Dakota. She explained that she'd spent her summers there as a child and it was beautiful that time of year. "I've never lived there in the winter though. I hear it can be rather daunting."

"Yeah, I've seen those blizzard scenes on the weather channel."

Nicole asked Jim about himself, and as he warmed up, he talked more freely. She found out that he wasn't the scary redneck Southern sheriff she'd seen in the movies. He had a B.A. in American Literature and a master's degree in Criminal Justice from the University of Florida, where he'd played baseball on a scholarship. He'd also spent two years in the minor leagues before he threw his arm out and taught school before going into law enforcement.

They'd been driving for about an hour when Jim said, "I have a confession to make."

"What is it?"

"Ordinarily, I would've had one of the deputies deliver the prisoner to Tallahassee. I wanted to give you a ride back because

I'm intrigued by this whole story of Martin Tabert and your search for his grave. It's a real historical mystery. Can I ask you more about that?"

Nicole could see that he had a sincere interest, so she told him everything she knew from her research and what her grandmother had told her. He kept asking about the details and dates.

"So, Martin's death was on February 1, 1922? You're positive about that?"

"Yes, that's in the official record . . . why does the exact date matter so much?"

"As long as I'm in a confessional mood, I'll tell you. I wanted to make sure that my grandfather wasn't involved in any way."

"Why would he have been involved?"

"My grandfather was a fisherman back in 1922. Out of the port at Apalachicola. He had a big family, twelve children, to feed. He was a decent enough man, given the times, I suppose, but the times were tough, and he skirted the law now and then. Anything to make a buck. Ran rum up from the Caribbean, smuggled illegal plumes out of the country, that sort of thing. I heard that he would occasionally do some work for Putnam Lumber in the off season—loading ships at the ports, driving freight and even prisoners, I suspect. It wasn't unusual. Most everyone in this part of Florida was connected in some way to Putnam. They ran the show down here."

"So, how do you know your grandfather wasn't involved in Martin's death in some way?"

"Well, when I heard about Martin Tabert's story from Doris at the Historical Center, I got to thinking, and I checked the fishing boat records, just to make sure. My father was a fisherman, too; he's retired now, but he still has all the old records. I went through them. The records show that my grandfather was down on the southwest coast at the time. Came back in late February with a hold full of snapper."

"Would it have made a difference to you if you'd found out that he'd been involved in some way in Martin's death?"

"I don't know. It probably would have given me a sick feeling in my gut."

"You get those?"

"From time to time."

He was quiet for a minute and then he said, "Truth be told, Florida has a long, sordid history of mistreatment and violence against Blacks and many poor white people too, like Martin. Chain gangs and convict work camps were a big part of our history. They fueled the boom times that benefitted a few of the wealthy. Why, if anyone dug up the railway and roadbeds that built Florida, they would find so many bones it would be embarrassing. People here have never come to terms with that history. We need to, or we'll never move ahead."

"I have noticed that people around here don't want to talk much about the convict labor history."

"No. The only history here is the Civil War. We're drowning in that bloody history. That was yesterday to most folks, but the 1920s, or anything since, including Jim Crow? That might as well be a thousand years ago."

"That's an interesting point of view."

"You mean from a Southern redneck sheriff."

"I didn't say that. But there is that stereotype."

He laughed, "Yeah, I don't always fit the stereotype. In fact, you better keep our conversation to yourself, or folks around here will think I'm too soft."

Now she laughed. "How did someone like you become sheriff of Dixie County, Florida?"

"Just stupid luck. I got pissed off at the way the former sheriff was running things down here—he was known to take some bills under the table from time to time. A committed segregationist, too. Ran against him and he just happened to pass away of a heart attack a month before the election. I still only beat him by a handful of votes."

She laughed again, and she glanced down and noticed that he wasn't wearing a wedding ring. She waited another thirty minutes, but she had to ask, "Are you married?"

"No, I've never been married. And I don't have any children either, if that's your next question."

He was quiet for a moment. "Everyone around here knows, so I might as well tell you too."

"What?"

"I had a pretty steady girlfriend for years. She died in a boating accident nearly five years ago."

"I'm sorry to hear that."

"How about you?"

"How about me, what?"

"Are you married?"

"No. No one special at all. I work too hard. I don't have much time for men. So far anyhow."

<hr>

Jim and Nicole drove to Edgar Seldon's house first. It was near the Gulf, just southeast of the town of Jena. As they drove, Jim explained to Nicole that Edgar was in his late nineties, although he reportedly still had his full faculties. He had worked for Putnam Lumber all over north Florida, mainly along the Gulf Coast. Mill work, not in the convict camps, but he was well connected at the time. If anyone knew anything, he might.

After they left the highway, they drove on a dirt road running its way through bogs and brush and up to a small one-story, green-clapboard house sitting on a mound. A sad gray mist hovered over the salt marsh as they got out of the car, making the house look like a giant bullfrog rising out of the swamp. A brown-and-white Chihuahua furiously announced their appearance. Edgar was at the door when they reached it. He had thin hair plastered back on a balding pate, a stubbed gray beard, and a weather-beaten face the color of worn leather. He wore a faded khaki shirt and blue jeans high at the waist. When he shook hands, however, it was with a strong grip, exuding a vitality that the years hadn't erased. He led them inside. The house was small with only three rooms and a worn carpet track between the kitchen and living area and a back bedroom. Shelves along every wall were stacked with mildewed newspapers and magazines. There was an odor in the house of dampness and urine. He showed them to a davenport, and he sat in a faded plaid recliner. He pulled a throw over himself. "My bones get cold these days," he explained.

Jim said, "I told you about Nicole and how she was looking to find someone who died back in the 1920s in one of the convict camps."

"Yes, yes, I'll do my best to help y'all out."

"The boy's name was Martin Tabert," Nicole said. "He was from North Dakota and came down here in the early winter of 1921. He spent some time in a convict camp somewhere in Dixie County before he was killed."

"From up north, you say."

"Yes. North Dakota."

"I remember hearing about one young feller from someplace in that north country. Farm boy. Sounds like he could be the one you're lookin' for."

"Was he killed in one of the camps?"

"Yes. Can't say if it was in Dixie County though. You gots to understand that Putnam Lumber had camps and mills all over north

Florida. Hundreds of them over the years. Cut the timber 'til it was a long way to haul it to the yard, then move the mill. Then move it again, and again. Stripped the giant cypress forests all across north Florida."

"What happened to the fellow you know about?"

"Like I was telling you, he was from up north, I do remember that clearly. Got killed in a camp, I know that too. Everyone knew the story on account of how he died."

Nicole leaned forward. "How was that?"

"The Captain of the camp took a dislike to him. Said he was a shirker. Whipped him something fierce. Damn near flayed him alive with that strap . . ."

Nicole interrupted. "That's what happened to Martin Tabert. The historical accounts document that." She looked at Jim hopefully. He nodded his head.

"Where was he buried?" Nicole asked.

"Put him in a shallow grave up towards Mingo. Some of the other convicts built a pen of logs over the grave to keep out the wild beasts. Din't want him to end up as a wild-boar-chewed cadaver."

"He was buried in the Mingo Cemetery?"

"I didn't say he was buried in the cemetery. It was near the town of Mingo, but out in the woods someplace."

"Would anyone know where it was?"

"Don't know that."

Nicole thought for a moment, "You said that everyone knew the story. There must be other people who know something, too."

"Yes, lots of folks knew the story. It was the way he died. You don't forget that. The axe and all. The story got around."

"I thought you said he was whipped to death?"

"I wasn't finished telling it."

"Telling what?"

"The story."

"Okay, what's the story then?"

"I'm gittin' to it if you jus' quit askin' so many questions."

"Sorry. Go ahead."

"Well, people said the Captain had a quirk of personality. Liked to see men rassle and fight neckid. Like the gladiators of old. It was his favorite entertainment. Couldn't get enough of it. One day he said that the boy from the North was shirkin'. Told the boy he would get a hundred lashes. Now, a hundred lashes would have surely killed him and all the men knew it. But the Captain was just tryin' to get to him. Tryin' to rile him. Using what they call that there psychology. Told him he would forgo the whippin' if'in he could lick the biggest man in the camp. The Captain picked out the biggest niggra in the camp—coal black, lookin' like he just stepped off the boat from Africa and standing over six hands high. Said whichever one lost would get the hundred licks. You can bet that got the niggra's attention. Ordered the two of them to strip down right then and there and go at it."

"Folks talked about that fight for years. How the two men pounded the hell out of each other. You see, they both knew they were fightin' for their lives. They was just a wallin' on each other—socken', scratchen', bitin'—'til they was a bloody sight to behold. Kickin' each other in the nuts 'til they was red and swelled up like rooster combs. First one would go down, then the other. The guards and convicts all gathered round, yellin' and cheerin' the men on. The thing is, the boy was smaller, but he somehow held his own. Maybe the niggra was weakened from so much time in the camps. Maybe he had the jungle fever. Who knows? Should have won easily, but he didn't. He finally went down with a flurry of kicks and punches and he was a strugglin' to git up. The boy jumped atop of him and poundin' him about the head with both fists and the blood a flyin'. Trouble was, once the Captain saw that the boy from the North might win, he threw a boxing axe on the ground near the niggra. He seen his chance and grabbed it, and the boy stumbled trying to gits away. The niggra runs after him, winds up, and cleaves him down the back of the head. They said the axe split the boy's skull in two from the top of his head right through his nose. The boy takes two or three steps and somehow lets out a yell, 'Lord, I'm comin', then falls stone dead."

"Jesus," Jim gasped.

"No one can forget a story like that once you hear it. That's one dadgum good story, ain't it? Why, I've wakin' many a night in a sweat, jus' thinkin' 'bout it," Edgar said.

Nicole sucked in air. "No, I don't expect you would forget such a story . . . it's not Martin Tabert's story though."

"No, not the one, eh."

"No."

As they were leaving, Jim said, "Sorry you had to hear that. If I had known that before, I would never have dragged you out here."

"No, don't apologize. I'm determined to follow up on every lead. This is what I get."

"It's a vicious story, though. Not something a lady should have to listen to."

"I've heard a lot of vicious stories."

Jim led Nicole up the driveway toward Netta Tuck's house. It was potted with puddles and overhung by moss. The house was old, ramshackled; once painted white, the paint now blistered with age. Rows of sheets and work shirts and diapers were flapping on the clothesline. A half dozen little Black children came running when they saw Jim approaching. "Sheriff Jim, Sheriff Jim," they yelled.

He knew them all by name and tousled their hair and horse-played with them a bit. The kids stared at Nicole until she smiled at them, and then they gathered around her too. Jim introduced her to all of them.

"Is Netta here?" he asked the eldest child, Ebony.

"Yes, sir."

They walked up and peered through a screen door with many holes neatly repaired with black thread. Nicole could see an elderly lady in a recliner. She wore a thin robe and she was sleeping. An old black and white television was playing loudly. Ebony shook the woman gently. "Aunt Netta, Sheriff Jim is here to see you."

"Oh, goodness. Let me get dressed properly."

Jim and Nicole stepped onto the plank porch, which was white and bleached like beach driftwood. It was cooler there in the shade, and Jim motioned for her to sit down on one of the wicker chairs. Later the screen door creaked, and Netta shuffled out in worn brown slippers. She'd put on a blue cotton dress and a floppy yellow hat. She was a heavy, small woman. Her face was wrinkled with age and one of her eyes was milky white. She smiled brightly when she saw Jim. "Mercy. My baby Jim," she cooed. After she was introduced to Nicole, she sat down in a cane rocking chair. She turned to Nicole. "I still call Jim 'baby,' even though he's old enough to have children of his own," she said. "I call all my young'uns baby. They still babies to me. Lordy, how the years do go by."

"Netta's brother worked on the fishing boat with my grandfather and father for years. She's known me since I was knee high," Jim explained.

He turned back to her. "Netta, Nicole is doing some research on her own family history. That's why I brought her here to see you. She needs some information on a friend of her grandmother. I told her you might know something."

"Well, well, that's mighty nice. Ain't nothin' more important than family. I don't recall no folk named Knutson. Where you from child?"

"I'm from the Chicago area originally, but I've lived on the east coast since I was ten. Maryland mostly."

"Maryland . . . let me see . . . there was a boy from Clara who moved up to Maryland." She paused. "Buck something . . . Buck Smith . . . yes, that was his name. Buck Smith. Moved about 1946. Right after the War. Don't s'pose you know him."

"No, I don't think I do."

"He might be dead now I reckon anyhow." She turned and yelled towards the kids, "Ebony, you get the sheriff and the lady somethin' to drink." She turned back to Nicole, "I thought about livin' in the city myself sometimes. But you know, I would miss these woods and the shade. And you can't do much fishin' in the city. Why, just the other day I caught the nicest mess of bream you ever seen down in the creek. Nice bream . . . fried 'em up . . . crispy . . . use bacon fat . . . nice bream." She seemed to drift off for a moment into her own thoughts.

Jim said, "Netta, Nicole here is looking for someone who might know something about a Martin Tabert. Martin was a boy from North Dakota killed in a convict camp back in the twenties."

Netta scowled.

"Now Netta, I know you don't like to talk about certain things that happened in the past, but this is important to Nicole. Her grandmother Edna is dying. She's ninety-eight and knew the Tabert boy when she was young, and she's wondering where he might be buried."

"I don't recollect anything about any white boy named Martin." She rocked faster, her slippers barely touching the floor.

"Please think, Netta. I remember hearing about your daddy being in one of those convict camps run by Putnam Lumber."

"No, no . . . don't remember nothin' 'bout that."

Then silence, only the sound of her rocker creaking in a fast rhythm.

"Well, if you can't remember, you can't remember," Jim said.

Nicole wondered if that was the end of it. Ebony brought out some raspberry Kool-Aid for them in tall frosty glasses, tinkling with ice cubes, and they thanked her and sat there for some time talking about the weather. Netta was taciturn, only occasionally adding a quiet "ah-hem." Eventually Jim brought the conversation back. "It's a shame you can't remember anything about the Martin boy. Seeing how Nicole flew all the way down here from her grandmother's bedside and all. Just too bad. I expect her grandmother needs some closure on this. Now she'll never know where her Martin is buried."

Netta clenched her lips tight and didn't say anything, staring off into space and occasionally shaking her head slightly. Her bosom rose and fell. Jim had an awkward look and studied his shoes. This was getting nowhere, Nicole thought. Another dead end.

Jim said, "I just feel bad for that Edna, not knowing and all."

Netta burst into tears, her heavy arms shaking. She looked up heavenly. "Oh Lordy, forgive me Lord, but I is have to tell." She turned to Jim and Nicole. "My papa made me swear on a Bible that I wouldn't say anything to anyone. I kept it in all these years. But I s'pect the Lord will forgive me, it's been so long."

She was quiet again for a moment. She sipped her Kool-Aid, taking her time, collecting her thoughts. "You see, the white folks threatened us. Told us that if we ever revealed where the body was they would get us. String us up where no one would find us or worse."

Netta paused and Nicole wondered if she had changed her mind about telling what she knew. Then she started up again. "It was back in the twenties. Oh, those chain gangs they had back then. All over Florida. Folks lived in fear of them. Worked you near to death. They'd pick up young men folk, din't need no reason. Loitering or vagrancy, they called it. Just folks without a regular job. Black folk, white folk, didn't matter, long as the person looked like they had a strong back. Sentence you to the convict camp. Oh mercy, the work they had to do. Choppin' trees, haulin' logs, buildin' roads. Why most of the roads in this county were built by those poor men. Used a whip to make 'em work. Just like when our kinfolk were slaves."

She looked up to the sky. "My papa Roy—he's been dead now some thirty years—was sentenced to ninety days for nothin'. Picked him up when he was coming back from fishin' for catfish in the Suwannee River. Said he was a vagrant. He served his ninety days but came back all skinny and back-scarred. Told the family 'bout a boy from up north whipped to death at the camp by the whippin' boss. I don't think I ever heard the name, but could have been your Martin boy. After he died, the whippin' boss told some of the Black folk to weight the body down and throw it in the swamp. The whippin' boss was scared that someone would see the body and charge him with murder. The body was so bad, skin flayed off in places from the whippin's, that he knew he could be in trouble. They did what they were told and threw the boy in the swamp, but it got playin' on Papa's mind. He knew the boy was a Christian. Wasn't right. The boy needed a Christian burial. So, when he was released a few days later, he snuck back there and pulled the boy out of the swamp at night. Th' rigor mortis had set in, but he managed to stuff him in a big burlap cotton bag and brought him to our house. They was gonna bury him the next day. My papa told me to stay away from that body."

She started sobbing. "I was ten and a curious little girl in those days. I woke up very early in the morning and walked out to the shed where the body was and pulled the burlap bag aside. I wish I had never done that to this day. I still have nightmares about it. Stunk like a dead coon in the sun. The worse was how he looked. Bloated up and no skin at all on his back. Jus' bloody flesh.

"They took him down to the church the next morning and said prayers over him. Buried him in a pine coffin nearest the river in the potter's field. An unmarked grave. Worried that if word got out they would dig up the body to throw it in the swamp again."

She took a sip of her Kool-Aid, her hand shaking. "Well, somehow word did get out," she said. "Someone said something, and it got around, and the white folks came and knocked on our door one night. That is when they said that if we ever told they would get us. The white folks made up some lie about them giving him a Christian burial and being buried in the Mingo Cemetery. When that story fell apart, they said the boy was buried in a field. All that was lies. We knew he was buried next to that river."

"Did you see exactly where the body was buried?" Nicole asked.

"Yes'm. I seen it. Many times when we went fishin' in the river I would sneak up there and lay a pretty piece of glass, or a mussel shell, or a few wild flowers on the spot."

"Can you show me?"

"No."

"Please, Netta," said Jim. "Show her where the spot is. She can hire a backhoe to go in there and dig up the body."

"No, you can't do that. I'm sorry. Someone should have said something long ago. That whole area by the river was washed out when Hurricane Easy hit in 1950. It blew the whole coast to tatters. We had over twenty inches of rain in three days. Half the country-side was under water and the river was running something fierce. It looked a mile across and whole trees were swept along and chicken coops and fence rails. Took everybody in that cemetery out to sea."

Nicole and Jim looked at each other and exchanged glances. They both knew it was the truth, a hard truth, but there was no escaping it.

"Thank you for telling us, Netta," Nicole said. "At least now we know, and I can tell my grandmother. And don't worry. I know for certain that the Lord will forgive you for breaking your promise not to tell."

"I'm sorry. Sorry it's too late."

Jim and Nicole got up to leave and they were just stepping off the porch when Netta said, "Wait." They stopped. "I got something for you," she said. She shuffled into the house. She was gone for quite a few minutes and shuffled back. She was holding something in her hand. "My daddy said that the boy had this in his pocket." She handed it to Nicole. It was a silver watch fob with some kind of design on it. Nicole used her skirt hem to rub off some of the dirt and tarnish. It looked like tall birds — cranes — dancing.

"We kept it in a cigar box all these years," Netta said. "It wasn't our property, so it wouldn't have been right to sell it. You take it and give it to your grandmother."

That evening Jim took Nicole out to an early dinner and then dropped her off at the Sun Shade Motel. He offered to drive her back to the airport at Tallahassee the next day, but she didn't want to impose further and said she would make arrangements to take an early bus. It was late, but she called the hospital to talk to Edna. A nurse answered, but when she asked to speak with Edna, the nurse told her that she would have the doctor call her. That worried her and she paced in her room until her phone rang.

"Is this Nicole?"

"Yes."

"Hi. This is Dr. Brownson calling. How are you?"

"I'm fine. How's Edna?"

"That's what I'm calling about. I'm afraid she's had a bit of a downturn again. Her EKG is unsteady. We're providing every care possible, but there's just so much we can do. She's very weak. To be honest, I don't think she has much longer."

"I'll be up there tomorrow."

Nicole was at the hospital the following evening. She walked briskly to Edna's room, hoping for the best. She peeked in the door. Edna's eyes were closed. Nicole tiptoed in and sat on a chair. After an hour or so, Edna opened her eyes. She appeared momentarily confused, but then smiled when she recognized her. "Nicole, you're back."

"Yes, Grandma."

"Where were you?"

"I flew back to Florida."

"Florida. Why?"

"I finally met someone who knew something about Martin Tabert. I have something for you." Nicole held out the watch fob with the dancing cranes. "Do you recognize this?"

Edna's eyes widened and her face broke into a smile and for a second Nicole saw the face of an innocent young teenage girl. Edna didn't say anything, but she slowly raised her trembling hand and Nicole gave it to her. She grasped it. "Oh, my Martin," she said, as tears gathered in her eyes. Nicole explained how she'd found it, as Edna quietly listened. Only when Nicole told her that Martin's grave had been washed out to sea did she speak. "He's back with nature then," she said. "He would have liked that."

"Yes, Grandma, I think you're right."

"And the Black folks gave him a real Christian burial?"

"Yes, they did."

"I feel better knowing that."

"Good."

"Thank you for going to all that trouble, Nicole. I love you so much."

"I love you too, Grandma."

The next day, as Nicole sat at her bedside holding her hand, Edna quietly drifted away.

Three days later, Nicole met her father at the airport in Devils Lake. She was happy to see him and she hugged him for a very long time. His body felt warm and comforting, like when she was a small child. They drove up to Munich together. It was a beautiful spring day, the sky saturated with light, and a warm southern breeze was melting the snow and releasing the fragrance of the rich black soil. Nicole felt happy to be with her father and they shared loving memories of Edna as they drove.

Edna's funeral was held at the Zion Lutheran Church. Nicole was surprised how many people were there, the entire church was full. She thought that was something very special, since pretty much everyone Edna's age was deceased. There were her three children and all the grandchildren, neighbors from the farm where she had lived for so many years, almost everyone from the town of Munich, and a van full of elderly people from the nursing home.

At her father's request, Nicole gave the eulogy. She spoke of the kindness of her grandmother and the love she gave to her children and grandchildren and the love she received in return. She talked about how her grandmother had lived a remarkable life. She'd seen the country develop from the lumbering ox team to the speed of jet travel. She'd eventually traveled around the world from her small town. Even in the last years of her life, she had a keen interest in current affairs and politics, and she'd voted in every presidential election from 1928 when she'd voted for Norman Thomas to 2000 when she'd voted for Al Gore. She talked about Edna's husband Ted, who brought joy to her life and she to his. Nicole talked briefly about Martin Tabert too, saying that he was her first love and that his death had been grievous for Edna, but she'd survived and found her own way in life. Nicole did not mention Torger by name, but said this: "Edna knew domestic violence and the evil that can possess people sometimes, but she never let it infect her soul, she stood up to it, and she herself showed only goodness and kindness to others."

After the funeral, they drove out to the cemetery in a long line of cars following the hearse. The cemetery was a few miles outside of town. There were a few pine trees surrounding the cemetery, but they were too few to stop the buffeting winds coming down from Canada for eternity. That would be fine with Edna, Nicole thought. She never did like to feel hemmed in.

After a few brief words at the gravesite, and before the dirt was thrown on the coffin, Nicole approached it and said a silent prayer. Only her father saw her pull something shiny and silver out of her pocket and drop it gently on top of Edna's coffin.

Later that day, Nicole sat at the Munich Café and Bowling Alley on Main Street with her father, eating cheeseburgers and fries. It was the sole remaining café in town. The place was small, but the ten booths and tables were mostly filled. There were three bowling lanes in the rear of the café, and one was being used, so the periodic crash of bowling pins added to the din of conversation. Nicole stepped outside to call Paige. She didn't answer. She texted her a message about the funeral. Paige called her back soon afterwards.

"I'm sorry I didn't answer when you called," she said. "I was sitting in on a subcommittee meeting and I couldn't leave."

"I understand."

"I'm sorry to hear about your grandmother. I know you were close. From everything you told me about her it sounds like she was a wonderful person. How was the funeral?"

"Sad . . . but in a way, not sad, too. She lived such a long life and in the end she died peacefully."

"That's good Nicole. When will you be back in D.C.?"

Nicole took a deep breath. "I'm not coming back Paige. I need to start a new life. Live differently. I'm not sure how yet, but I know I'm changing. I'm not the person I used to be."

There was a silent pause. "Are you still there?" Nicole asked.

"Yes. I'm sorry you're not coming back, but it doesn't surprise me. You haven't seemed happy about your work for a long time."

"No, I haven't been. It weighs on me. Some of the things I did were wrong. I'm beginning to see that now. I want to try to make amends. Can you do me a favor and have my things boxed up? I'll send a moving company to pick them up."

"Sure. Where are you moving?"

"I'm moving to North Dakota for the time being. At least until I get things sorted out."

"You're kidding. What would you do there?"

"I'm not sure yet, but I heard they need an attorney on the Spirit Lake Indian Reservation up here. I may take something like that for a while."

"Wow, that's quite a change. I hope you realize that once you get off the track like that, you can never come back. Not in D.C. anyway. I hope you haven't gone off the deep end."

"I know. I hope I haven't gone off the deep end either. Or maybe I did go off the deep end, but now I feel like I'm fighting my way back up to the surface."

"You're talking a little strange."

"Yeah, I guess I am. I'm definitely looking at things differently. It seems I've developed a penchant for cardiologists and red-neck southern sheriffs too."

"What's that about?"

"Nothing. I'll tell you later. I have to go. I'm having lunch with my dad right now. I'll be in touch about the moving. Take care. Bye." Nicole hung up. It felt like a huge relief, and Nicole was gripped by a sudden feeling of happiness.

Later that day, Nicole called a reporter for the *New York Times*. "I'm Nicole Knutson. I work for the Office of Legal Counsel in the U.S. Department of Justice. Well, I used to work there. I would like to meet with you. I have some photographs that I think you would be interested in seeing."

EPILOGUE

A few have protested, a few have been sick with shame, but a million people have been ignorant of the system or have closed their eyes to what was going on about them, have shrugged their shoulders and turned away carelessly.

"Tragedy of Convict Camp Stirs Florida; Saw
Tabert Lashed," *New York World*, April 2, 1923

The Tabert family was notified of Martin Tabert's death by a typed letter from Putnam Lumber Company to Ed Tabert dated February 2, 1922:

> Dear Sir: This is to advise that Martin Tabert, who was sentenced Dec. 15th, in Tallahassee, Leon County, for a term of three months, died in our camp on the 1st of fever and other complications. This company has all convicts from the above County leased, is the reason he came here. We were unable to get any trace of his people until he was buried here yesterday. We understand you are his brother. For your information, the boy was given a Christian burial in a cemetery near and had a minister officiate same.[6]

The assertion that Martin had been given a Christian burial with a minister officiate was a lie. The stated cause of death was also a lie.

The family was perplexed because after they'd sent the fifty dollars for the fine and the letter was returned, they'd assumed that Martin had found some other way to secure his release. But they could not do anything other than to try to get more information from the company. Putnam Lumber was not cooperative.

The next they heard was in July 1922. Convict Glen Thompson, now released, sent a letter addressed to the Munich postmaster:

> Dear Sir: Would you please find out whether the parents or kinfolks of Martin Tabert know or care to know the particulars of Martin's death in February of this year. I was an eyewitness in the boy's death and I am doubting whether any particulars were sent to the folks."[7]

The family corresponded with Glen Thompson and found out the terrible truth about Martin's death.

In the late summer of 1922, Benjamin Tabert and his sons walked into the law office of States Attorney Gudmunder Grimson

Gudmunder Grimson who served as Special Asssistant Attorney General in the Tabert case.
Photo courtesy of State Historical Society of North Dakota, Collection 10120, Folder 17, Item 316.

Tabert investigating committee at Florida Legislature, Tallahassee, Florida. Photo courtesy of State Historical Society of North Dakota, Collection 10120, Folder 17, Item 298.

and told him about Martin's beating death in the swamps of Florida. Grimson was a man of Icelandic origin and had grown up on a farm in Cavalier County, North Dakota. He was a young attorney, but already thought of as a man with integrity. He would later become a Supreme Court Judge in North Dakota.

Grimson took the case and traveled to Florida to investigate Martin's death. He took affidavits from witnesses and brought back a report which roused people in North Dakota.[8] A subscription of $4,000 was soon raised from state citizens to prosecute the case. The North Dakota legislature passed a resolution in February 1923, demanding a full investigation by the Florida legislature of the allegations that the Leon County Sheriff and lumber camp operators had conspired to convict men for minor offenses. Grimson also secured the attention and support of the *New York World*, and Tabert's plight was detailed by journalist Samuel D. McCoy.[9] The press coverage of the trial helped to draw attention to the plight of convicts in the South. The paper was later awarded a Pulitzer Prize for the articles on the Tabert case and their campaign to abolish the leasing system of prisoners.

The pressure from Grimson and embarrassment by the press forced legislative and grand-jury investigations in Florida.

An indictment was issued by the grand jury:

Indictment for Murder in the First Degree

T.W. Higginbotham . . . in the County of Dixie, on the 27th day of January, A.D. 1922, . . . with a deadly weapon, to-wit, a leather strap about three feet long, about three inches wide and weighing about six pounds . . . did strike, beat, bruise, wound and ill-treat the said Martin Tabert with the leather strap aforesaid thereby and thus inflicting in and about the head, body, and limbs of the said Martin Tabert diverse mortal wounds, bruises, centusiens, lacerations and fractures . . . and from which said mortal wounds . . . the said Martin Tabert did languish and languishing did afterwards, to-wit . . . die.[10]

Higginbotham was tried at Lake City, Columbia County, Florida in June 1923. Grimson assisted in the prosecution as a Special Assistant Attorney General. He later reported:

Opposing lawyers incited bitter local feeling against me by calling me a hick, a damn Yankee, an outsider . . . Defense lawyers abused me day after day, and I kept smiling back at their insults until my face hurt . . . One of the star witnesses, Jerry A. Poppell, died suddenly of poisoning on his way to testify. Another witness, a colored woman, was shot and killed a few hours before she was due to appear.[11] Putnam Lumber officials accused him of meddling and said he should go back to North Dakota and slop his pigs.[12]

Baliff Daugherty during Whipping Boss trial, Cross City, Florida.
Photo courtesy of State Historical Society of North Dakota, Collection 10120, Folder 17, Item 301.

Doc Jones testified that Martin had died of syphilis and Higginbotham denied that he flogged Tabert excessively, but on July 7 the jury found Higginbotham guilty of second degree murder. The judge sentenced him to twenty years in the state prison. Subsequently, the Florida Supreme Court granted him a new trial on the basis of a technicality. His lawyers were able to get the second trial moved to a more favorable jurisdiction at Cross City in Dixie County, where Putnam Lumber wielded enormous influence. He was acquitted. Higginbotham was never imprisoned for the murder of Martin Tabert and continued to work for Putnam Lumber

Company. He was later indicted in another murder, that of Lewis "Peanut" Barker, an African American turpentine worker in 1926.

The investigations forced Florida legislators to confront the structural problems with Florida's penal system. Over time, the situation of Florida convicts was improved. Florida legislators voted for the cessation of whipping as a means of punishment in May 1923. They also voted for the abolishment of the convict lease system. A state-run road labor system took its place, and although abuses continued—as did lynchings—in the South, the anger and indignation fueled by the Tabert case coming to light contributed to change over time, thanks to a few people who had the conviction and integrity to speak up.

Group of correspondents covering Tabert Whipping Boss trial, Cross City, Florida. Photo courtesy of State Historical Society of North Dakota, Collection 10120, Folder 17, Item 307.

Alice O'Brien, the daughter of Putnam Lumber Company found-
er William O'Brien, was sent to Florida to investigate the convict
camps after the death of Martin Tabert. She reported to the press,
"There is no truth to reports that Tabert was flogged to death in one
of the Putnam Company's camps." She later became president of
Putnam Lumber Company and a prominent St. Paul, Minnesota, so-
cialite. She enjoyed yachting and spending winters on her 72-foot
yacht out of Captiva Island, Florida.

As of the date of publication of this book, no one has ever
been prosecuted for authorizing the torture of detainees post 9/11,
under the administration of President George W. Bush and Vice
President Richard Cheney, many of whom were later shown to be
innocent individuals picked up by mistake.

Martin Tabert of North Dakota
(*New York World*, April 24, 1923)

By Marjory Stoneman Douglas (April 7, 1890–May 14, 1998)
(A ballad, to be sung in a minor key, but at the end with shouts.)

Martin Tabert of North Dakota is walking Florida now.
O children, hark to his footsteps coming, for he's walking soft and slow.
Through the piney woods and the cypress hollows
A wind creeps up and it's him it follows —
Martin Tabert of North Dakota, walking Florida now.

They took him out to the convict camp, and he's walking Florida now.
O children, the tall pines stood and heard him when he was moaning low.
The other convicts they stood around him
When the length of the black strap cracked and found him, —
Martin Tabert of North Dakota, — and he's walking Florida now.

They nailed his coffin boards together and he's walking Florida now.
O children, the dark night saw where they buried him, buried him, buried
    him low.
The tall pines heard when they went to hide him
And the wind crept up to moan beside him,
Martin Tabert of North Dakota. And he's walking Florida now.

The whip is still in the convict camp, For Florida's rising now.
Children, from Key West to Pensacola you can hear the great wind go.
The wind he roused when he lay dying,
The angry voice of Florida crying,

> "Martin Tabert of North Dakota,
> Martin Tabert of North Dakota,
> Martin Tabert of North Dakota,
>   You can rest from your walking now."

ENDNOTES

[1] Folksong originally collected by Zora Neale Hurston in *Of Mules and Men,* J.P. Lipppencott Co., 1935.

[2] Ibid.

[3] Affidavit of Max Grimm, as reported in Vivien Miller, "The Icelandic Man Cometh: North Dakota State Attorney Gudmunder Grimson and a Reassessment of the Martin Tabert Case," *Florida Historical Quarterly*, Vol. 81, No. 3, Winter 2003.

[4] Letter from John Gardner to John Tabert, January 29, 1923, Gudmunder Grimson Papers, records of the State Historical Society of North Dakota, Collection Number: 10120.

[5] Affidavit of A.B. Shivers, Gudmunder Grimson Papers.

[6] Gudmunder Grimson Papers.

[7] Ibid.

[8] Gudmunder Grimson and Irving Wallace, "Whipping Boss," *North Dakota History* 31, April 1967.

[9] "Murder, 'Convict Flogging Affairs,' and Debt Peonage: The Roaring Twenties in the American South," by Vivien Miller, in *Reading Southern Poverty between the Wars 1918–1939*, edited by Richard Godden and Martin Crawford, University of Georgia Press, 2006.

[10] Gudmunder Grimson Papers.

[11] Gudmunder Grimson and Irving Wallace, "Whipping Boss," page 133.

[12] Grimson and Wallace, page 132.

BIBLIOGRAPHY

Ayers, Edward L. *Vengeance and Justice: Crime and Punishment in the 19th Century American South* (Oxford University Press, 1984).

Blackmon, Douglas A. *Slavery by Another Name: The Re-Enslavement of Black Americans from the Civil War to World War II* (Doubleday, 2008).

Carper, Gordon N. "Martin Tabert, Martyr of an Era," *Florida Historical Quarterly* 52 (October 1973).

Constitution Project (Georgetown Public Policy Institute). Task Force on Detainee Treatment, *The Report of the Constitution Project's Task Force on Detainee Treatment*, 2013.

Drobney, Jeffrey A. "Where Pine and Palm Are Blowing: Convict Labor in the North Florida Turpentine Industry, 1877–1923, *Florida Historical Quarterly* 72, No. 4 (April 1994).

Dubofsky, Melvyn. *We Shall Be All: A History of the Industrial Workers of the World* (Abridged, University of Illinois Press, 2000).

Genovese, Edward D. *The Southern Tradition: The Achievement and Limitations of an American Conservatism* (Harvard University Press, 1994).

Godden, Richard and Crawford, Martin. Ed., *Reading Southern Poverty Between the Wars 1918–1939* (The University of Georgia Press, 2006).

Grimson, Gudmunder Papers, *Records of the State Historical Society of North Dakota*, Bismarck, North Dakota, Collection Number: 10120.

Grimson, Gudmunder, as Told to Irving Wallace, "Whipping Boss," *North Dakota History* 31 (April 1967).

Jahoda, Gloria, *The Other Florida* (Charles Scribner and Sons, 1967).

Hampsten, Elizabeth. *Settlers' Children: Growing Up on the Great Plains* (University of Oklahoma Press, 1991).

Handy-Marchello, Barbara. *Women of the Northern Plains: Gender & Settlement on the Homestead Frontier 1870–1930* (Minnesota Historical Society Press, 2005).

Jones, Jacqueline. *The Dispossessed: America's Underclasses from the Civil War to Present* (Basic Books, 1992).

Lauriault, Robert N. "From Can't to Can't: The North Florida Turpentine Camp, 1900–1950, *Florida Historical Quarterly* 67, No. 3 (January 1989).

Mayer, Jane. *The Dark Side: The Inside Story of How the War on Terror Turned into a War on American Ideals* (Anchor Books, 2008).

Miller, Vivian. "The Icelandic Man Cometh: North Dakota State Attorney Gudmunder Grimson and a Reassessment of the Martin Tabert Case," *Florida Historical Quarterly* 81, No. 3 (Winter 2003).

Oshinsky, David M. *Worse Than Slavery: Parchman Farm and the Ordeal of Jim Crow Justice* (The Free Press, 1996).

Powell, J.C. *The American Siberia; Or, Fourteen years' Experience in a Southern Convict Camp* (Homewood Publishing Company, Copyright 1891, 1893).

Shofner, Jerrell H. "Forced Labor in the Florida Forests 1880–1950," *Journal of Forest History* 25, No. 1 (January 1981).

Spivak, John. L. *Hard Times on a Southern Chain Gang*, (The University of South Carolina Press, 2012, originally published 1932).

Ste. Claire, Dana. *Cracker: The Cracker Culture in Florida History* (The Museum of Arts and Sciences, Daytona Beach, Florida, 1998).

Stock, Catherine McNicol. *Main Street in Crisis: The Great Depression and the Old Middle Class on the Northern Plains* (The University of North Carolina Press, 1992).

Wyman, Mark, *Hoboes: Bindlestiffs, Fruit Tramps, and the Harvesting of the West* (Farrar, Straus and Giroux, 2010).

ABOUT THE AUTHOR

Author photograph
by Nancy Vang and Kham Lee Vang

Paul Legler is a former lawyer turned writer. He grew up on a small farm in North Dakota and was educated at the University of North Dakota, University of Minnesota, and Harvard University. Legler worked as a poverty and civil rights attorney, Senior Policy Analyst at the Malcolm Wiener Center for Social Policy, Harvard University, and policy adviser in President Clinton's Administration. He currently lives in Minneapolis, Minnesota.

ABOUT THE PRESS

North Dakota State University Press (NDSU Press) exists to stimulate and coordinate interdisciplinary regional scholarship. These regions include the Red River Valley, the state of North Dakota, the plains of North America (comprising both the Great Plains of the United States and the prairies of Canada), and comparable regions of other continents. We publish peer reviewed regional scholarship shaped by national and international events and comparative studies.

Neither topic nor discipline limits the scope of NDSU Press publications. We consider manuscripts in any field of learning. We define our scope, however, by a regional focus in accord with the press's mission. Generally, works published by NDSU Press address regional life directly, as the subject of study. Such works contribute to scholarly knowledge of region (that is, discovery of new knowledge) or to public consciousness of region (that is, dissemination of information, or interpretation of regional experience). Where regions abroad are treated, either for comparison or because of ties to those North American regions of primary concern to the press, the linkages are made plain. For nearly three-quarters of a century, NDSU Press has published substantial trade books, but the line of publications is not limited to that genre. We also publish textbooks (at any level), reference books, anthologies, reprints, papers, proceedings, and monographs. The press also considers works of poetry or fiction, provided they are established regional classics or they promise to assume landmark or reference status for the region. We select biographical or autobiographical works carefully for their prospective contribution to regional knowledge and culture. All publications, in whatever genre, are of such quality and substance as to embellish the imprint of NDSU Press.

We changed our imprint to North Dakota State University Press in January 2016. Prior to that, and since 1950, we published as the North Dakota Institute for Regional Studies Press. We continue to operate under the umbrella of the North Dakota Institute for Regional Studies, located at North Dakota State University.